# "MAKES THE SHARK FROM JAWS LOOK LIKE A PET GOLDFISH . . .

**Like JAWS, BEAST will keep readers on the edge of their beach chairs."**
*USA Weekend*

Straight from the cutting edge of today's science and the logs of mariner legend comes an immense horror—a creature that rises up from the well of an ocean gone mad with an insatiable hunger and an endless lust to kill.

And when the beast strikes, and strikes again and again, one man leads a harrowing and desperate struggle for survival amid a threatened Bermuda paradise. His name is Whip Darling, a down-and-out deep-sea expert who doesn't know where he'll get his next meal . . . or whether it will get him first.

# BEAST

It owes its very existence to its favorite prey: us.

## A Book-of-the-Month Club Special Dual Edition

. . . ase turn the page
. . . more reviews. . . .

D0125092

# "JUST WHEN YOU THOUGHT IT WAS SAFE TO GO BACK IN THE WATER,

Peter Benchley has written another thriller about a set of jaws looming up out of the deep. . . . BEAST is most satisfying to read."
*The New York Times*

"Benchley is in high gear. . . . He's a fine, smooth writer, taut of technique, inventive of language."
*The Washington Post*

"What we have here is a big beast—a big, *big* beast—that's hungry and ticked off."
*The Cleveland Plain Dealer*

"Exciting and tersely written."
THE ASSOCIATED PRESS

# BEAST

## Peter Benchley

FAWCETT CREST • NEW YORK

A Fawcett Crest Book
Published by Ballantine Books
Copyright © 1991 by Peter Benchley

This is a work of fiction. Names, characters, places and inci-
dents are the product of the author's imagination or are used
fictitiously. Any resemblance to actual events, locales or persons, living or dead, is entirely coincidental.

Library of Congress Catalog Card Number: 91-10579

ISBN 0-449-22089-3

This edition published by arrangement with Random House,
Inc.

Manufactured in the United States of America

First Ballantine Books Edition: July 1992

*For the Squid Squads*

1979

*Billy Mac, Garbage Bob,*
*The Duke, Columbus Mould,*
*Captain Fathom*

1990

*George Bell, Clayton Benchley,*
*Nat Benchley, Adrian Hooper,*
*Kyle Jachney, Stan Waterman,*
*Michele Wernick, Donald Wesson,*
*John Wilcox*

*And, of course, for the Tuckers:*
*Teddy, Edna and Wendy*

"She [Scylla] has twelve splay feet and six lank scrawny necks. Each neck bears an obscene head, toothy with three rows of thick-set crowded fangs blackly charged with death. . . . Particularly she battens on humankind, never failing to snatch up a man with each of her heads from every dark-prowed ship that comes."

—HOMER, *The Odyssey*

# PART ONE

# 1

IT HOVERED IN the ink-dark water, waiting.

It was not a fish, had no air bladder to give it buoyancy, but because of the special chemistry of its flesh, it did not sink into the abyss.

It was not a mammal, did not breathe air, so it felt no impulse to move to the surface.

It hovered.

It was not asleep, for it did not know sleep, sleep was not among its natural rhythms. It rested, nourishing itself with oxygen absorbed from the water it pumped through the caverns of its bullet-shaped body.

Its eight sinuous arms floated on the current; its two long tentacles were coiled tightly against its body. When it was threatened or in the frenzy of a kill, the tentacles would spring forward, like tooth-studded whips.

It had but one enemy: All the other creatures in its world were prey.

It had no sense of itself, of its great size or of the fact that its capacity for violence was unknown in other creatures of the deep.

It hung more than half a mile below the surface, far beyond the reach of any sunlight, yet its enormous eyes registered faint glimmers, generated, in terror or excitement, by other, smaller hunters.

Had it been observable to the human eye, the animal would have been seen as purplish maroon, but that was now, at rest. When aroused, it would change color again and again.

The only element of the sea that the animal's sensory system monitored constantly was temperature. It was most comfortable in a range between 40 and 55 degrees Fahrenheit, and as it drifted with the currents and encountered thermoclines and upwellings that warmed or cooled the water, it moved up or down.

It sensed a change now. Its drift had brought it to the scarp of an extinct volcano, which rose like a needle from the ocean canyons. The sea swept around the mountain, and cold water was driven upward.

And so, propelled by its tail fins, the beast rose slowly in the darkness.

Unlike many fish, it did not need community; it roamed the sea alone. And so it was unaware that many more of its kind existed than had ever existed before. The balance of nature had been disrupted.

It existed to survive. And to kill.

For, peculiarly—if not uniquely—in the world of living things, it often killed without need, as if Nature, in a fit of perverse malevolence, had programmed it to that end.

FROM AFAR, THE boat might have been a grain of rice on a vast field of blue satin.

For days, the wind had blown steadily from the

southwest. Now, in the past few hours, it had faded—withered, retreated—and the stillness was uncertain, as if the wind were catching its breath and shuffling like a weary fighter before deciding where to launch its next assault.

Howard Griffin sat in the cockpit, one bare foot resting on a spoke of the wheel. The boat, deprived of the driving force of the wind, rocked gently in the long swells.

Griffin glanced up at the flapping sails, then checked his watch and cursed himself for a fool. He hadn't counted on this, hadn't anticipated a calm. He had plotted their course, their schedule, on the presumption of southerly winds.

Naïve. Stupid. He should have known better than to try to outguess the weather.

They were already hours behind schedule, thanks to having spent the entire morning in the Royal Navy Dockyard waiting for a customs officer to finish showing an apprentice how properly to search a fifty-two-foot Hatteras for contraband.

They should have been well at sea by now. Instead, as Griffin turned and looked back off the fantail, he could see the tall channel marker at the end of Eastern Blue Cut, a white speck glistening in the oblique light of the lowering sun.

He heard the kettle whistling below, and after a moment his wife came up through the hatch and handed him a cup of tea. He smiled his thanks and, as the thought suddenly came into his mind, he said, "You look terrific."

Startled, Elizabeth smiled back. "You're not so bad yourself."

"I'm serious. Six months on a boat, I don't know how you do it."

"A delusion." She bent down and kissed the top of his head. "Your standards have gone to hell."

"Smell good, too." Soap and air and skin. He looked at her legs, the color of oiled oak, not a stretch mark or a varicose vein to betray age or two children born more than fifteen years ago, just a single white scar where she had barked her shin against a concrete post one night down in the Exumas. He looked at her feet, brown and knobby and callused. He loved her feet.

"How am I ever gonna wear shoes again?" she said. "Maybe I'll get a job at the Barefoot Bank and Trust Company."

"If we ever get there." He gestured at the luffing mainsail.

"The wind'll go round again."

"Maybe. But we don't have time." He leaned forward, toward the ignition key, to turn on the engine.

"Don't."

"You think I like it? The man's gonna be at the dock Monday morning, and we better be there too."

"One second." She held up a hand, staying him. "Just let me check."

Griffin shrugged and sat back, and Elizabeth went below. He heard a burst of static as she adjusted the radio, then Elizabeth's voice as she spoke into the microphone. "Bermuda Harbour Radio, Bermuda Harbour Radio, Bermuda Harbour Radio . . . this is the yacht *Severance*."

"Yacht *Severance*, Bermuda Harbour Radio . . ." came back a voice from fifteen miles to the south. "Go to six-eight, please, and stand by."

"*Severance* going to six-eight," Elizabeth said, and there was silence.

Griffin heard a little splash off the stern of the boat. He looked overboard and saw half a dozen gray chubs swarming on a patch of yellow sargasso weed, competing for the tiny shrimps and other creatures that took shelter among the floating stalks and bladders. He liked sargasso weed, as he liked shearwaters, which spoke to him of freedom, and sharks, which spoke to him of order, and dolphins, which spoke to him of God. Sargasso weed spoke to him of life. It traveled on the water, pushed by the wind, bearing food for small animals, which became food for larger animals, and so on up the food chain.

"Yacht *Severance,* Bermuda Harbour Radio . . . go ahead."

"Yes, Bermuda. We're sailing north for Connecticut. We'd like to get a weather forecast. Over."

"Right, *Severance.* Barometer three-oh-point-four-seven and steady. Wind southwest ten to fifteen, veering northwest. Seas three to six feet tonight and tomorrow, with winds northwest fifteen to twenty. Scattered showers possible over open water. Over."

"Many thanks, Bermuda. *Severance* standing by on sixteen."

Elizabeth reappeared through the hatch and said, "Sorry."

"Me too."

"This wasn't the way it was supposed to end."

"No."

What was supposed to happen, how they had envisioned their return, was that they would ride a south wind all the way up the coast, and when they cleared Montauk Point, with Fishers Island ahead and Stonington Harbor just beyond, they'd run up all the burgees and pennants and flags from all the countries and yacht clubs and marinas they'd visited in the last half-year. When they reached the Stonington breakwater, the wind would back a little bit around to the east so they could march triumphant down the harbor with everything flying proud and beautiful. Their kids would be waiting on the dock with Elizabeth's mother and Griffin's sister and her kids, and they'd have a bottle of champagne and then strip the boat of all their personal things and turn it over to the broker for sale.

One chapter of their life would end, and the next would begin. With all flags flying.

"There's still hope," Griffin said. "This time of year, a northwest wind doesn't last." He paused. "It better not, or we'll run out of fuel and tack back and forth till we die of old age."

He turned the key and pushed the button that started the engine. The four-cylinder diesel wasn't particularly noisy, but it sounded to him like a locomotive. It wasn't particularly dirty, but it smelled to him like midtown Manhattan.

Elizabeth said, "God, I hate that thing!"

"It's a machine. How can you hate a machine? I don't like it, but I can't hate it. You can't hate a machine."

"I can so. I'm a terrific-looking person. You said so yourself. It's in the Constitution: Terrific-looking people can hate whatever they want." She grinned and went forward to haul in the jib.

"Think positively," he called after her. "We've had a lot of sailing. Now we'll do a little motoring."

"I don't *want* to think positively. I want to be angry and disappointed and spoiled. And I'd appreciate it if you'd be angry too."

"What do I have to be angry about?" When he saw that the jib was down, Griffin put the boat in gear and pointed the bow into the breeze, which had begun to freshen. The oily calm had been wiped off the swells and replaced by the dappling of little waves. "I'm shacked up with the most beautiful crazy woman in the Atlantic, I've got a boat worth enough money to let me spend a year looking for a decent job, and I'm getting horny. What more could a guy ask?"

Elizabeth came aft and started on the mainsail. "So that's the bottom line, is it? You want to fool around."

"That I do," Griffin said. He stood and helped her with the big sail, steering with his foot to keep the bow pointed to windward. "But there's one tiny little problem."

"What's that?" She stood on one foot and let the toes of the other trace a circle on Griffin's calf.

"Someone to drive the boat."

"Turn on the automatic pilot."

"Great idea . . . if we had one."

"Yeah. I thought maybe saying the words would make one happen."

"You are disturbed," he said. "Gorgeous but nuts." He leaned between folds of the sail and kissed her. Then he reached for a length of bungee cord to secure the sail. His foot slipped off the wheel, and the boat yawed off the wind. A wave struck the starboard quarter and splashed cold spray down Elizabeth's legs. She yelped.

"Nice work," she said. "You sure know how to drown romance."

Griffin spun the wheel to starboard and brought the bow back into the wind. The boat's motion was uncomfortable now, as it plowed into the short, choppy seas. He said, "Maybe we should wait for a fairer breeze."

"Well . . . it's nice to know your heart's in the right place." She smiled at him and wiggled her butt and went below.

Griffin looked to the west. The sun had reached the horizon and was squashing into an orange ball as it slipped off the edge of the world.

The bow dipped under a wave, rose up and slapped the next wave hard. Spray flew aft like a chill rain. Griffin shivered, and was about to call out to Elizabeth, to ask for his slicker, when she reappeared, wearing her own slicker and carrying a cup of coffee.

"Let me take her for a while," she said. "You get some sleep."

"I'm all right."

"I know, but if the wind doesn't go round, this is bound to be a long night." She slipped around the wheel, into the seat beside him.

"Okay," he said, and he lifted one of her hands off the wheel and kissed it.

"What was that for?"

"Change of command. Old sea custom. Always kiss the hand of your relief."

"I like that."

He stood up, ducked under the boom and went to the hatch. "Wake me if the wind dies," he said.

Below, he consulted with the loran, took its numbers to a chart on the gimballed table in the cabin and pinpointed their position. He used a ruler to draw a pencil line from their position to Montauk Point, then matched the line to the compass rose on the chart.

He poked his head up through the hatch and said, "Three-three-oh oughta do it." In the past few minutes the sky had darkened so that the light from the binnacle now cast a reddish glow under Elizabeth's chin. Her yellow slicker shone orange, and her auburn hair shimmered like charcoal embers.

"You *are* beautiful," Griffin said, and he backed down into the cabin and went into the head. As he peed, he listened to the engine and to the sounds of the water rushing by the wooden hull. His ears were alert to strange noises, but he heard none.

He walked forward, peeled off his shirt and shorts and tucked himself into one of the two small bunks in the fo'c'sle. In port, they slept together in the after cabin, but at sea it was better for whichever one was sleeping to sleep forward, to keep in touch with the motion of the boat, to sense a change in the weather, a shift in the wind, just in case. . . .

The pillow smelled of Elizabeth.

He slept.

The engine droned on. Injectors pumped fuel into the cylinders, pistons compressed the fuel to combustion, and a thousand explosions every minute turned the shaft that held the propeller that drove the boat north into the night.

A pump drew seawater through a fitting in the hull and passed it through the engine, cooling it, and fed it aft to be flushed overboard with the engine's exhaust.

The engine was not old, had had less than seven hundred hours on it when they bought the boat, and Griffin had nursed it like a cherished child. But the exhaust pipe was harder to tend. It exited the engine compartment aft and nestled tightly beside the propeller shaft, under the floor of the after cabin. It was of steel, good steel, but for a thousand hours or more of engine use it had carried tons of salt water and acrid gases. And when the engine was not running, when the boat was sailing or tied to a dock, salt residue and molecules of corrosive chemicals had lain in the exhaust pipe and begun gradually to eat away at the steel.

The minuscule hole in the exhaust pipe could have been there for weeks. They had had fair winds all the way up from the Bahamas and had used the engine only to power in and out of St. George's Harbour and Dockyard, and routine pumping of the bilges would have removed any excess water. But now, with the engine running steadily and the heat-exchanger pump working full time and the boat punching into the sea rather than sailing gently with it, thus stressing its innards, the hole was growing. Bits of rusted metal flaked away from its edges, and before long it was the diameter of a pencil. Water that had dripped into the bilges now flowed.

Elizabeth steered with her feet and leaned back against the cushions in the cockpit. To her left, in the west, all that remained of the day was a sliver of violet on the rim of the world. To her right, a crescent moon was rising, casting a streak of gold that tracked her on the surface of the sea.

No souls, she thought as she looked at the moon. It was an Arab idea—she had read of it in *The Discoverers,* one of a score of books she had for years been meaning to read and had at last devoured in these past six months—and she decided she liked it: The new moon was an empty celestial vessel setting out on a month's journey to collect the souls of the departed, and as the days passed it swelled and swelled until, finally, engorged with souls, it disappeared to deposit its cargo in heaven, then reappeared, an empty vessel, and began again.

One reason she liked the conceit of a ship of souls was that for the first time in her life she was beginning to think she understood what a soul was. She was not a profound person, had always deflected serious conversations before they could plumb too deeply. Besides, she and Griffin had always been too busy living to pause and reflect.

He had been on the fast track at Shearson Lehman Brothers, she in the private banking division of Chemical Bank. The eighties had been a time when they had gathered toys: a million-dollar apartment, a half-million-dollar house in Stonington, two cars with heated seats and light bulbs in the backseat ashtrays. The money came in, the money went out: twenty thousand dollars for private-school tuition, fifteen thousand a year for eating out a couple of times a week, twenty thousand for vacations, fifty thousand for maintenance and upkeep.

Twenty thousand here, twenty thousand there—they used to joke—and pretty soon you're talking about real money.

It *was* a joke, because the money just kept coming in.

And then one day the tap was turned off. Griffin was laid off. A week later, Elizabeth was given a choice: half time at half salary, or quit.

Griffin's settlement would have allowed them to live for a year, no frills, while he looked for another job. But another job (undoubtedly at less money) would have meant climbing onto the same treadmill, a few paces back of the pack.

The other option was to take their severance money and buy a boat and see if, in fact, there was more to the world than *confit de canard* and designer fizzy water.

They kept the house in Stonington, sold the apartment in New York and put the proceeds in a trust to fund the children's education.

They were free, and with freedom came excitement and fear and—day after day, almost minute after minute—discovery. Discovery about themselves, about each other, about what was important and what was dispensable.

It could have been a disaster, two people confined twenty-four hours a day to a space forty feet long by twelve feet wide, and for the first couple of weeks they wondered. They got in each other's way and carped about this and that.

But then they became competent, and with competence came self-assurance, and with self-assurance, self-esteem and appreciation for one another's strengths.

They fell in love again, and, just as important, came to like themselves again.

They had no idea what they would do when they got

home. Maybe Griffin would try for another job in the money business, though from everything they'd read— mostly in the Caribbean edition of *Time*—the money business was in the dumper. Maybe he'd try to find work in a boatyard. He loved tinkering, didn't even mind varnishing and sewing sails.

And she? Maybe she'd teach sailing, maybe try to join the staff of an environmental group. She had been horrified by what they had seen of the destruction of the reefs in the Bahamas and of the wildlife in the Windwards and Leewards. They had snorkeled over barren bottoms littered with the sea-bleached shells of dead conchs and the shattered carapaces of spiny lobsters. Around island after island they had seen the ocean environment despoiled and destroyed. And because they had had time to think and observe, they had come to understand more fully the cycle of poverty breeding ignorance breeding poverty breeding ignorance. She had concluded that there might be something she could do, could contribute—as a researcher or a lobbyist. She still had contacts with a lot of the rich people she had dealt with at Chemical.

It didn't matter. They'd find something. And whatever they found would be better than what had been before, for they were new people.

It had been a wonderful trip, with not a single regret.

Well, that wasn't quite true. There was one regret— that they had had to turn on the engine. She hated its relentless rumble, the absurd gurgle as the exhaust pipe dipped in and out of the water, the vile smell of the fumes eddying over the stern and swirling in the cockpit.

The hole in the exhaust pipe had begun to grow, as tiny bits of rusty, weakened metal had flaked away. With each surge of the boat, with each slight heave from side to side, there was movement, not only of the hull but of everything within it—not much, not noticeable, but enough to cause strain, enough to aggravate weakness.

An eye could not have seen the hole grow, but now, as the boat's bow stuttered between two short, choppy seas, the exhaust pipe was seized by a slight torsion. It buckled and tore, and then all the water from the cooling pump poured into the bilges. And because the pipe was broken, when the boat's stern dipped and the exhaust outlet submerged, there was nothing to keep the sea from rushing in.

Elizabeth was sleepy. The boat's motion was the worst kind of soporific: staccato enough to be unpleasant but not violent enough to force her to stay alert. Perhaps she should wake Griffin.

She looked at her watch. No. He'd been asleep for only an hour and a half. Let him have another half hour. Then he'd be fresh and she could get some sleep.

She slapped herself in the face and shook her head.

She decided to sing. Impossible to fall asleep singing. Scientific fact. So she sang the first few bars of "What Are You Doing the Rest of Your Life?"

A wave lapped over the stern of the boat and soaked her.

No problem. The water wasn't cold. It would—

A *wave*? How does a wave come over the stern of a boat when you're heading into the sea?

She turned and looked.

The stern was four inches from being awash. As she watched, it dipped again, and more water rushed aboard and spread over the cushions.

Adrenaline shot up her back and down her arms. She sat still for a moment, willing herself to stay calm, to gather data. The annoying gurgle from the exhaust pipe had stopped. Fumes no longer swirled over the stern.

The seas on either side of the boat looked higher. The boat's motion was sluggish, wallowing, ass-heavy.

She reached forward of the wheel, lifted a plastic cover and flicked the switch that turned on the bilge pump. She heard the electric motor start, but something was wrong with the sound. It was distant, faint and laboring.

"Howard!" she shouted.

No answer.

"Howard!"

Nothing.

A length of bungee cord was looped over the boom, and she hooked each end around a spoke of the wheel, securing it, and went down through the hatch.

A stench of exhaust fumes choked her and burned her eyes. It was coming up through the floor.

"Howard!"

She looked into the after cabin. Six inches of water covered the carpet.

Griffin was in a dark, foreboding dream when he heard his name called from what seemed a great distance. He willed himself awake, sensing that something was wrong, wrong with him, for his head hurt, his mouth tasted foul, he felt drugged.

"What is it?" he said, and he rolled his legs over the edge of the bunk. He looked aft and saw, through a bluish haze, Elizabeth running toward him and shouting something. What was she saying?

"We're sinking!"

"Come on. . . ." He blinked, shook his head. Now he could smell the exhaust, recognize the taste.

Elizabeth peeled back the carpet in the main cabin and lifted the hatch covering the engine compartment. By now Griffin was standing over her. They saw that the engine was half underwater. The batteries were still dry, but the water rose as they watched.

Griffin heard sloshing in the after cabin, saw the water and knew what had happened. He said, "Shut down the engine."

"What?"

"Now!"

Elizabeth found the lever and choked off the engine. The rumbling died, and with it the circulating pump. No new water was being forced aboard, and they could hear the comforting electric whine of the bilge pump.

But there was still an open wound in the stern.

Griffin grabbed two dish towels from the sink and a shirt from a hook, and he handed them to Elizabeth. "Stick these up the exhaust pipe. Tight. Tight as you can."

She ran up through the hatch.

Griffin reached into a drawer and found a crescent wrench. He knelt on the deck and adjusted the wrench to one of the bolts holding the batteries to their mounts. If he could get the batteries out of the engine compartment, raise them a couple of feet, a foot even, he could give the bilge pump time to stop the water from rising. He had meant to move the batteries, after he read a cautionary article in one of the boating magazines about how dangerously dependent modern boats had become on sophisticated electronics. But that would have involved some reconstruction beyond his talents, which would have meant dealing with island labor, which would have delayed them.

Delayed them from what?

He cursed and heaved against the first bolt. It was corroded, and the wrench skidded off.

With its way gone, the boat slewed broadside to the sea and fell into a rhythm of steep, jerky rolls. A cupboard door flew open, and a stack of plates skidded out and crashed to the deck.

He tightened the wrench and leaned on the handle.

The bolt moved. He managed half a turn, then the wrench handle butted against the bulkhead. He yanked the wrench off, refitted it and turned again. The water rose.

In the cockpit, Elizabeth lay facedown on the fantail, spread-legged, her feet braced against the roll. One of the dish towels was balled in her fist, and she felt along the hull for the two-inch opening in the exhaust outlet. She could barely reach it with the tips of her fingers, and she tried to jam the towel inside. The pipe was too big, the towel too thin. It slipped out of the hole and floated away.

She heard a new sound, and paused to decipher it. It was the sound of silence. The bilge pump had stopped.

Then she heard Griffin's voice below. "Bermuda Harbour Radio . . . this is the yacht *Severance* . . . Mayday, Mayday, Mayday . . . we are sinking . . . our position is . . . *Fuck!*"

Elizabeth pulled the shirt from under her chest and balled it with the second dish towel, and again felt for the hole in the stern.

The boat yawed. Water rushed over the stern, and she skidded. Her feet lost their grip. She was falling. Her arms flailed.

A hand grabbed her and pulled her back, and Griffin's voice said, "Never mind."

"Never *mind*!? We're sinking!"

"Not anymore." His voice was flat. "We've sunk."

"No. I don't—"

"Hey," he said, and he gathered her to him and held her head against his chest and stroked her hair. "The batteries're gone. The pump's gone. The radio's gone. She's gone. What we've got to do is get the hell off before she slips away. Okay?"

She looked up at him and nodded.

"Good." He kissed her head. "Get the EPIRB."

Griffin went forward and uncovered the raft lashed to the cabin roof. He checked to make sure all its cells were inflated, checked the rubberized box screwed to the deck plates, to reassure himself that no one in some out-island port had stolen their flares or fishing lines or cans of food. He felt his belt to make sure his Swiss Army knife was secure in its leather case.

A five-gallon plastic jug of fresh water was tied to the boat's railing, and he untied it and set it in the raft. He debated going below to retrieve the small outboard motor stowed forward, then decided: Forget it. He didn't want to be caught below when the boat sank.

As he undid the last of the raft's lashings, Griffin felt a weird satisfaction: He wasn't panicking. He was acting precisely as he should—methodically, rationally, thoroughly.

Keep it up, he told himself. Keep it up. And maybe you've got a chance.

Elizabeth came forward. She carried the plastic bag containing the boat's papers, their passports and cash, and in her other hand the EPIRB, the emergency beacon, a red box covered with yellow Styrofoam, with a retractable antenna on one end.

The deck was awash now, and it was easy for them to heave the raft over the low railing into the sea. He held the raft with one hand and with the other steadied her as she jumped aboard. When she was seated in the bow, he stepped off the sailboat's deck and dropped into the stern of the raft. He sat, flicked on the switch on the EPIRB, pulled out the antenna and fitted the device into an elastic strap on one of the rubber cells.

Because the raft was light and the northwest wind was brisk, it moved quickly away from the crippled sailboat.

Griffin took Elizabeth's hand, and they watched in silence.

The sailboat was a black silhouette against the stars.

The stern sank lower, then slowly disappeared. Then, suddenly, the bow rose up like a rearing horse and slipped backward down into the abyss. Enormous bubbles rushed to the surface and burst with muffled booms.

Griffin said, "Jesus . . ."

# 3

IT WAS ALERT, had been for several moments, and its sensory receptors were processing signals of increasing danger.

Something large was approaching, from above, from where its enemy always came. It could feel vast quantities of water being displaced, feel the pressure waves.

It prepared to defend itself. Chemical triggers fired throughout the great body, sending fuel to the masses of flesh. Chromatophores ignited within the flesh, and its color changed from maroon to a lighter, brighter red—not a bloodred, for so permeated was its blood with hemocyanin that it was in fact green, but a red designed by Nature purely for intimidation.

It withdrew and cocked its two longest, whiplike arms, then turned and backed around to face the direction from which its enemy was coming.

It was not capable of fear; it did not consider flight.

But it was confused, for the signals from its enemy were unusual. There was no acceleration, no aggression. Most of all, there were none of the normal sounds of its enemy echolocating, no clicks or pings.

Whatever was coming moved erratically at first and then angled downward without pause.

Whatever it was, it passed and continued into the deep, trailing strange noises. Creaks and pops. Dead sounds.

The creature's color changed again, and its arms uncocked and unfurled with the sea.

Random drift had brought it to within a hundred feet of the surface, and its eyes gathered flickering shimmers of silver from the stars. Because light could signal prey, it allowed itself to rise toward the source.

When it was twenty feet from the surface and its motion was beginning to be affected by the roll above, it sensed something new—a disturbance, an interruption in the flow of the sea, moving and yet not moving, floating with the current, on the water but not part of it.

Two impulses drove the creature now, the impulse to kill and the impulse to feed. Hunger dominated, a hunger that had become more and more urgent as it searched in vain for prey in the deep. Once, hunger had been a simple cue, a signal to feed, and it had responded routinely, feeding at will. But now food was a quest, for prey had become scarce.

Again the animal was alert: not to defend itself, but to attack.

# 4

THEY HAD NOT spoken.

Griffin had fired a flare, and, holding hands, they had watched the yellow arc and the burst of orange brilliance against the black sky.

Then they had returned their gaze to the spot where the boat had been. A few bits of flotsam had drifted by—a seat cushion from the cockpit, a rubber fender—but now there was nothing, no sign that the boat had ever existed.

Elizabeth felt a tightness, a rigidity, in Griffin's hand, and she cupped it in both of hers and said, "What are you thinking?"

"I was doing the old 'if only' routine."

"What?"

"You know: if only we'd left a day earlier or a day later, if only the wind hadn't gone around, if only we hadn't had to start the engine . . ." He paused, and then his voice was bitter. ". . . if only I hadn't been too goddam lazy to get underneath the floor and check that pipe . . ."

"Don't do this, Howard."

"No."

"It wasn't anybody's fault."

"I suppose." She was right. Or even if she wasn't, what he was doing was useless. Worse than useless.

"Hey!" he said, forcing brightness. "I just thought of

something. Remember when Roger sold us the insurance? Remember we wanted the cheapest policy we could get, and he said no, we could never rebuild a wooden boat that big these days for anything like that amount, and he made us go the whole way? Remember that?"

"I guess."

"Sure you do. The point is, the boat is insured for four hundred and fifty thousand dollars. We could *never* get that on a sale."

Elizabeth knew what he was doing. She was glad, and she was about to say something, when the raft dipped off the top of a wave and slid into a trough.

They were capsizing. She knew it, they couldn't stop it. She screamed.

Then the raft evened out and bobbed gently up the next wave.

"Hey," Griffin said, and he edged over to her and put his arm around her shoulders. "It's okay. We're fine."

"No," she said into his chest. "We're not fine."

"Okay, we're not fine. What are you scared of?"

"What am I scared of?" she snapped at him. "We're in the middle of the ocean in the middle of the night in a raft the size of a bottle cap . . . and you ask what am I scared of? How about *dying*?"

"Dying from what?"

"For God's sake, Howard . . ."

"I'm serious. Let's talk about it."

"I don't want to talk about it."

"You got something better to do? Come on." He kissed her head. "Let's bring the demons out and crush them."

"Okay." She took a deep breath. "Sharks. Call me a wimp, but I'm terrified of sharks."

"Sharks. Good. Okay. We can forget about sharks."

"*You* can, maybe."

"No. Listen. The water's cold. The Japanese and the Koreans have fished most of them out anyway. And if some big shark does come around, as long as we stay in the raft we don't look, smell or feel like anything he's used to eating. What else?"

"Suppose a storm . . ."

"Okay. Weather. Not a problem. The forecast is good. We're not in hurricane season. Even if a northeaster does come up, this raft is next thing to unsinkable. Worst can happen, it tips over. If it does, we right it again."

"And float around till we starve to death."

"Not gonna happen." Griffin was pleased, for he found that the more he talked, the more he was able to push his own fears away. "One, the wind is pushing us back toward Bermuda. Two, there are ships in and out of here every day. Three, worst case, by Monday afternoon the kids and what's-his-name from the brokerage will report us missing, and Bermuda Harbour Radio knows all about us. But it won't get to that. This baby is beeping its heart out for us." He patted the EPIRB. "First plane that goes over will call out the cavalry. Probably already has."

Elizabeth was silent for a moment, then said, "You believe all that?"

"Sure I believe all that."

"And you're not scared."

He hugged her and said, "Sure I am."

"Good."

"But if you don't do something with fear—talk it away, change it—it eats you up."

She put her head down into his chest and breathed through her nose. She smelled salt and sweat . . . and comfort. She smelled twenty years of her life.

"So . . ." she said. "You want to fool around?"

"Right!" he laughed. "Capsize in a fit of passion."

They stayed like that, huddled together, as the raft drifted slowly south on the breeze. Overhead, stars seemed to dance in crazy unison, twisting and dipping with the motion of the raft but always moving inexorably westward.

After a while, Griffin thought Elizabeth had fallen asleep. Then he felt tears on his chest.

"Hey," he said. "What is it?"

"Caroline," she replied. "She's so young. . . ."

"Don't, hon. Please . . ."

"I can't help it."

"You should try to sleep."

"Sleep!?"

"Okay, then. Let's play Botticelli."

She sighed. "Okay. I'm thinking of . . . a famous *M*."

"*M*. Let's see. Is he a . . . famous French—"

Elizabeth suddenly started. She sat up and turned toward the bow. "What was that?"

"What was what?"

"That scraping noise."

"I didn't hear anything."

"Like fingernails."

"Where?"

She crawled forward and touched the rubber on the forward-most cell of the raft. "Right here. Like fingernails scraping on the rubber."

"Something from the boat, maybe. Forget it. A piece of wood. All sorts of floating crap out here. Could've been a flying fish. Sometimes they'll come right in the boat."

"What's that smell?"

"What smell?" Griffin took a deep breath, and now he did smell it. "Ammonia?"

"That's what I thought."

"Something from the boat."

"Such as?"

"How do I know? We had a bottle under the sink. . . .
Unless something's spilled in here." He turned and
faced the stern of the raft and unzipped the lid of the
rubberized box. It was too dark to see, so he bent over
to smell inside the box.

He heard a noise like a grunt, and the raft bounced
and lurched to one side. He was knocked off his knees,
and the tins in the box rattled together, and the deck
plates beneath him creaked and squealed against the
rubber, and he heard some vague splashing sounds—
probably of the raft slapping against confused wavelets.

"Hey!" He steadied himself with one hand on each
side of the raft. "Careful there."

There was no alien odor in the box. He zipped it
closed. "Nothing." But the smell of ammonia was
stronger now. He turned back to face the bow. "I don't
know what—"

Elizabeth was gone.

Gone. Just . . . gone.

He had a split second's sensation that he had gone
mad, that he was hallucinating, that none of this was
happening, that none of it had ever happened, that he
would soon awake in a hospital after a month-long
coma induced by an automobile accident or a lightning
strike or a slab of cornice fallen from an office building.

He called out, "Elizabeth!" The word was swallowed
by the breeze. He called again.

He sat back and took a deep breath and closed his
eyes. He felt dizzy and nauseated, and his pulse thun-
dered in his ears.

After a moment, he opened his eyes again, expecting
to see her sitting in the bow and eyeing him quizzically,
as if wondering if he'd had a fit.

He was still alone.

He got to his knees and hobbled around the entire

raft, hoping—imagining—that she had fallen overboard and was clinging to a dangling loop of lifeline.

No.

He sat back again.

Okay, he thought. Okay. Let's look at this rationally. What are the possibilities? She jumped overboard. She suddenly went out of her mind and decided to swim to shore. Or to kill herself. Or . . . or what? She was kidnapped by terrorists from the Andromeda Galaxy?

He screamed her name again, and again.

He heard a scraping noise, felt something touch the rubber beneath his buttocks.

She was there! Under the raft! She must have fallen over and gotten tangled in something, maybe some debris from the sailboat, and now she was under the raft fighting for air.

He leaned over the side and stretched his arms under the raft, feeling for her hair, her foot, her slicker . . . anything.

He heard the scraping noise again, behind him.

He withdrew his arm and shoved himself back inside the raft and looked forward.

In the yellow-gray light from the sliver of moon he saw something move on the front of the rubber raft. It seemed to be clawing its way up the rubber, scrambling to come aboard.

A hand. It had to be a hand. She had freed herself from the tangle and now, exhausted, half-drowned, was struggling to climb aboard.

He flung himself forward and reached out, and when his fingers were an inch or two away from it—so close that he could feel its radiant coolness—he realized that it wasn't a hand, that it wasn't human.

It was slimy and undulant, an alien thing that moved toward him, reaching for him.

He recoiled and scrambled toward the stern of the

raft. He skidded, fell. The shift of his weight caused the bow to rise up, and he knew a second of relief as the thing disappeared.

But then he watched, horrified, as it reappeared and inched upward until finally it was entirely atop the rubber cell. It straightened up, fanned out, looking now, he thought, like a giant cobra. Its surface was crowded with circles, each quivering with a life of its own and dripping water like ghastly spittle.

Griffin screamed. No word, no oath, no curse or plea, just a visceral shriek of terror, outrage, disbelief.

But the thing kept moving forward, always forward, compressing itself into a conical mass and slithering toward him, walking, it seemed, on its writhing circles; and as each circle touched the rubber it made a rasping sound, as if it contained claws.

It continued to come. It did not hesitate or pause or explore. It came as if it knew that what it was searching for was there.

Griffin's eyes fell on the oar in the raft, tucked under the cells on the starboard side. He grabbed it and held it like a baseball bat, and he raised it above his head and waited to see if the thing would come closer.

He braced himself on his knees, and when he judged that the moment had come he shouted, "Son of a *bitch*!" and slammed the oar down upon the advancing thing.

He was never to know whether the oar struck the thing or whether, somehow, the thing had anticipated it. All he would know was that the oar was torn from his hands and held aloft and crushed and rejected, cast away into the sea.

Now the thing, sensing exactly where Griffin was, moved more rapidly along the rubber.

Griffin stumbled backward, fell into the stern. He pushed himself back, and back, and back, desperate to squeeze into the tiny space between the cells and the deck plates. He reached—insanely, ridiculously—for his Swiss Army knife, fumbling with the snap on the leather case and mewling a litany of "Oh God . . . oh Jesus . . . oh God . . . oh Jesus."

The thing hovered over him, twitching and spraying him with drops of water. Each of its circles twisted and contorted itself as if in hungry competition with its neighbors, and in the center of each was a curved hook which, as it reflected rays of moonlight, resembled a golden scimitar.

That was the last Griffin knew, save for pain.

WHIP DARLING TOOK his cup of coffee out on the veranda, to have a look at the day.

The sun was about to come up; already there was a pink glow in the eastern sky, and the last of the stars had faded. Soon, a slice of orange would appear on the horizon, and the sky would pale and the wind would make up its mind what it was going to do.

Then he'd make up his mind, too. He should put to sea, try to raise something worth a few dollars. On the other hand, if he stayed ashore, there was always work to do on the boat.

The wind had gone around during the night. When he had come up from the dock at twilight, the boats anchored in the bay had been facing south. Now their bows were a phalanx arrayed to the northwest. But there were no teeth to the wind; it was little more than a gentle breeze. Any less, and the boats would have lain scatterways and swung with the tide.

He saw a splash in the bay, then another, and heard a fluttering sound: baitfish, a school of fry running for their lives and skittering over the glassy surface.

Mackerel? Jacks? Little puppy sharks finishing their dawn patrol before returning to the reefs?

Mackerel, he decided, from the vigor of the swirls and the relentlessness of the chase.

He loved this time of day, before the din of traffic began across in Somerset, and the growl of sightseeing boats in the bay and all the other noises of humanity. It was a time of peace and promise, when he could gaze at the water and let his memory dwell on what had been, and his imagination on what might yet be.

The screen door swung open behind him, and his wife, Charlotte—barefoot and wearing the summer cotton nightgown that showed the shadow of her body—came out with her cup of tea and, as she did every morning, stood beside him so close that he could smell the spice of sleep in her hair. He put an arm around her shoulder.

"Mackerel in the bay," he said.

"Good. First time in . . . what?"

"Six weeks or more."

"You going out?"

"I expect so. Chasing rainbows is more entertaining than chipping paint."

"You never can tell."

"No." He smiled. "And there's always hope. Anyway, I want to retrieve the aquarium's lines."

He finished his coffee, poured the dregs onto the grass, and as he turned to go inside, the first rays of the sun flashed over the water and bounced off the white-washed house. He looked at the dark blue shutters, paint flaking, slats cracked and sagging.

"Lord, this house is a mess."

"They want two hundred apiece to do the shutters," said Charlotte, "three thousand for the lot."

"Thieves," he said, and he held the door for her.

"I suppose we could ask Dana. . . ." She paused.

"Not a chance, Charlie. No more. She's done enough."

"She *wants* to help. It's not like—"

"We're not there yet," he said. "Things aren't that bad."

"Maybe not yet, William." She went into the house. "But almost."

" 'William' now, is it?" he said. "It's pretty early in the day for your heavy artillery."

William Somers Darling was named after the Somers who settled Bermuda by shipwreck in 1609. Sir George Somers had been on his way to Virginia when his *Sea Venture* struck Bermuda, which Darling regarded as a triumph of seamanship, since to hit Bermuda in the middle of a billion square miles of Atlantic Ocean was akin, he felt, to breaking one's leg by tripping over a paper clip on a football field. Still, Somers wasn't the first or the last: It was a safe guess that the twenty-two square miles of Bermuda were ringed by more than three hundred shipwrecks.

Most Bermudians, black and white, were named after one or another of the early settlers—Somers, Darling, Trimingham, Outerbridge, Tucker and a dozen more. The names harkened to history, rang with tradition. And yet, as if in rebellion against mother-country pretension, most Bermudians, black and white, soon cast off one or two of their names and assumed a nickname that had to do with something they looked like or something they'd done or some affliction.

Darling's nickname was "Buggywhip," in commemoration of the weapon with which his father had regularly thrashed him.

His friends called him Whip, and so did Charlotte, except when they argued or discussed something she considered too serious for levity. Then she called him William.

He was a fisherman, or, rather, he had been; now he was an ex-fisherman, for being a fisherman in Bermuda had become about as practical a profession as trying to be a ski instructor in the Congo. It was hard to make a living catching something that wasn't there.

They could live comfortably if not lavishly on twenty or twenty-five thousand dollars a year. They owned the house—it had been in his family, free and clear, since before the American Revolution. Upkeep, including cooking gas and insurance and electricity, cost five or six thousand dollars a year. Boat maintenance, which he and his mate, Mike Newstead, did themselves, cost another six or seven thousand dollars. Food and clothing and all the other magical incidentals that appeared from nowhere and ate money, consumed the rest.

But twenty thousand dollars might as well have been a million, because he wasn't making it. This year was half gone, and so far he'd made less than seven thousand dollars.

His daughter, Dana, was working downtown in an accounting firm, making good money instead of going to college, and she tried to help. Darling had refused, more brusquely than he meant to but unable to articulate the confusion of love and shame that his child's offer had triggered in him.

For a while, Dana had succeeded in stealing some of their bills from their mailbox and paying them herself. When, inevitably, she had been discovered and confronted, she had advanced the matter-of-fact defense that since the house was going to be hers one day, she saw no reason why she shouldn't contribute to its maintenance, especially since the alternative was for them to go to the bank for mortgage money, which would only burden her with payments later on.

The argument had slipped away from reason into dark regions of trust and mistrust and had ended in hurt and anger.

Maybe Charlotte was right. Maybe things *were* that bad. Darling had seen a folder from the bank in a pile of mail on the kitchen table, but before he could ask about it, it had vanished, and he had put it out of his mind. But now he forced himself to wonder: Was she already talking about mortgages or loans? Would they have to let the bank get its hooks into them?

No. He wouldn't let it happen. There had to be ways. The Newport-Bermuda race was coming up in ten days, and a friend in the dive business was overbooked for charters during the layover and had asked Darling to pick up a few for him. They'd be good for a thousand dollars apiece, maybe five thousand in all.

Then there was the aquarium retainer, which paid his fuel costs in exchange for his bringing them exotic animals he fished up from the deep. At four dollars a gallon he burned up thirty-two dollars' worth of fuel every hour he was away from the dock. The aquarium also paid a bonus if he caught something spectacular. He never knew what he'd catch. There were common things down there, like little toothless sharks with catlike eyes, and rare things, like anglerfish, which lured their prey with bioluminescent dorsal stalks and ate it with needle teeth that seemed to be made of crystal. He knew that in the abyss there were unknown critters, too, animals no one had ever seen. Those were the challenge.

Finally, there was always the chance—about as long as winning the Irish Sweepstakes, but never mind, a chance—that he'd find a shipwreck with some goodies on it.

In the kitchen, he ate a banana while he warmed up some of last night's barracuda. There were two barometers on the wall, and he consulted both. One was a standard aneroid instrument with two pointers, one of which you set by hand, the other responding to atmospheric pressure. He tapped the glass. No change.

The other barometer was a tube of shark-liver oil. In good weather the oil was clear, a light amber color. In times of change or dropping pressure, the oil clouded. His faith was in the shark-oil barometer, for it wasn't a machine, and he distrusted machines. Machines were made by man, and man was a chronic screwup. Nature rarely made mistakes.

The oil was clear.

He decided to go to sea. Maybe there was a robust grouper out there waiting to be caught, a wanderer from times gone by. A hundred-pound fish could net him four or five hundred dollars. Maybe he'd run into a school of tuna.

Maybe . . .

Darling's mate, Mike Newstead, showed up a little after seven. Darling liked to joke that a geneticist would have prized Mike as the ultimate Bermudian, for he contained every ethnic strain ever represented in the colony. He had the short, curly hair of a black, the dark red skin of an Indian—a memento of eighteenth-century Tories bringing Mohawk Indians to the island as slaves—the bright blue eyes of an Englishman (but almond-shaped like an Asian's), and the taciturn resignation of a Portuguese. He was thirty-six, five years younger than Darling, but he looked ageless. His face had always been sharp-featured and deeply furrowed, as if hacked from some mountain stone. A stranger might have guessed his age at anything from thirty to fifty.

Some people still referred to him, behind his back, as Tutti-Frutti, but nobody called him that to his face anymore, for he stood six foot four and weighed well over 220 pounds, not a gram of which was fat. Though Mike was slow to anger, he was said to possess an explosive temper that was kept in check by his diminutive Portuguese wife, and by Darling, whom he loved.

Darling considered him the perfect mate. Mike didn't like to make decisions, but rather preferred to be told what to do. He responded instantly and unquestioningly to commands—as long as he respected his commander. He didn't talk much—he barely spoke, in fact—and if he had any opinions, he kept them to himself. He communicated most intimately and joyfully with Darling's most hated enemies: machines. Utterly unschooled, he seemed to intuit the workings of engines and motors, be they powered by diesel oil, gasoline, kerosene, air or electricity. He talked to them, soothed them, cajoled them and seduced them into doing what he wanted.

Darling poured Mike some coffee, and they went outside and stood on the dock and watched a cormorant wheeling over the bay in search of food.

"I guess we'll go pull the aquarium's traps," Darling said. "We leave 'em down too long, critters might die or get eaten . . . traps could break away."

"Aye."

"Might take along some bait . . . just in case."

Mike nodded, finished his coffee and went to the freezer in the toolshed to fetch some mackerel for bait.

Darling boarded the boat and started the big Cummings diesel and let it warm up.

The *Privateer* was a shrimp dragger that Darling had bought at a yard in Houma, Louisiana, and had converted to an all-purpose Bermuda workboat. Her name back then had been *Miss Daisy,* but he had known at first sight she was not a Miss Daisy. She was big and broad and strong, steel-plated, steel-bulkheaded, steel-decked, a safe, stable platform that rode good weather comfortably and challenged bad weather with defiance, slamming into the seas as if daring them to hole her or pop her rivets.

She'll knock you down, he'd say, but she'll never drown you.

She had a dry and roomy house, two compressors, two generators and racks for twenty scuba tanks.

Darling was as superstitious as the next man, but he defended himself against the offense of changing the boat's name by declaring that since she had been mis-named to begin with, all he had done was give her her right name.

Still, just to be on the safe side, on the bulkhead inside the wheelhouse he had nailed a little obeah figurine from Antigua, and in times of trial—such as the day when a small cyclone made up directly over Bermuda and the wind went from 8 to 120 knots in five minutes and blew like the howling hounds of hell for an hour—he'd give it a rub.

Mike hopped aboard and cast off fore and aft. Darling put the boat in gear and eased out of Mangrove Bay and around the point to Blue Cut.

Settling himself onto a hatch cover in the stern, Mike muttered at a recalcitrant pump motor as he cradled it in his lap.

Darling had set the aquarium's line to the northwest, about six miles offshore, in five hundred fathoms of water. He could have found five hundred fathoms closer on the south shore, for there the reefs ended and deep water began only a mile or two from land. But for some reason the creatures that interested the aquarium seemed to live only off the northwest edge.

Now, as they cruised among the reefs, the water was calm but with enough of a ripple to cut the glare and give definition to the different colors of the corals, which gave Darling leave to wander away from the cut and thread his way through the high heads. There was truth to the old rule that the darker something was, the deeper it was, so as long as he could see the yellow villains beneath the surface, he could avoid them.

Standing on the flying bridge, cooled by the northwest breeze and warmed by the young sun, Whip Darling felt himself a happy man. He could forget, for a moment, that he didn't have any money, and could dream dreams of vast wealth. He allowed himself to fantasize about stacks of silver coins and serpentine chains of gold. Sure, it was fantasy, but it was reality, too, it had been known to happen: the Tucker treasure, the Fisher treasure from the *Atocha,* the billion-dollar bonanza from the *Central America.* Who could say it couldn't happen again?

And gold and silver weren't the only treasures waiting to be discovered. There were animals, unknown and unimagined, especially in the deep, that might change people's ideas about everything from biology to evolution, that might give clues to cures for everything from arthritis to cancer. Finding one or two of these creatures wouldn't fill Darling's pocketbook, but they were the things that nourished his spirit.

His gaze drifted from the white sand holes to the crevices in patches of reef, and always his eyes searched for the telltale signs of a shipwreck that could be as old as the time of the first James.

Nobody knew when the first ship had come to grief on the Bermuda volcano: at least as far back as Elizabeth, because there was evidence that a hapless Spaniard had passed an unplanned holiday there during the reign of the Virgin Queen. The man had spent a lot of time and trouble carving an inscription on a rock that was still legible: F.T. 1543.

Bermuda had always been a ship trap, and it still was, even with all the modern miracles like RDF, loran and satellite navigation, because the volcano, albeit extinct, protruded from the bottom of the sea like a wand full of electromagnetic anomalies. Machines, electronic or magnetic, seized up and went berserk around Bermuda. Nothing worked, not reliably. Compasses reeled back and forth like drunks. A mariner who asked a loran where he was might well be told he was in the mountains above Barcelona.

The whims of the Bermuda volcano helped spawn the legends of the Bermuda Triangle, for when the mind of man got hold of a nugget of truth and twisted it into a pretzel of fancy, it conjured up everything from Atlantis to UFOs to omnivorous monsters living in the core of the planet.

Darling didn't object to people indulging themselves in nonsense about the Bermuda Triangle, but it seemed to him a waste of time. If people would make an effort to learn about the wonders that *did* exist, he thought, their appetite for dragons would be well satisfied. Seventy percent of the earth's surface was covered by water, and ninety-five percent of that seventy percent had never been explored by anybody. Instead, man kept spending billions of dollars to explore places like Mars and Neptune, to a point where it was an established fact that we already knew more about the back side of the moon than we did about three-quarters of our own home. Crazy.

Even he—a nobody in a tiny, pissant corner of no-where—had in his twenty-five years on the ocean seen enough to know that the sea sheltered ample dragons to fuel the nightmares of the entire human race: thirty-foot sharks that lived in the mud, crabs as big as motorcars, finless fish with heads like horses, viper eels that ate anything including each other, fish that went fishing with little lanterns that hung down off their eyebrows, and so on.

These days, the Bermuda ship trap snared one or two victims every couple of years, usually a Liberia- or Panama-registered tanker, owned by a partnership of dentists or podiatrists from someplace like Altoona, Pa., whose Taiwanese captain spoke not a word of English. He would leave Norfolk, say, and set his course for the Straits of Gibraltar and turn on his automatic pilot. Then he'd go below to drink tea or have a nap or get a shiatsu massage, without bothering to notice an insignificant blip on his chart some six hundred miles to the east of North Carolina.

A couple of nights later, the airwaves would suddenly be flooded with S.O.S. calls. Sometimes, if the night was still and clear, Darling had only to walk out his back door and look to the north or northwest, and there on the horizon would be the lights of the stranded vessel.

His first thought always was, Lord, don't let her be laden with oil. His second was, If she has got oil, Lord, don't let her have a hole in her.

Back in the old days, the reefs were capturing so many ships that an industry arose of people who made their living rowing out and salvaging stricken ships. Some weren't content to wait; they wanted to make their luck, and they'd wave phony lights to lure ships onto the reefs.

Darling had always been amused by what he regarded as a nice irony: Mariners had made Bermuda a ship trap. They could have avoided Bermuda; the trouble was, they needed it.

Until the 1780s, there was no such thing as reliable

longitudinal navigation. Sailors could tell their latitude by the angle of the sun off the horizon, had been doing it for a thousand years with cross-staffs, astrolabes, octants and sextants. But to tell where they were on the east-west axis they needed an accurate—truly accurate—chronometer. And there wasn't one.

Bermuda was a known fixed point in the ocean, and once they found it, they knew exactly where they were. And so, they would leave the West Indies or Hispaniola or Havana and sail north in the Gulf Stream, then northeast, until they reached 32 degrees north latitude. Then they would turn east and look for Bermuda, which would give them the course to set for home.

But if they ran into a storm, with winds so fierce and seas so high that they couldn't see, or if there was a fog, or if their navigator was a bit addled, by the time they finally did see Bermuda, the chances were they would be *on* Bermuda.

Charlotte had once read Darling a line a poet wrote: ". . . many a midnight ship and all its shrieking crew." He liked the words, because they spawned in him a vision of what it must have been like aboard one of the old-timers facing doom: sailing along, safe as a bird on the wing, the sounder up in the bow dropping his lead and getting no bottom, then all of a sudden—what's that?—the sound of surf—*surf?* how can there be surf in the middle of the ocean?—and they strain their eyes but they can't see, and the boom of the surf grows louder—and then the sounding lead does find a bottom, and there's that moment of horror when they know. . . .

Today, Darling saw no signs of shipwreck in the shallow water, but what he did see—for it was all he saw—drew the happiness out of him like a syringe pulling blood: one parrotfish, a needlelike garfish tail-walking across the surface, half a dozen flying fish that spooked away from the boat's bow, and a few meandering breams.

Reefs that had once teemed with life were as empty as a train station after a bomb scare.

He felt as if he were witnessing a funeral for a way of life . . . his way of life.

Soon the shallows sloped away, to forty feet, sixty feet, a hundred feet, and he stopped looking at the bottom and began to search for his buoy.

It was where he had left it, which half surprised him, because over the past year or two desperate fishermen had begun to abandon the code of honor that said, No man touches another man's pots. And even without human intervention, the baits were so deep that some great survivor could have taken and run with them—a six-gill shark, perhaps, or a big-eyed thresher—and dragged the traps miles away before breaking loose.

"Coming up on it," Darling called down to Mike, who put his pump motor aside and reached for the boat hook.

The orange-and-white buoy slid down the side of the boat, and when it reached the stern, Mike snagged it and pulled it aboard and walked it forward and wrapped the rope around the winch.

Darling put the boat in neutral, letting it wallow in the gentle sea, and came down from the flying bridge.

"Go you," Mike said, and Darling pushed the lever and turned on the winch, and as the rope began to come up, Mike fed it into a fifty-five-gallon plastic drum.

They had put down three thousand feet of polyethylene rope, with the buoy on top and twenty-five pounds of sash weights to keep it on the bottom. Starting at two thousand feet, they had attached, at every hundred-foot interval, a twenty-foot length of forty-eight-strand stainless-steel airplane cable, and at the end of each cable was one of the aquarium's gimmicks. Some were small wire boxes, some were contraptions of fine-mesh net. Most had bits of gurry inside to attract whatever creatures lived down in the dark. Because Darling didn't know—nobody knew—what those creatures might be or what they liked to eat, he had indulged his theory about ocean scavengers—whatever stinks most works best—and had baited the traps with the rankest, rottenest flesh he could find.

Into a few of the traps he had put no bait at all, just Cyalume chemical lights, following another of his theories—that light was such a novelty in a world of perpetual night that some animals might be drawn to it out of curiosity.

His hope was to bring the animals up alive and keep them alive in a cold-water tank on the boat. Every week or so, a scientist from the aquarium would come to examine the catch, and the creatures that were rare or unknown he would take back to study in the laboratory in Flatts.

Darling estimated that twenty percent of the animals survived the trip and the transfer to the aquarium—not a great number, perhaps, but as good a cheap way as possible to gather new species.

And it paid his fuel bills, which really mattered these days.

Darling held the lever and kept his eye on the rope. It was taut, squeaking and spitting water, but it should be, considering the weight of half a mile of rope and twenty-five pounds of lead and the traps and the cables and the baits.

He put his foot on the bulwark to steady himself against the wallow and looked over the side, down into the blue gloom, hoping to see some big fish cruising by.

Not bloody likely, he thought. If there were any such left in the sea, they had long since departed Bermuda.

"Something's not right," Mike said. He had a hand on the rope, feeling the tension with his fingertips.

"What?"

"She's stuttery. Feel." Mike passed the rope to Darling and stepped back to take the winch lever from him.

Darling felt the rope. It was trembling erratically. There was a thud to it, like an engine misfiring.

The rope was marked in hundred-fathom sections, and as the third mark passed, Darling held up a hand, telling Mike to slow the winch, and bent over the side to see the first trap come into view. If it was fouled around the rope, he wanted to clear it before it banged against the boat. Some of the tiny abyssal animals were so delicate that any slight trauma would kill them.

He saw the glint of the first stainless-steel swivel holding the length of cable, saw the cable, and then . . . nothing.

The trap was gone.

Impossible. The only animal large enough to take it was a shark, but there was nothing in the trap to interest a shark. And if one of them had taken a run at it, he would have taken the whole rig with him, rope and all. There was no way a shark could have broken the cable.

He let the winch bring the cable up to him, and he unsnapped it from the rope and looked at the end. Then he held it up to Mike.

"Busted?" Mike asked.

"No. If she'd popped, the strands'd be all frizzy, like a head of hair when you stick your finger in a light socket. Look: These strands are still as tight as in the factory."

"So?"

Darling held the end of the cable close to his eyes. It had been sheared off, cut as clean as if by a scalpel. There were no gnaw marks, no worry marks.

"Bit," he said. "Bit clean through."

"Bit?"

Darling looked out over the water. "What in the name of Christ has a mouth that can bite through forty-eight strands of stainless steel?"

Mike said nothing. Darling gestured for him to start the winch again, and in a moment the second cable came up.

"Gone," he said, for that trap had vanished, too, that cable bitten through.

"Gone," he said again as the next cable appeared, and the next and the next. They were all gone.

Now he saw the sash weights coming, and there was something strange about them, so he told Mike to stop the winch, and he pulled the last of the rope up by hand.

"Sweet Jesus," he said. "Look here."

One of the traps had been wrapped around the weights, embedded into them so hard it was as if everything had been melted together in a furnace.

They pulled the gnarled mass up and set it on the deck; it was a confusion of steel reinforcing rod, wire and lead.

Mike stared at it for a long moment, then said, "Jesus, Whip. What kind of sumbitch do that?"

"No man, for sure," said Darling. "No animal, neither. At least, no animal I've ever seen."

# 6

THEY DIDN'T SPEAK as they disassembled the rig, coiling the lengths of cable and securing them with twist ties, discarding the chemical lights, jamming the final fathoms of rope into the plastic drum.

Darling was running through the catalog of creatures in his head, trying to think of what might have the power and the inclination to destroy that rig.

He even considered Mike's thought that it might have been a man, some fisherman who was angry, resentful, jealous—although what Whip Darling had these days that anybody'd be jealous of he couldn't imagine. Or maybe just somebody bent on destruction for its own sake. No. He didn't think that any man could do it, and he was certain that nobody'd bother. There was no logic to it.

So what did that leave? What could have bitten through a cable woven of forty-eight strands of stainless steel?

Part of him hoped that they'd never know.

He wasn't a stranger to the fact that Nature had a dark side. Once, more than two decades ago, he had been crew on a tanker off South Africa when, out of nowhere—an easy sea and a steady barometer—had come a rogue wave that had put a hundred-foot wall of water in front of the ship. The captain had never seen such a thing, no one on board ever had, and because they didn't know what to do they steamed directly into the wall of water, which closed over the ship, drowning it, sending it plunging to the bottom. If Darling hadn't been sent up to the crow's nest three minutes earlier to fetch something, he would have gone down with the ship. Instead, he had washed overboard and drifted on a hatch cover for two days until a coastal freighter picked him up.

Another time, in Australia, he and some mates had jumped ship after discovering that the captain was addicted to ouzo and boys, and had embarked on a feckless treasure hunt in the outback. They had met up with a family on holiday in a little caravan, and one afternoon they came back to find the whole family dead, killed by a taipan, a snake that attacks for the sake of attacking, that kills for the sake of the kill.

Darling had gradually concluded that Nature wasn't to be trusted; often enough, she revealed a sinister side.

Mike had had no such experiences, and he was not happy with the unknown. He didn't mind so much not having answers himself, but he didn't like it when Whip didn't have them. He hated to hear Whip say, "I don't know." He preferred the security of knowing that somebody was in charge, somebody knowledgeable.

So now he was worried.

Darling saw the signs of anxiety. Mike refused to look him in the eye; he was coiling the lengths of cable too meticulously. Darling knew he would have to ease the man's misery.

"I take it back," Darling said. "I think it was a shark."

"What makes you think so?" Mike asked, wanting to believe, but needing some convincing.

"Had to be. I just remembered, *National Geographic,* some sharks can put out twenty tons per square inch when they bite. That'd be more than enough to cut those cables."

"Why wouldn't he run with it?"

"Wouldn't have to. No hooks in it. He just swims round and round and bites the wires off one by one." Darling was even beginning to convince himself.

Mike thought for a moment, then said, "Oh."

Darling looked up at the sky. He felt an odd desire, a desire to quit and go home. But the sun was still climbing, it wasn't yet noon, and he'd already burned up twenty-five or thirty dollars' worth of fuel. If they went home now, he'd be out of pocket fifty bucks with nothing to show for it but an awkward explanation to the aquarium. And so he forced himself to say, "What say we try for a day's pay?"

Mike said, "Good enough," and together they began to rig a deep line with some big baited hooks.

Maybe they'd catch something worth selling, maybe just something worth eating. Even if they just caught *some*thing, it would be better than heading back to the dock and acknowledging another day's defeat.

The thought depressed him. These days, the act of fishing itself, which once had been enjoyable even when he was skunked, had become depressing. He likened it to journeying back to the place where you were raised, where you had had good times and good memories, and finding that it had been paved over and made into a parking lot.

All fishing did nowadays was remind him of how good things used to be.

He had read all the old accounts of what Bermuda had been like when the first settlers arrived. The island was overrun then by birds and pigs. The birds belonged, and some of them, like the cahows, were so dumb that they'd land on people's heads and wait to be grabbed and put into the cook pot. The pigs didn't belong. Some had been put ashore by ships' captains, in anticipation of a time when castaways would need nourishment. Others swam ashore from shipwrecks, and they thrived on birds and eggs.

But what had entranced the old-timers, what accounted for the almost religious enthusiasm in their accounts, was the sea life. Everything was around Bermuda, everything from turtles to whales, and in numbers inconceivable to people from the Old World, where even by the seventeenth century a great many species had been slaughtered almost to extinction.

Darling wasn't one to indulge in weepy bushwa about the good old days. He saw change as inevitable and destruction as part of it, especially when man got into the mix, and that was the way things were.

But what did infuriate him, what shamed and disgusted him, was the change he had seen in Bermuda in only twenty years. By his reckoning, Bermuda had been ruined in the lifetime of a house cat.

In the late sixties and early seventies, he could still go out on the reefs and catch his dinner. There were lobsters under every rock, schools of parrotfish, angelfish, triggerfish, surgeonfish, damselfish, hogfish, porgies, even occasional groupers. When he worked on a shipwreck, goatfish dug in the sand beside him, rays skittered across the bottom, and there was always the tiny danger that some nearsighted wrasse would take a bite from his earlobe. More than once, reef sharks had chased him off a wreck, nibbling at the tips of his flippers.

Just over the edge in deeper water were whole colonies of groupers—Nassau groupers, spotted groupers, black groupers and now and then a 500- or 600-pound jewfish. There were moray eels and tiger sharks, bull sharks and hinds and snappers. Turtles poked their heads up like little children swimming on the surface.

And in the deep, to put out a slick and drift was an invitation to excitement. Wahoo fought with barracudas for the bait. Bonitos and Alison tuna swarmed around the back of the boat. Billfish cruised the slick, their dorsal fins cutting the water like scythes, and the big, fast pelagic sharks flashed beneath the boat and showed off the shiny blue of their backs.

A good day was a thousand pounds of rockfish and a thousand more of tuna, and the hotels took pride in listing the prime special of the day as fresh Bermuda fish.

No more. Some of the hotels still listed Bermuda fish, but not with pride, for what they served now, all that was left, was trash, the fish that had survived because nothing wanted them. If a fisherman caught a grouper of any size, it was an event that made the paper.

Bermuda's ocean was one step from being as lifeless as the western eddies of Long Island Sound.

Darling listened with bitter amusement to the explanations of the fishermen. Pollution! they cried, and to that he replied: Bullshit.

What had killed Bermuda's fishing industry—he believed, he knew, he felt he could document—was fishermen. Not only Bermuda fishermen, but the species in general. People. People who weren't content with making a living and wanted to make a killing, treating the ocean as if it were a deep pit to be strip-mined. He had even given them a scientific name: *Homo assholus*.

Well, they'd made a killing all right, but not the way they thought.

And the chief villain was a piece of equipment they had invented: the fish trap.

In times past, fishermen had *fished*—with hand lines—and what limited their catch was their grit. They stopped when they fell down in a stupor, their hands swollen like a convention of sausages.

Then someone thought of putting down wire cages with bait inside and buoys to the surface. The fish would swim in and, thanks to the construction of the traps, not be able to find their way out again.

Soon, everybody was putting traps down, as many as they wanted. There was supposed to be a limit, but nobody paid any attention to it.

And did they catch fish! So many fish that they threw away all but the best—dead or dying, but who cared?—and if the price went down because there were too many, why, no sweat, they just caught more.

Darling had never used traps, didn't like them, not from some high moral purpose but because to him trapping wasn't fishing, it was killing and scooping up, not entertaining in the least. And, he thought, if you can't enjoy what you do for a living, then find something else to do. He had no intention of ending his days sitting in the yard with a cat in his lap and a bird on his shoulder, telling visitors that he had lived a long life and had hated every minute of it.

The first problem with the traps was that they did their job too well. They caught everything—big, small, young, old, pregnant, whatever. A hand-line fisherman could pick and choose among his catch and put back fish that were too small or too young or too loaded with roe or simply not what he was fishing for. But with traps, by the time the fish had been jammed together in the wire for a few days, and bruised and shocked and scarred and abused by one another and by the cage itself, they had little chance of surviving even if the fishermen took the trouble to put them back, which most of them didn't.

The second problem was lost traps. If the buoy broke away or the rope chafed off or a storm sea pushed the trap over the edge into the deep and it sank beyond reach, the trap would keep on killing. The fish inside would die and become bait for more fish, which would come in and be trapped and die and become bait for more fish, forever and ever, amen.

Everybody had a remedy. They tried biodegradable string to hold the traps' doors shut, even biodegradable doors, on the theory that if a trap got lost, eventually the material would rot away and the door would open and the fish could get out. But "eventually" was so long in coming that whole generations of animals could be wiped out before the doors would magically pop open.

Darling had found lost traps on the bottom that looked like a Tokyo subway car at rush hour, jam-packed with everything from eels to parrotfish to octopus to crabs. The sight saddened and enraged him, for while he was not a sentimentalist about death, this was death to no purpose whatever—an ultimate waste. More than once, he had stopped the boat and lost time and money diving down to deep traps and slashing off the floating lines and cutting away the doors with wire snips. The perplexed, exhausted and wounded prisoners—some with scales scraped away by the wire, some with open sores from frantic fights—would meander within the now-open trap for several moments, as if unable to believe their sudden good fortune, and only when he moved away would they seem to share some silent cue and burst free.

Finally, in 1990, about ten years too late, the Bermuda government had outlawed trap fishing and paid off the island's seventy-eight commercial fishermen—richly enough, Darling thought, though the fishermen complained loudly that the amounts were too paltry to compensate them for the loss of a God-given right.

The sanctimonious outcry against the loss of rights infuriated Darling. *What* rights? Where was it written that any man had a right to kill off all the fish in Bermuda? By such logic, he felt, bank robbery should be a protected profession: If a man has a right to feed his family, and if what he does costs an insurance company a few hundred thousand dollars a year, well, that's the cost of freedom.

Now that traps were outlawed, the hope was that the fish would come back, but Darling had his doubts. Bermuda was not like the Bahamas, a chain of seven hundred islands that had a chance to replenish each other if one or another was fished out—though some Bahamians seemed even more hell-bent than Bermudians on destroying themselves. They had taken to fishing with Clorox: pump a little into a reef, and all the fish and lobsters come out in the open where they're easy to scoop up. Of course, Clorox killed the reef, too, all of it, forever. But a man had to make a living.

Bermuda was a single rock in the middle of nowhere. What was there was there, and what wasn't never would be.

And as if man weren't working fast enough to turn Bermuda into a wasteland, Nature was throwing her wrecking ball at the island. Darling had a friend, Marcus Sharp, stationed at the U.S. Navy base, who knew something about meteorology and had showed him some NOAA figures concluding that the water temperature around Bermuda had risen by two degrees in the last twenty years.

Some scientists said it was because of the burning down of the Amazon jungle and the burning up of too much fossil fuel. Others said it was part of a natural rhythm, like the coming and going of the ice ages. But the reason wasn't as important as the fact: It was happening.

To a man in a city, two degrees might be nothing. To corals in the sea, two degrees spelled the difference between life and death. Ten percent of Bermuda's corals were already dead. Darling saw the evidence every day—big patches of bleached reef, like a boneyard. If ten percent became twenty percent, if then *all* the corals disappeared, gradually Bermuda would erode away, for corals were the island's shield against the open ocean.

Coral polyps weren't the only animals affected by the temperature rise. Some creatures had vanished, some had gone deeper, and some new ones had sprung up. There was a new burrower, for example—a microscopic worm or louse that lived in the sand. When divers disturbed the sand, the burrowers were liberated, and they fixed themselves to human skin and dug in. They excreted a poison that caused pustulant sores and an infernal itching that lasted for a week.

The last horse in the troika of destruction was the foreigners. While Bermudians were killing off their reef fish, the Japanese and the Koreans were massacring the deep-water species. They were out there every day, setting thirty-mile-long nets to intercept the migrators, and they were getting everything: tuna and billfish, mackerel and wahoos, sharks and bonitos and jacks and porpoises.

Those fishermen who didn't use nets used long lines— miles and miles of line, with baited hooks every few feet, which accomplished the same thing: They killed everything, without selection or discrimination.

Darling thought of it as equality of slaughter.

Fishing had once given Darling a feeling of vitality, an appreciation of and wonder at the richness and diversity of life.

Now all it made him think of was death.

It took them an hour to bait and set their deep line. When it was down, Darling snapped a rubber buoy into a loop at the end of the line and tossed it overboard, letting it drift with the tide as the breeze pushed the boat to the southeast.

Mike opened a tin of Polish ham and a bottle of Coke and took them aft and sat on the hatch cover and tinkered some more with the pump motor.

Darling went into the wheelhouse and ate an apple while he listened to the radio to hear if anyone was catching anything anywhere. One captain reported that he had raised a shark. Another, a charter-boater way out on Challenger Bank, had caught a few Alison tuna. No one else had seen a thing.

The sun had just begun to slide westward off its peak when they pulled in the line. They took turns—one on the winch, the other feeling the line—and exchanged hopeful guesses.

"Feel him?"

"Coupla coneys."

"Gummy shark, maybe."

"Tapioca fish."

"I say a pair of snappers."

"Don't you wish. . . ."

The eight hooks had caught two small red snappers, their eyes popped and their bladders squeezed out through their mouths by the sudden loss of pressure. Darling tossed them into the bait box and looked at the sky, then at the sea. Not a fin, not a feeding bird. Nothing. "Well, then, to hell with it," he said, and he wiped his hands on his pants and went forward to start the engine.

He was about to step inside the cabin when he heard Mike say, "Look there." He was pointing to the southern sky.

A navy helicopter was heading their way from the south.

"Wonder where he's going," Darling said.

"Nowhere. They never do. Just loggin' time."

"Maybe." Darling waved as the helicopter passed overhead and continued northward. Mike was probably right. Except for occasional search-and-rescue jobs, there was so little work for navy pilots that they often had to fly back and forth around the island just to keep up their proficiency and their flying hours.

But this pilot wasn't idling, he was heading north into the vast nowhere, and with speed on too.

"I don't know," Darling said. "Unless he's late for supper up in Nova Scotia, I'd say he's on a mission with some clout to it."

He turned into the wheelhouse and picked up the radio microphone.

"Huey One . . . Huey One . . . Huey One . . . this is *Privateer* . . . come back. . . ."

# 7

LIEUTENANT MARCUS SHARP had been shooting baskets that Friday—fantasizing himself in a *manó a mano* with Larry Bird—when the operations officer called him inside and said that a British Airways pilot on his way to Miami had picked up an emergency signal twenty miles north of Bermuda.

The pilot hadn't seen anything, the ops officer said, which wasn't surprising considering that he was traveling more than five hundred miles an hour more than six miles above the ocean, but the signal had been loud and clear on his VHF radio. Someone was in trouble down there.

The guys in the tower at the naval air station had

checked with Miami, Atlanta, Raleigh/Durham, Balti-
more and New York to see if any planes were overdue.
Then ops had called Bermuda Harbour Radio and
asked for any reports of vessels missing, overdue or in
distress.

Everything seemed copacetic, but they couldn't take
a chance—they had to follow up on the signal.

Sharp had quickly showered and pulled on his flight
suit, while the operations officer had rounded up a co-
pilot and a rescue diver for him and made sure one of
the helicopters was gassed up. Then he had scribbled
down the coordinates reported in by the B.A. pilot,
stuffed a chocolate bar and some gum into his pockets
and trotted across the apron to the waiting chopper.

As he had lifted off from Kindley Field and banked
around to the north, for the first time in weeks Marcus
Sharp felt alive. His juices were flowing, his pulse was
up, he was interested, he had a goal to focus on. Something was happening—not much, not exactly what he'd
call action, but *any*thing was better than the nothing
that had become his routine.

Maybe, he thought as he corrected his course to the
northwest, maybe they'd actually find someone in the
water, someone in danger. Maybe they'd even have to
accomplish something . . . for a change.

Sharp's problem wasn't only that he was bored. It
was more complicated than that, worse than boredom:
He had a weird, amorphous sense that he was dying, not
physically but in other, less tangible, ways. He had always needed adventure, courted danger, thrived on—
felt he could not survive without—change. And life had
always provided nourishment enough.

The navy recruiter at Michigan State had recognized
the need in Sharp for action and had played to it. Here
was a kid who had broken both legs—one skiing, one
hang-gliding—and yet had persisted in both sports; a

certified scuba diver since the age of fourteen whose hero was not Jacques Cousteau but Peter Gimbel, the man who had made the first underwater films on great white sharks and the wreck of the *Andrea Doria;* a dreamer who wanted to build an ultralite airplane and fly it across the country; a restless quester whose ambition was to affirm himself not by accumulating wealth but by testing his own limits. On the navy's psychological-profile test, he had listed three men he admired: Ernest Hemingway, Theodore Roosevelt and James Bond—all "because they were doers, not observers, they *lived* their lives." (Sharp noted that, like him, the navy wasn't persnickety about making distinctions between legend and reality.)

The recruiter persuaded Marcus that the navy offered him a chance to spend his career doing what others could hope to do only on occasional vacations. He could pick his specialty, change it regularly, "stretch his envelope" on the sea and in the sky and, in the process—almost incidentally—contribute to the nation's defense.

He signed up before graduation and, in June of 1983, he entered Officer Candidate School in Newport, Rhode Island.

The first few years met all his expectations. He became expert in underwater demolition. He qualified as a helicopter pilot. He served a stint of sea duty and actually saw combat, in Panama. When his mind caught up with his body and he developed adult interests, he spent a year studying meteorology and oceanography on an exchange tour in Halifax.

Life for Sharp was rich, varied and fun.

But in the past year and a half, variety and fun had ceased to satisfy.

Part of his problem, he knew, was an unwillingness to confront the specter of becoming a grown-up. He was twenty-nine and hadn't given much thought to thirty, certainly hadn't been afraid of it, until a few months before, when he had been rejected in his application to join the navy's elite, high-risk, high-demand amphibious guerrillas, the SEALs. He was too old.

But at the core of his discontent lay the only thing close to tragedy that Marcus Sharp had ever known.

He had fallen in love with a United Airlines flight attendant, a skier and scuba diver, and they had been all over the world together. They were young and immortal. Marriage was a possibility but not a necessity. They lived in and for the present.

And then one September day in 1989, they were snorkeling off a beach in North Queensland. They had heard routine warnings about dangerous animals, but they hadn't been worried. They had been swimming with sharks and rays and barracudas; they could take care of themselves. The sea was a world not of danger but of adventure and discovery.

They had seen a turtle swimming by, and they had followed it, trying to keep up with it. The turtle had slowed and opened its mouth, as if to eat something, though they saw nothing, and they glided up to it, entranced by its grace and efficiency in the water.

Karen had reached out to touch it, to stroke its shell, and as Sharp watched she suddenly convulsed and arched her back and clawed at her breast. Her snorkel slipped from her mouth. Her eyes went wide and she screamed, tearing at her own flesh.

Sharp grabbed her and pulled her to the surface and tried to get her to speak, but all she could do was shriek.

By the time he got her to shore, she was dead.

The turtle had been feeding on sea wasps, box jellyfish all but invisible in the water, colonies of nematocysts so toxic that a brush with them could stop a human heart. And so it had.

When Karen had been buried in Indiana and Sharp's grief had begun to scar over, he had found himself possessed by darker thoughts, thoughts of the randomness of fate. It wasn't a matter of injustice or unfairness—he had never thought of life as fair or unfair; it simply *was*. But fate was capricious. They were not immortal; nothing was forever.

He had become plagued by the emptiness of his life, the lack of focus. He had done many things, but to no purpose.

He had an image of himself as a steel ball on a pinball machine, popping in and out of one hole after another, going nowhere.

The navy had given him the best billet available, a two-year tour in Bermuda—sunny, comfortable, undemanding and only two hours from the U.S. mainland. Quiet, however, was not what Sharp needed. He needed action, but now action alone wasn't enough: There had to be a point, a purpose to it.

In Bermuda, he had found nothing much to do except shuffle papers and occasionally fly around in a helicopter and hope that someone needed rescuing.

From time to time, he thought of quitting the navy, but he had no idea what he would do. Civilian life had few slots for helicopter pilots expert in blowing up bridges.

Meanwhile, he volunteered for any task that would keep his mind off himself.

He was heading northwest now, intending to set a search pattern from the northwest to the north to the northeast and then the east, all on the north side of the island. He turned his UHF radio to 243.0 and his VHF to 121.5, the two frequencies over which emergency equipment broadcast. He flew at five hundred feet.

Six miles off the island, where the reefs ended and the

water changed from dappled turquoise to deep ceru-
lean, he heard a beep—very faint, very distant, but persistent. He looked at the co-pilot, tapped his earphones,
and the co-pilot nodded and gave him a thumbs-up sign.
Sharp scanned his instruments, turning the helicopter
slowly from side to side until he found the direction in
which the beeping from his radio direction finder was
loudest. He took a bearing from the compass.

Then a voice came over his marine radio.

"Huey One . . . Huey One . . . Huey One . . . this is
*Privateer* . . . come back."

"*Privateer* . . . Huey One . . ." Sharp smiled. "Hey,
Whip . . . where you at?"

"Right underneath you, lad. Don't you keep your
eyes on the road?"

"Had my eyes on the future."

"Going for an outing?"

"B.A. pilot picked up an EPIRB signal a while ago.
You hear anything?"

"Not a peep. How far out?"

"Ten, fifteen miles. I've got it on one-twenty-one-five
now. Whatever it is, northwest wind's pushing it back
this way."

"Maybe I'll chase your wake."

Sharp hesitated, then said, "Okay, do that, Whip.
Who knows? Might use your help."

"Done and done, Marcus. *Privateer* standing by."

Good, Sharp thought. If there was a boat sinking out
there, Whip would arrive a lot faster than any vessel
summoned from the base. If it was an abandoned
boat, a lifeboat, say, SOP would call for him to put a
diver down to investigate. The weather was decent, but
putting a diver down from a helicopter in the open
ocean under any conditions involved risk. He wouldn't
hesitate to go himself, but he didn't relish putting a
nineteen-year-old down into the sea all alone. Whip

could check it out for him while he went in search of floaters. If they found people, alive or dead, he'd have to put the diver down, and he wanted the boy to be fresh.

Besides, maybe there'd be something worthwhile for Whip if nobody claimed it. A raft. A radio. A flare gun. Something worth selling or using, something to get Whip money or save him money. And Sharp knew Whip needed it.

Besides, Sharp thought, I owe him one.

One? Hell, he owed Whip Darling about a hundred.

Whip had saved Sharp's sanity, at a time when there was a better-than-even chance of his becoming a blob, an addict of entertainments like *Surf Nazis Must Die* and *Amazon Women on the Moon*. His weekends had become unbearable. He had dived with every commercial tour group on the island, ridden a motorbike around every square inch of the place, visited every fort and museum, spent money in every saloon—he had no moral objection to becoming a drunk, but he had no tolerance for liquor and didn't like the taste of it—and seen every movie in the base video store except those involving the ax murder of baby-sitters. He read for hours every day, till his eyes rebelled and his ass atrophied. He was on the brink of doing the unthinkable— taking up golf—when he met Whip at a base function.

He had listened, fascinated, to Whip's discourse on the techniques of discovering shipwrecks and had asked enough intelligent questions to secure an invitation to come out on the boat some Sunday . . . which had quickly become every Sunday and most Saturdays. As he listened to Whip, he learned, and, curiously, he found himself becoming ashamed of his education. For, here was a man with six years' schooling who had taught himself to be not just a fisherman and a diver but a historian and a biologist and a numismatist and . . . well, a walking encyclopedia of the sea.

Sharp had offered to contribute to the cost of Darling's fuel and been turned down; he had offered to help paint the boat and been accepted, which pleased him because it made him feel like a participant instead of a parasite. Then Whip had shown him photographs of what old shipwrecks looked like from the air, and suddenly—as if a door had cracked open, lighting a corner of his mind he had not known was there—he saw the prospect of new interests, new goals.

Whip taught him not to look for the classic fairy-tale image of a shipwreck—the ship upright and ready on its keel, sails rigged, tricorn-hatted skeletons sitting where they died gambling over a stack of doubloons. The old ships had been wooden, and, for the most part, the ones that hit Bermuda sank in shallow water. Storm seas broke them to pieces, and centuries of moving water had dispersed them and pressed them into the bottom, and the bottom had absorbed them and corals grew on them, taking the dead to their bosoms.

There were three main telltales, Whip had said, to a shipwreck on the bottom. When a ship was driven over the reefs—flung by the wind, shoved by a following sea—it would crush the reef, kill the fragile corals and leave a scrub mark that, from a couple of hundred feet in the air, would look like a giant tire track.

A sharp eye might see a cannon or two, overgrown and coral-encrusted and looking like not much more than an unlikely mass in an unnaturally straight line. There was truth to the old saying that nature doesn't like straight lines. But the presence of a cannon didn't always mean the ship itself was nearby, because when a vessel was in its last throes, often the crew would heave everything heavy overboard to keep her from capsizing. It was possible to find a cannon here, an anchor there, and no ship at all if the sea had carried her miles away before slamming her down and busting her to bits in her last resting place.

What *was* a dead giveaway—visible from the air but most difficult to identify—was a ballast pile, for Whip insisted that where a ship dropped her ballast was where she had died. Yes, her deck might have drifted away, or her rigging, carrying a survivor or two, but her heart and soul—her cargo, her treasure—lay with her ballast. Usually, the old-timers ballasted with river rocks from the Thames or the Ebro or one of the other rivers near their home ports. The rocks were smooth and round and small enough for a man to lift. Think of cobblestones, Whip told Sharp, because all the cobblestones in places like Nantucket had been ballast stones, carried in the bowels of a ship to keep her upright on her way over from England, then replaced with barrels of oil for the journey home.

So what Sharp conditioned himself to look for was a gathering of very round stones all piled together, often in a white sand hole between dark coral heads, for Whip had taught him that an old ship would have struck the coral head and stuck there until another sea came along and broke her loose and cast her innards into the sand, which would embrace them and cover them over.

Now Sharp never missed a chance to fly, and whenever he flew—whether supposedly to keep his hours up, or to train new pilots, or to test new equipment—he always kept an eye out for shipwrecks. He flew as low as possible, yawing back and forth to keep the sun's rays at a cutting angle through the shallow seas, and if one of his crew ever asked what the hell he was doing, he would reply with something vague like, Putting her through her paces.

So far, he had found two ballast piles, two shipwrecks. One, Whip said, had been explored in the sixties. One was new. They'd go have a dig on it one of these days.

The beeping was loud and regular now, and Sharp could see something yellow sliding up and down the rolling seas. He pushed the collective-power-control lever down, and dropped the helicopter to a hundred feet.

It was a raft, small and empty and apparently undamaged. He circled it, careful to stay high enough so that the downdraft from his rotors didn't start it spinning or capsize it off the top of a wave.

"*Privateer* . . . Huey One . . ."

"Yeah, Marcus . . ." came Whip's voice.

"It's a raft. Nobody aboard. Just a raft. Could've fallen off a boat. Some of those EPIRBs are salt-water activated."

"Whyn't you let me pick it up with my davit? I'll cruise around, see if there's any swimmers, then bring it to shore. Nobody has to get wet."

"You got it. It's three-four-oh from where you were. Should be here in an hour or so. Meantime, we'll set a search grid and swing back and forth till fuel sends us home."

"Roger that, Marcus."

"False alarm, I guess. But the land of the free and the home of the brave is grateful to you anyway, Whip."

"My pleasure. *Privateer* standing by. . . ."

# 8

MAYBE THE DAY isn't a dead loss after all," Darling said as he climbed the ladder to the flying bridge.

"Why's that?" Mike was stowing the last of the coiled wire leaders.

"Got us a chance to pick up a raft. If she's a Switlik and nobody's name's on her, there's a couple thousand, maybe more."

"Somebody'll claim it. They always do."

"Probably . . . the way our luck's been running."

They raised the raft in less than an hour, and Darling made a slow circle around it, studying it like a specimen on a laboratory slide.

"Switlik," he said, pleased.

"Looks brand-new off the shelf, like nobody was ever on it."

"That, or they were rescued right quick." Darling saw none of the normal signs that people had spent time in the raft: no dirt, no scuff marks from rubber shoes, no fish blood from anything they'd caught, no bits of clothing.

"Sharks got 'em?" Mike said.

Darling shook his head. "Shark would've bit through the rubber, collapsed one of the cells, maybe burred it with his skin. You'd see it."

"What, then?"

"Whale, maybe." Darling kept circling as he pondered that possibility. Killer whales had been known to attack rafts, dinghies, even big boats. Nobody knew why, because they'd never gone on and attacked the people; there had never been a true case of an orca eating a human being. Perhaps they just got to playing with a raft and, like a kid who had grown too fast, they didn't know their own strength.

Humpback whales had killed people, but always by accident. They had come up to rafts out of curiosity, to see what they were, and gotten underneath and given a flip with their tails, and people had been flung to death.

"No," Darling said, dismissing the thought. "Everything would be upside down and akimbo."

Mike said, "Could be she just slipped off the deck and fell in the ocean."

"Then what turned on the EPIRB?" Darling pointed to the Styrofoam-cased beacon. "That's not automatic. Somebody turned it on."

"Maybe a ship picked the folks up and they forgot to turn it off."

"And nobody bothered to report in to Bermuda?" Darling paused. "Gun to my head, I'd say their boat sank out from under 'em, and they tossed the raft in the sea and jumped for it and missed and drowned themselves."

Mike seemed to like that answer, so Darling didn't articulate the hazy idea he had of another option. No point in stirring up bad thoughts in Mike. Besides, speculation was usually bullshit.

"Well, the good news is," Darling said, "she's a brand-spanking-new Switlik, worth enough to keep the wolves at bay for a little while."

They snagged the raft with a grappling hook, fixed the rope to the block-and-tackle rig on the davit, turned on the winch and hauled it aboard.

Mike knelt down and poked around, opening the supply box in the bow, feeling under the rubber cells.

"Best turn off the EPIRB," Darling said as he removed the hook and coiled the rope. "Don't want a lot of pilots baffled by emergency signals when they should be caring for their hangovers."

Mike flicked the switch on the beacon and pushed the antenna back inside. He stood up. "Nothing. Nothing missing, nothing wrong."

"No." But something was bothering Darling, and he continued to stare at the raft, comparing the inventory of what he saw to what he knew he should be seeing.

The oar. That was it. There wasn't any. Every raft carried at least one oar, and this one had been meant to have oars; there were oarlocks. But no oar.

And then, as the boat shifted slightly, his eye was attracted to sunlight glinting off something on one of the rubber cells. He bent over and put his face close to the rubber. There were scratch marks, as if a knife had cut the rubber but hadn't gone all the way through, and around each scratch mark, shining in the sun, was a patch of some kind of slime. He touched his fingers to the slime and raised them to his nose.

"What?" Mike said.

Darling hesitated, then decided to lie. "Sunburn oil. Poor buggers were worried about their tans."

He had no idea what it was. It stank of ammonia.

Darling called Sharp on the radio and told him he had the raft and intended to keep searching, a bit farther to the north. A person in the water, alive or dead, had no sail area, so he or she wouldn't have traveled nearly as far as the raft had—might, in fact, have moved in the opposite direction from the raft, depending on the current.

And so they drove north for an hour—ten miles, more or less—then turned south and began to zigzag from southwest to southeast. Mike stood on the bow, his eyes on the nearby surface and the few feet below it, while Darling scanned the distance from the flying bridge.

They had just turned eastward, away from the sun, when Mike called out, "There!" and pointed off the port side.

Twenty or thirty yards away, something big and glisteny was floating in a tangle of sargasso weed.

Darling slowed and turned toward it. As they closed on it, they saw that the thing, whatever it was, was not man-made. It bobbed slowly and had a wet sheen and quivered like Jell-O.

"What the hell is *that*?" said Mike.

"Looks like a six-foot jellyfish snarled itself in the weed."

"Damn! Don't want to run into him."

Darling put the boat in neutral and watched from the flying bridge as the thing slid down the side. It was a huge clear jelly oblong, with a hole in the middle, and it appeared to have some sort of life, for it rotated as if to expose new parts of itself to the sunlight every few seconds.

Mike said, "No jellyfish *I've* ever seen."

"No," Darling agreed. "Beats me. Spawn of some kind, I guess."

"Want to pick some up?"

"What for?"

"The aquarium?"

"No. They never asked me for spawn. If it *is* spawn, let's let the critters live, whatever they are."

Darling resumed his course to the southeast. By the time they reached the area where they had recovered the raft, they had found two seat cushions and a rubber fender.

"Wonder why Marcus didn't see these," Mike said as

he brought the fender aboard. "It's not like they were underwater."

"A helicopter is a wonderful contraption, but you got to fly it *real* slow over open water or you overwhelm the scanners in the human eye." Darling looked out over the water. There were no signs of life, present or past. "That's it, then."

He took a bearing on the dim hump in the distance called Bermuda, and headed for home.

By six o'clock, they had left the deep behind, the ocean swell had faded and the water's color had changed from blued steel to dark green. From the flying bridge they could see sand holes on the bottom and dark patches of grass and coral.

"Who's that?" Mike asked, pointing to a boat silhouetted against the lowering sun.

Darling shaded his eyes and looked at the boat, appraising the rake of the bow and the shape of the house and the size of the cockpit.

"Carl Frith," he said.

"Hell's he doing? Trolling?"

"In the shallows? Not bloody likely."

They kept looking. They could see movement aboard the boat, which rolled as if it were taking on a weight and then rolled back as if releasing it.

"You don't think . . . ?" Mike began. "Nah, he's not that stupid."

"Stupid? Maybe not," Darling said as he turned toward the boat and pushed his throttle forward. "But how about greedy?"

Mike glanced over at Darling. There was a set to Whip's jaw, a cold and squinty hardness to his eyes.

Carl Frith had been a trap fisherman, and one of the noisiest protesters when traps were outlawed. He was always bleating about freedom, independence and the rights of man, despite having received over $100,000 from his settlement with the government—enough for any man, Darling thought, enough to let him change over to line fishing or charter fishing or start another business altogether. But it was beginning to look as if Carl Frith wanted to have it both ways.

Because they were approaching from the northwest, upwind, they got to within a hundred yards of Frith before he heard *Privateer*'s engine. They had a clear view of him reaching underwater with his boat hook and snagging the sunken buoy, pulling the rope up to his winch, hauling the big fish trap aboard his boat, opening the door and emptying the catch into the fish hold.

"Miserable sonofabitch," Darling said.

"Gonna run him down?"

"Gonna fillet the bastard."

"Good enough."

Darling felt a rage rising in the pit of his stomach. He didn't care that what Frith was doing was illegal: As far as Darling was concerned, most laws were whores assigned to serve politicians. What burned him—outraged him, sickened him—was the mindless selfishness of the man, the headlong rush at destruction and waste. And it wasn't only that Frith was still trap fishing, he was using submerged buoys so that the marine police wouldn't see them on the surface. A passing boat might catch the buoy in its propeller and cut it away, or a storm might shift the trap so Frith couldn't find it. Either way, the trap would be lost on the bottom, where day after day, week after week, it would kill and kill and kill.

Frith heard him coming now. He had a trap hung over the side, and as soon as he turned and saw *Privateer* bearing down on him, he pulled a knife from a sheath at his belt and cut the rope holding the trap, and the trap splashed into the water and sank away.

Darling kept up speed until he was ten yards from Frith's small boat, and then he turned sharply and pulled back on the throttle, throwing a wake that slammed into Frith's boat and staggered the man.

"Hey!" Frith shouted. "What you think you're doin'?"

Darling let his boat wallow beside Frith's. He leaned on the railing of the flying bridge and looked down. Frith was in his fifties, big-bellied and bald. His skin was as dark and worn as an old saddle, his teeth yellow from nicotine.

Darling said, "Just come by to see what you're up to, Carl."

"None of your concern."

"Wouldn't be fishing, would you?"

"Don't worry about it."

"Wouldn't be *trap* fishing?"

"Piss off, Whip."

"Let's see, Carl . . ." Darling's smile was icy. "I expect you're getting mostly . . . what? . . . parrotfish and breams. Right?"

Frith said nothing.

Darling turned to Mike. "Have a look, Michael, see what he's got."

Mike started down the ladder from the flying bridge. Frith pulled his knife and held it up. "Nobody comes aboard my boat."

From his perch on the ladder, Mike leaned over and looked down into Frith's fish hold. Then he looked up at Darling and nodded.

Darling kept smiling and said, "Parrotfish and breams. Gonna cut 'em up and sell 'em to the hotels, right, Carl? Sell 'em as fresh Bermuda fish? Get maybe a couple bucks a pound?"

"You can't prove anything," Frith said. He spread his arms and gestured at the empty cockpit. "Traps? Where do you see traps?"

"I don't have to prove anything, Carl, I'm not gonna report you."

"Oh." Frith relaxed. "Well, then . . ."

Mike looked startled, but he kept quiet.

"You know what parrotfish and breams do, Carl? They eat the algae that grow on the corals, they clean the reefs. Without them, the coral suffocate and die."

"Come on, Whip . . . one man, a few traps, don't make—"

"Sure, Carl." Darling let his smile fade. "One man who took a hundred thousand dollars from the government and gave his word he'd stop fishing, one man who doesn't need the money but's too pigheaded to do anything else, one man who doesn't give a shit . . ."

"Hey, fuck you, Whip."

"No, Carl," Darling said. "Fuck *you*." He spun his wheel to the right and leaned on his throttle, and *Privateer* jumped ahead and to the right, slamming into Frith's boat, its steel bow shearing off Frith's wooden swim step.

Frith screamed, "Hey! Goddam—"

Darling kept turning, his bow pushing Frith's stern around. Frith ran forward and turned the key and pushed the button to start his engine. The engine coughed, protested, turned over.

Darling reversed his engine, backed around and aimed his bow at Frith's stern. He struck Frith's fantail, crushing it.

Then Frith was in gear, pulling away, trying to escape.

Mike climbed the ladder and stood beside Darling on the flying bridge. "Gonna sink him?"

"He's gonna sink himself." Darling looked back into

the sun: It was still well above the horizon, still a brilliant yellow ball.

Frith fled, heading east. Darling stayed ten yards behind, threatening collision but not forcing it, heading Frith off whenever he tried to turn, pressing him ever eastward.

"I don't get it," Mike said.

"You will."

"You're driving him to the cut."

"Not exactly *to* it."

Mike thought for a moment, and then he got it, and he smiled.

For five more minutes Darling chased Frith, always checking the sun behind him and the reefs ahead. Then, gently, he pulled back on his throttle. *Privateer* slowed, and Frith gradually drew away.

Frith looked back and saw that he was gaining. He shouted something that was snatched away by the wind, and he threw Darling the finger.

Darling pulled his throttle back into neutral, and *Privateer* stopped. "Bye, Carl," he called. "Have a nice day." He pointed off the bow. Not five feet away, barely covered by water, was the first of a ragged phalanx of yellow coral heads.

"Think it'll work?" Mike said. "He knows these reefs."

"No man knows these reefs, Michael, if he can't see."

Carl Frith dodged one coral head, then another.

Take it easy, he told himself. You may only draw three feet, but some of these buggers aren't a foot deep.

He throttled back, slowing down, letting his breath catch up with his heart.

Damn him, the self-righteous bastard. Who was Whip Darling to tell a man how to make a living? Whip wasn't doing such a good job of it himself, from what he'd heard. You'd think he'd have some sympathy. Parrotfish important? Breams? That was a laugh. They were trash fish, everybody knew that.

Whip was just pissed off 'cause he hadn't had any traps to stiff the government for.

Never mind. No problem. Whip had said he wasn't about to report him, and, whatever else there was about Whip, he was a man of his word. He wanted this to be personal, Frith would keep it personal. He'd go out one day and maybe just cut away Whip's buoys, all that horseshit he did for the aquarium. Not even man's work.

Anyway, it was obvious Whip wasn't too serious, or he would've done more than just chase him up into the shallows. No big deal. All he had to do was turn around and . . .

Frith looked to the west. He couldn't see anything, just the blinding yellow flashes of the sun on the dappled sea. No definition to the water, no coral heads, nothing. It was like looking at a sheet of tinfoil at high noon.

He realized he was trapped. He couldn't go eastward because there the coral heads actually broke water. He couldn't go west because he couldn't see: Blind, he was guaranteed to tear the bottom out of his boat. And the tide was falling, he remembered that from this morning when he had checked the tide tables to be sure he could find his buoys.

He could wait till sunset—and what? Try it in the dark? Forget it.

He'd have to wait till morning. He'd put his anchor down and wait, have a beer and a sleep and . . .

But he didn't dare. If the wind came up, he might be forced to move in the middle of the night. What was the wind supposed to do? He hadn't bothered to check, it hadn't seemed important.

He couldn't see Whip's boat: It was out there somewhere in the sunlight. He shouted, "God damn you! . . ."

Darling watched Frith's boat slow down, then stop. He imagined Frith thinking everything was fine, then turning around and looking into the sun.

"He'll wait till morning," Mike said.

"Not Carl. He hasn't got the patience."

They stayed for a few more minutes, drifting at the edge of the shallow reef.

"Maybe you're right," Darling said, and he reached for his throttle.

Just then, they heard Frith's engine roar.

"Nope," Mike said, grinning.

They listened to the sound of the engine across the still water, heard it rev up then die off, advancing and retreating.

"He's searching," Darling said. "Like a blind man."

A moment later they felt a little tremor in their feet, sent by the water through the *Privateer*'s steel plates, and then they heard a low grinding kind of noise, followed suddenly by the yowl of Frith's engine.

"He did it," Darling said, and he laughed and slapped Mike on the shoulder. "Ran himself up on that reef, hard and fast."

"Want me to call the police?" Mike asked. "They can send the rubber boat."

"Let him swim. He could use the workout." Darling turned his boat to the west. "Besides, we got a duty to do."

"What's that?"

"Wreck the bastard's traps."

"He'll report us," Mike said. Then he paused. "No, now I think of it, I don't guess he will."

* * *

By the time Darling rounded the point into Mangrove Bay, the blue of the sky was fast turning violet, and the departed sun had tinted the western clouds the color of salmon.

A single light bulb burned on the dock, and beneath it, moored to a piling, was a white twenty-five-foot outboard motorboat with the word POLICE stenciled on the side in foot-high blue letters.

"Christ," Mike said, "he's reported us already."

"I doubt it," said Darling. "Carl's a fool, but he's not crazy."

Two young policemen stood on the dock, one white, one black, both wearing uniform shirts, shorts and knee socks. They watched as Darling eased the boat against the dock, and they passed Mike the bow and stern lines.

Darling knew the policemen, had no problem with them—no more than he had with the marine police in general, whom he regarded as ill-trained, under-equipped and overburdened. These two he had taken to sea with him on their days off, had helped them learn to read the reefs, had shown them shortcuts to the few deep-water channels in and out of Bermuda.

Still, he chose to remain on the flying bridge, sensing instinctively that altitude reinforced his authority.

He leaned on the railing and raised a finger and said, "Colin . . . Barnett . . ."

"Hey, Whip . . ." Colin, the white cop, said.

Barnett said, "Come aboard?"

"Come ahead," said Darling. "What brings you fellas out of a night?"

"Hear you found a raft," Barnett said.

"True enough."

Barnett stepped aboard and pointed to the raft lying athwart the cockpit. "That it?"

"That's the one."

Barnett shone a flashlight on the raft and leaned down to it. "Lord, it stinks!"

Colin stayed where he was and said hesitantly, "Whip . . . we gotta take it."

Darling paused. "Why's that? Somebody claim to have lost it?"

"No . . . not exactly."

"Then it's mine, isn't it? . . . First law of salvage: finders keepers."

"Well . . ." Colin seemed uneasy. He looked at his feet. "Not this time."

"That so." Darling waited, feeling a roil of anger in his stomach, fighting it down. "What, then?"

"Dr. St. John," Colin said. "He wants it."

"Dr. St. John." Now Darling knew he was bound to lose, and his temper was bound to win. "I see."

Liam St. John was one of the few men in Bermuda whom Darling took the trouble to loathe. A second-generation Irish immigrant, he had gone away to school in Montana and graduated from some diploma mill that awarded him a doctorate. Exactly what the doctorate was in, nobody knew and he never said. All anybody knew for certain was that little Liam had left Bermuda pronouncing his name "Saint John" and had returned pronouncing it (and insisting everyone else do, too) "SINjin."

Armed with an alphabet appended to his name, St. John had rallied a few powerful friends of his parents and besieged the government, arguing that certain disciplines, such as maritime history and wildlife management, were being grossly mishandled by amateurs and should be turned over to certified, qualified experts— which meant him, since he was the only status-Bermudian with a doctorate in anything other than medicine. Never mind that his degree was in an unknown field, probably something utterly useless like Druid combs.

The politicians, who were unconcerned with shipwrecks and nettled by loudmouthed fishermen, were pleased to remove both from their agendas, and for Dr. Liam St. John, Ph.D., they created the new position of minister of cultural heritage. They didn't bother with a precise job description, which suited St. John just fine, for he defined and expanded the job as he went along, assuming more and more authority and enforcing rules and regulations of his own making.

As far as Darling was concerned, all St. John and his regulations had done was turn hundreds of Bermudians into criminals. He had decreed, for example, that no one was permitted to touch any shipwreck without first securing a license from him and agreeing to pay one of his staff two hundred dollars a day to supervise work on the wreck. The result was that nobody ever reported finding anything, and if they did dig up some coins or artifacts, gold earrings or Spanish pottery, they hid them until they could smuggle them out of Bermuda.

Thanks to the minister of cultural heritage, Bermuda's heritage was being sold in galleries on Madison Avenue in New York.

Scientists who had once regarded Bermuda as a prime deep-water laboratory, a unique speck of land in the mid-Atlantic, no longer bothered to come, because St. John insisted that all discoveries be turned over to and examined by his staff, who prepared papers (always pedestrian, usually erroneous) for him to deliver at academic conclaves.

For almost a year, Darling and his diver friends had fantasized about ways to get rid of St. John. Someone had suggested reporting a shipwreck find and taking St. John to have a look at it and then sinking the boat. (It was said that St. John didn't know how to swim.) The idea was vetoed, largely on the grounds that St. John would never go himself: He'd send one of his stooges.

Someone else suggested they just kill him—hit him on the head and dump him in the deep. But although everyone agreed that the result was desirable, no one volunteered to do the deed.

Darling wouldn't have been surprised, however, if it were to happen some night—if St. John were simply to vanish. Nor would he have been crestfallen at the news.

"Colin," he said, "I want you to do me a favor."

"Name it."

"You go back and tell Dr. St. John that I'll give him the raft. . . ."

"Okay."

". . . if he'll come over here himself and let me shove it up his ass."

"Oh." Colin looked at Barnett, then at his feet again, then, reluctantly, at Darling. "You know I can't do that, Whip."

"Then we got us a problem, don't we, Colin? 'Cause there's something else you can't do, and that's take the raft."

"But we *have* to!" There was a wailing note in Colin's voice.

Barnett stepped away from the raft and came forward and stood at the bottom of the ladder, looking up.

As Darling looked down at him, he saw movement in the shadows aft. It was Mike, moving silently toward the rack where they kept the clubs and gaff hooks for subduing big fish.

"Whip," Barnett said, "you don't want to do this."

"That raft is mine, Barnett, and you know it." Darling wanted to say more, wanted to say that it wasn't a matter of the raft, wasn't even just a matter of principle, it was also a matter of the two or three or four thousand dollars, dollars that could make a difference, dollars he was not going to let Liam St. John steal from him. But he said none of it; he was not about to whine to a policeman.

"Not if St. John wants to study it like he says."

"Prick doesn't want to study it. He wants to keep it. He knows what it's worth."

"That's not what he says."

"And since when has he become a frigging paragon of truthfulness?"

"Whip . . ." Barnett sighed. Something made him look aft—a glimmer of light, maybe, or a sound—and he saw Mike standing in the darkness, holding across his chest a three-foot gaff with a honed four-inch hook on the end. "You know what we're gonna have to do."

"Yep. Go back and tell Dr. St. John to suck eggs."

"No. We're gonna go back and get a dozen more coppers and come back and take the raft."

"Not without somebody getting bruised."

"That may be, Whip, but think about it: That happens, you're gonna end up in jail, we're gonna end up with the raft, and who's gonna get the last laugh? Doctor St.-fucking-John."

Darling looked away, across the dark water of Mangrove Bay, at the lights of the cars crossing Watford Bridge, at the glow of lanterns on the veranda of Cambridge Beaches, the hotel nearby, where some bygone singer was warbling along with the band, telling the world he did it His Way.

Darling wanted to fight, wanted to rage and defy and storm around. But he swallowed it, because he knew Barnett was right.

"Barnett," he said at last, and he started down the ladder, "you are the soul of wisdom."

Barnett looked over at Colin, who let out a big breath and smiled back at him.

"Dr. *SINjin* wants my raft," Darling said as he strode

aft and took the gaff from Mike, "Dr. *SINjin* shall have my raft."

He stepped over to the raft and raised the gaff above his shoulder and slashed downward at the bow. The hook plunged through the rubber, and, with a pop and a hiss, the cell collapsed.

"Whoops!" Darling said, "sorry," and he dragged the raft toward the bulwark. He slammed the hook into another cell, and it deflated, and he hauled the sagging rubber up onto the bulwark. Something small fell from the raft and hit the steel deck with a click and rattled away. He withdrew the hook and stepped back and drove it through the aftermost cell. He yanked upward and held the raft in the air over the police boat. The muscles in his shoulders were afire, and the sinews in his neck stuck out like wires.

"Whoops!" he said again, and he dropped the raft into the police boat, where it landed in a heap of hissing rubber. He turned back to the two policemen and dropped the gaff on the deck and said, "There. Dr. St. John can have his bloody raft."

The policemen looked at one another. "Okay," said Colin, as he quickly stepped off onto the dock. "We'll tell Dr. St. John that's how you found it."

"Right," said Barnett, and he followed Colin. "Looks to me like a shark got it."

"And there *was* a sea on," Colin said. "You couldn't go into the water after it, sharks all around. . . . 'Night, Whip."

Darling watched as the policemen piled the raft in the stern of their boat and started their motor and backed away into the darkness. He felt drained and slightly nauseated, half-pleased with himself and half-ashamed.

"There's always the dive charters during the big race layover," Mike said. "They'll turn us a pretty dollar."

"Sure," said Darling. "Sure."

* * *

As they cleaned up the boat, stowing gear and swabbing down the deck, Darling felt something small and sharp under his foot. He picked it up and looked at it, but the light was bad, so he dropped it into his pocket.

"See you in the morning?" Mike said when he was ready to go ashore.

"Right. We'll give the aquarium the bad news, see if they want to trust us with more gear. If not, we'll start chipping paint."

" 'Night, then."

Darling followed Mike up the path to the house, waited till Mike had started his motorbike and driven away, then shut off the outside lights and went inside.

He poured himself a couple of fingers of dark rum and sat in the kitchen. He debated turning on the news but decided not to: All news was bad news, by definition, otherwise it wasn't worth putting on the TV. And he didn't need any more bad news.

Charlotte came in, smiled and sat down across the counter from him. She took a sip from his glass, then reached for one of his hands and held it between hers.

"That was childish," she said quietly.

"You saw?"

"Police don't stop by every evening."

He shook his head. "Whoreson Irish bastard."

"What did you accomplish?"

"D'you know how sick it makes me feel to feel so helpless? I had to do *some*thing."

"Did it make you feel better?"

"Sure."

"Really?"

"Sort of . . ." He looked at her. She was smiling. "Okay, you're right. I'm an old fart with a baby's brain."

"Well . . . you're cute anyway." She leaned across the counter and took his chin and drew him toward her.

As he rose up to kiss her, something stabbed him in the thigh, and he yipped and jerked backward and fell into his seat.

"What?" she said.

"I've been punctured." He reached into his pocket and pulled out the thing he had stepped on and put it on the counter.

It was a crescent-shaped hook, not of steel but of some hard, shiny, bony substance.

"What have I gone and stabbed myself with now?" He picked it up and pressed it into the counter, trying to bend it. It wouldn't bend.

"It looks like a claw," said Charlotte. "Tiger, maybe. Or even a fang. Where'd you find it?"

"Fell out of that raft," he said. He hesitated as he recalled the marks he had seen on the raft, like cuts in the rubber. He looked at Charlotte, then at the thing, and he frowned and said, "What the hell . . . ?"

IT HUNG IN the deep and waited.

Motionless, invisible in the blackness, it searched with its senses for the vibrations that would signal the approach of prey.

It was accustomed to being served, for the cold, nutrient-rich water at a thousand feet had always been host to countless animals of all sizes. It had never known, never needed, patience, for food had always been abundant. It had been able to nourish its great body by reflex, without struggle or severe exertion.

Its skills were those of a killer, not a hunter, for it had never needed to hunt.

But now the rhythmic cycles that propelled the creature through life had been disrupted. Food was no longer abundant. Because it had no capacity for reason, knew no past and no future, it was confused by the discomfort caused by the unfamiliar sensation of hunger.

Instinct was telling it to hunt.

It felt an interruption in the flow of the sea, a sudden irregular static in the water's pulse.

Prey. In numbers. Passing by.

They were not near, they were somewhere distant, somewhere above.

The creature drew quantities of water through the muscular collar of its mantle, then expelled it through the funnel in its belly, driving itself up and backward with the force of a racing locomotive.

It homed on the signals and thrust itself through the water with spasmodic expulsions from its funnel. It recognized the signature of the signals: fish, many fish, many big fish.

Chemicals coursed through its flesh, altering its colors.

When it judged itself close enough, it spun and faced the direction where its prey should be. Its huge eyes registered a flash of silver, and it lashed out with its whips. The clubs at the ends of the whips fastened on flesh, their toothed circles tore at it, the crescent-shaped hooks erect within each circle slashed it to shreds. Within seconds, all that remained of the fish was a shower of scales and a billow of blood.

The creature's hunger was not allayed, however—it was increased. It needed more, much more.

But the pressure wave generated by the displacement of so much water by the movement of a body so huge had alarmed the school of bluefin tuna, and they had fled in phalanx.

And so the searching whips found nothing. The shorter arms at the base of its body gradually ceased moving; the gnashing beak closed its jaws and withdrew into the body cavity.

Hunger now consumed the creature, but exhaustion also restrained it. Vast amounts of energy had been expended, and yet it had found too little with which to fuel its enormous needs.

It drifted, hungry and confused.

The bottom far below was ridged, and the current that swept up from the abyss propelled the creature slowly along a slope to a plateau at five hundred feet. The cool water eddied here, so the creature rose no farther.

On another slope, up ahead, was something large and unnatural, something that its senses told it was dead, except for the routine life forms that grew upon it.

The creature ignored it, and waited, gathering strength.

# 10

LUCAS COVEN WAS so annoyed, and so impatient to get this day over and done with, that he put his boat in gear and leaned on the throttle before the winch had the anchor snugged up. He heard the big steel flukes thud against the hull, and he could envision the nasty gouges in the fiberglass, which made him even angrier.

He was always doing this, getting himself in over his head and then, captive of his bullheaded pride, refusing to back off. He was a fisherman, for God's sake—had been, anyway—so where did he get off playing Jacques bloody Cousteau?

It was his mouth that betrayed him every time. He swore that if he made it through today without a calamity or a lawsuit, he'd never go into a bar again—or, if he did, he'd sew his lips together and drink his vodka through a straw.

Once clear of Ely's Harbour, he turned south. He looked down from the flying bridge to make sure his two passengers hadn't fallen overboard or speared one another or dropped something serious on a foot. They were down there on the stern assembling their diving gear—compasses, knives, computers, octopus regulators, buoyancy vests, still cameras, video cameras—good God, they had enough gear to equip an astronaut for a month on the back side of the moon.

They had said they were expert divers, had insisted on

showing him their Advanced Open-Water cards. But in Lucas's mind, people who decked themselves out in all that machinery weren't divers, they were shoppers. Sure, diving could be complicated, if you wanted to mess with all that chemistry, but it didn't have to be. A savvy person made it simple: Wear a bathing suit so nothing grabs you by the balls, flippers for your motor, a mask so you can see, a tank of air to breathe, a few pounds of lead to keep you down, a depth gauge in case you get absentminded.

Besides, that girl, Susie, looked like she didn't *need* gear—she had a set of lungs on her that should take her to a thousand feet on a single breath. Gear just spoiled the picture, covered up all the golden-brown skin, the mane of yellow hair that when he first saw it had made him catch his breath. She was a prime candidate for that *Sports Illustrated* special issue.

But they were high-tekkies, these two. Like most everybody these days, they relied on electronic doodads to do their work for them. Common sense and gut instincts were becoming a thing of the past.

Well, he hoped one of them, the boy or the girl, still had a ration of common sense, because where they were going, the only thing the costly toys might do was provide a record for the coroner.

That thought brought Lucas another fit of anger. Maybe he'd pay someone to remove his vocal cords.

His first mistake had been to go to the Hog Penny Pub for his five o'clock smile. He never went to any of the tourist bars on Front Street: The drinks were overpriced and undergenerous. But a pretty girl had stopped on her motorbike to ask him directions, and she'd said she went to the Hog Penny every day, and why didn't he come by for a drink later on, and so he'd shaved his face and changed his shirt and dropped by. Naturally, the girl never did.

His second mistake had been to hang around long enough to destroy a twenty-dollar bill, because even at tourist prices, twenty dollars bought him enough fuel to generate heat in his belly and tamp down his native quietness.

His third—and by far most serious—mistake had been to put his mouth where it didn't belong, into a conversation between two young people he didn't know.

He'd been dazzled by the girl from the moment he saw her, but he had no ambitions about her because the boy she was with was just as good-looking as she was, in his way, just as tall and blond and tan. Lucas imagined them to be a matched pair from some scientific stud farm, programmed to breed a race of beauties. They looked so much alike, they could have been brother and sister . . .

. . . which, he later learned, was exactly what they were: twins, just out of college, down here staying in their parents' house out by the Mid-Ocean Club. He gathered that their father was some big-shot tycoon in the broadcast business up in the States.

Because Dr. Smirnoff had Lucas well in tow by now and was deluding him that he was as smooth as Tom Cruise, Lucas began to fancy that he might actually have a chance with this heart-stopper. Her getup alone should have been warning enough: No girl with a real-gold Rolex watch, a gold pinky ring and one of those five-dollar golf shirts with the fifty-dollar polo player on it—let alone the satin skin and teeth as perfect as piano keys—was likely to give a thought to some scraunchy, ragged-haired boat-jockey in tattered jeans. But Dr. Smirnoff was driving.

They were consulting a set of decompression tables, wondering aloud if they should have decompressed after their last dive and planning how deep they could go on tomorrow's dives—all of which should have rung alarm bells in Lucas's head since, first of all, no visitors were ever taken on deep dives in Bermuda and, second, deep diving wasn't something sensible people did by choice.

Lucas didn't say a thing while the two discussed the depths of the various shipwrecks they had been on, comparing the *Constellation* to *l'Herminie,* the *North Carolina* to the *Virginia Merchant.* None of them lay deeper than forty feet—breath-hold range for anybody but a consumptive. He wasn't tempted to correct them when they talked about the *Cristóbal Colón* versus the *Pollockshields,* two iron ships so shallow you had to take care not to hit them with the boat.

He had found his opening when the boy—Scott, his name was—said something like, "The boat guy said the deepest wreck around's the *Pelinaion.*"

"Where is it?" asked Susie. "Will he take us to it?"

Lucas leaned forward and turned his head toward them and said, " 'Scuse me. None of my business, but I'm afraid somebody's pulling your chain."

"Really?" Susie's eyes opened wide, and Lucas decided that she had the longest eyelashes he'd ever seen.

"Yep. Like I say, none of my business, but I hate to see you get a bum steer."

"What is, then?" said Scott. "The deepest wreck."

"The deepest shipwreck in Bermuda," Lucas said with a smile, *so* charming, pleased to find that his mouth was working even though his lips felt kind of numb, "is the *Admiral Durham.* It's off the South Shore. Leastways, the deepest one anybody's ever seen."

"How deep is that?" Scott had a look that said he didn't believe a word of this but that he had nothing better to do just now than humor Lucas Coven.

"She starts at a hundred and ninety, then angles down the slope to about three hundred."

Susie said, "Wow!"

Scott said, "Gimme a break. . . ."

Looking back, Lucas wished he'd said something terminal like, "Piss off, Junior," something that would have sunk the expedition right then and there.

But Susie had given Scott a punch on the shoulder and said, "Scott! Listen, for once in your life," which meant she was interested.

So Lucas had let his mouth keep running.

"She ran up on the South Shore in a storm and hung there a day or more while they tried to pull her off. They got her free okay, but she was holed so bad that before they could patch her she filled up and went, slid back down the hill."

"And you've seen it," Scott said.

"Once, years back. She's not so easy to find."

"What was it like?" Susie asked, all eager.

"Gets your blood to racing. I call her the Widowmaker." He didn't, but it sounded good. "For a long time you don't see anything at all. Then all of a sudden she looms up out of the deep, and your first thought is, Man, I must be narcked. 'Cause what you see is a great iron ship that looks to be sailing right up at you. Then, what downright convinces you that you've got the vapors is that there's this no-kidding locomotive train engine lying right beside her, fallen off the bow. Just about the time your head clears, it's time to go. You only get about five minutes at that depth."

"I don't believe it," said Scott.

Lucas said, "That's your privilege," and motioned for a refill.

Susie put a hand on Lucas's arm, actually touched him, and, with a glance at her brother that told him to keep quiet, said, "Our treat," and gestured to the bartender to give them a couple of beers and Lucas another vodka.

That was the moment when Lucas knew he had them. And because he was enjoying himself and trying to figure out where to take Susie when they managed to ditch Scott, he didn't think the time would come when he wished he hadn't.

When the drinks came, Susie said, "Excuse us a minute," and she took Scott's arm and led him off by some empty tables. They stayed over there, whispering, for three or four minutes, gesturing at one another, and when they came back it was Scott who started the ball rolling.

There had been no stopping it.

Did Lucas think he could find the *Admiral Durham* again?

Probably, with the new electronics on the boat.

Would he be willing to try?

What for?

Because (Susie said) they were bored with the diving around Bermuda; they'd seen nearly everything, and they wanted to get some *real* diving in before the summer was gone and they were both trapped indoors in jobs or grad school or whatever. Also, they couldn't go to some other island to dive right now, because they were waiting for their parents to come down from New York.

Well . . . he didn't know, he was pretty busy.

They'd make it worth his while.

He had to be honest with them, he said, he had a charter party on hold for tomorrow. (*Charter party!* Where had he come up with *that?* He'd never taken a charter party out in his life; he had no idea what you did with one or how much you charged them.) He wished he could help them, they seemed like nice kids and all, but he couldn't sacrifice that charter fee.

And how much was that?

Well . . . full day . . . fifteen hundred (a fat figure, plucked out of the air).

No problem. In fact, if he could guarantee to put them on the shipwreck, they'd pay two thousand. But if he didn't find it (Scott was playing Mr. Big-Time Hard-Nose), they'd ride for free.

Fair enough, but Lucas had to ask, were they sure they were up to a two-hundred-foot dive? Ever done it before? Did they know about the bends, which could cripple or kill them; about nitrogen narcosis, the notorious "rapture" that could cause them to lose their bearings . . . about all the other stuff that happened at depth?

Oh sure, they were supercareful, they knew all the chemistry and physics. And if they hadn't actually gone to two hundred feet before, they'd both been down well over a hundred (Scott was positive, Susie pretty sure), and there wasn't really that much difference, was there, only nine or ten stories of an office building.

And three more atmospheres of pressure, Lucas thought—three steps up on the squeeze ladder, three times the chance of a mishap that could end in a funeral. But he didn't say anything because by now he was convinced Susie had eyes for him, and besides, Scott was running on about their expertise.

Scott listed all the places they'd dived and in what kinds of weather. They brandished their C-cards and logbooks listing every time they'd gotten their feet wet.

Okay, then, he'd take them, but he'd have to send them down the anchor line alone, he couldn't go with them 'cause he didn't have a mate and he couldn't leave the boat unmanned—safety was his first concern, he had a reputation around the island. 'Cause if the boat should happen to break away, they didn't want to have to swim to shore after a two-hundred-foot dive . . . unless they cared to spring for another couple of hundred to hire a mate for the day.

Susie said, Gosh, they didn't need a nursemaid, they'd swim right down the old anchor line, take a lot of pictures and be back before he knew it.

Scott said, So let's raise a glass to the dive of a lifetime.

And they had done just that, several glasses, in fact, until the time came when Lucas decided to make his move on Susie and suggested they slip away for a quiet dinner somewhere.

She had laughed at him—not a nasty laugh but a kind of sweet motherly laugh that he couldn't get mad at— and ruffled his hair and said, See you tomorrow.

Lucas gave Southwest Breaker a wide berth. There was no breeze to speak of, just a light sou'westerly, but the sea still boiled around the treacherous fang of rock sticking up from the bottom, yearning to puncture passersby.

Fresh air cleared Lucas's head, a handful of peppermints killed the taste of rot in his mouth and a breakfast beer restored him to where he could look on the bright side of things.

Two thousand dollars was more than he could make in a month netting flying fish or helping a chummy haul water.

Maybe the kids had done some bragging, maybe they had too much faith in all their Mickey Mouse gear, but they certainly were being careful, checking and rechecking every hose and fitting.

He could tell, looking down at them, that they were nervous, which was healthy. They might eat up air so fast they'd never get near the bottom, but that wasn't his worry.

The day was looking promising, after all. With luck, he could be back at the dock by lunchtime. If they were successful, if he gave them the dive of a lifetime, Susie might yet come around. You never knew.

The reef line was close on the South Shore, deep water came fast, so it wasn't long before Lucas started looking to array his landmarks. He had written them down—no reason, but now a piece of good luck—the one and only time he'd been out to this wreck, which had to be ten years ago.

There was a purple house with twin tall casuarinas directly behind it. His eye was supposed to line up those trees straight as a rifle sight, at the same time triangulating so that the main building of the peach-colored cottage colony to the westward sat at the feet of Gibbs Hill Lighthouse.

The tide was running offshore, so Lucas drove a little bit to sea, then turned and pointed the bow at the shore while he powered slowly up and adjusted the landmarks.

Landmarks weren't foolproof, though, with a shipwreck this deep. You couldn't see it from the surface, you had to take your marks after you'd swum up from it, and maybe by then the boat had swung at anchor.

And close wasn't good enough with the *Admiral Durham*. The light was dim down there, visibility probably no more than thirty or forty feet at best, and with five minutes' bottom time—which meant five minutes from the time you left the surface till the time you started up from the bottom—you didn't have leisure to go hunting around. Lucas had to anchor *on* it, drop the hook on the deck and let it drag along till it found a purchase on a rail or some chain or maybe even that rusty old commode that squatted on the foredeck, the one he'd had his picture taken sitting on.

He switched on his fish-finder and set the depth of its read and shaded the screen with his hand. The readout of lines and lumps showed nothing, a void, between the surface and the bottom. He turned the wheel, nosing the boat a couple of points to port, then a couple to starboard, and suddenly it was there, a giant hulk rising up from the bottom.

Lucas jockeyed the boat until the hulk was dead center on the screen. Then he nudged forward a hair, enough to compensate for the current gripping the anchor and bowing the line, and pushed the button that released the anchor.

He closed his eyes and wished the anchor all the way down, seeing it in his mind dropping through the darkening blue and striking steel with a hearty clang.

# 11

THE CREATURE WAS in a state close to hibernation. Its respiration—the ingestion and expulsion of water—had slowed to fifteen cycles per minute. Its color had dulled to a grayish brown. Its arms and whips floated freely, like gigantic snakes.

And it was gaining strength, as if sucking sustenance from the cool and silent darkness.

Suddenly the silence was broken by sound vibrations, which showered down upon it and were amplified by the salt water. To a human ear, the sound would have been thick, resonant, metallic, the sound of solid steel striking hollow steel with weight and velocity.

To the creature, the sound was unknown . . . alien and alarming, and so its respiration increased, quickly doubled. Its arms curled, its whips cocked. Its color changed, brightened, brown hues vanishing, replaced by purples and reds.

It located the noise as coming from above, so it began to rise up the slope toward the large and unnatural and lifeless thing it had sensed there earlier.

The sound began again, but altered, a series of short staccato bumps. Then it stopped altogether.

The creature moved toward the unnatural thing, then hovered over it, searching for the source of the sound. Any sound, any change whatever in the normal rhythms of the sea, could mean prey.

And the need that was overwhelming it, now that it was moving and consuming energy, was hunger.

# 12

LUCAS STOOD ON the bow and let the anchor rope run through his hands until he saw the piece of tape marking fifty fathoms. Then he took a turn around a cleat and watched the swing of the bow and the angle of the rope. If he gave it too little scope, there was a risk that it would pull the anchor free; too much, and traveling time for the divers would be too long and they'd run out of air.

Might as well give them a sporting chance, he thought, now that the two thousand dollars was as good as in his pocket.

When he was satisfied with the set, he cleated off the

rope and went aft. "Dive, dive, dive!" he said, grinning at Scott and Susie, who looked like heroes from one of those comic books.

They were wearing matching wetsuits, blue with yellow chevrons the color of their blond hair, and strapped to their legs were red-handled knives big enough to fell a buffalo. Their Italian flippers were so long that the kids looked like some kind of weird mutant ducks. Both of them were lashed up with straps, buckles and snaps.

"You're sure you found the *Durham*?" said Scott.

"You didn't hear the anchor bong on the deck down there?"

They didn't know whether to believe him or not, so they just smiled, both looking antsy.

Lucas ushered them down onto the swim step off the stern. Susie's tan seemed to have faded, and her face had taken on an ashy hue.

"You okay?" Lucas asked, touching her arm.

"Yes . . . I guess."

"You don't have to go. There's no shame."

"We're going," Scott said. "She'll be fine."

Lucas looked at Susie, who nodded.

"It's your party." Serious now, Lucas said, "Swim on the surface up to the anchor line. Get a grip on it and check everything out and wait till you're all calm and cool. I don't care if it takes a week, there's no rush, I don't want you going down there all anxious. When you're ready, one of you go first, the other right behind, and I tell you, *fire* for the bottom, don't dally. You got precious little time as it is. Any spare time you got, use it to come up nice and slow."

They nodded and cleaned their masks and put them on. Lucas passed them their cameras: a video in a housing for Scott, a Nikonos V for Susie.

They gave one another the thumbs-up sign.

"Hey!" said Lucas, and they looked up at him. "One

last thing: Don't go frightening anything down there."
He smiled, to show he was making a little joke.

They didn't smile back.

As soon as they hit the water, they inflated their vests
and lay on their backs and kicked against the tide toward the bow of the boat.

Lucas walked forward and stood looking down as
they gathered at the anchor line. They fiddled with this
and checked that and said something back and forth.
Then they put their mouthpieces in, vented their vests
and dropped beneath the surface.

Lucas looked at his watch: 10:52. By eleven o'clock
he'd either be two thousand dollars richer or in a mess
he didn't want to think about.


The creature had twice covered the length and
breadth of the large, unnatural thing. The sound vibrations had ceased, and no other signs of prey had followed.

Its eyes registered faint light above. Here the cool
water was blending with warmer, so it moved away
from the unnatural thing and began to drop back into
the darkness.

But then it sensed movement again, something coming closer, and a sound that signaled a life form.

It dropped back atop the unnatural thing, its great
body resting in shadows, waiting.

As the movement drew near and the rasping sound of
living things respiring grew louder, the creature's color
began to change.


Scott pulled himself down the anchor rope hand over
hand, the video camera snapped to his weight belt
trailing behind him. He was in dim nothingness now,
surrounded by blue. He paused to check his air gauge—

2,500 pounds, plenty—and his depth gauge—120 feet. He saw no shipwreck below him, no bottom.

The feeling was eerie, lonely, but not frightening, for there was solace in the tautness of the anchor line. *Some*thing was down there; the anchor had caught in it. If it was the shipwreck, fine; if not, well . . . they'd save two thousand dollars. He still hadn't figured out how to explain to the old man the thousand-dollar cash advances he and Susie had each taken on their credit cards.

Where was Susie?

Scott turned and looked back up the anchor line. She **was** way above, hanging on the rope at fifty or sixty feet—afraid, maybe, or having trouble with her ears.

There was nothing he could do for her. As long as she was above him, she'd be okay. Coven could look after her.

He rinsed a patch of fog from his mask, tipped downward and kicked for the bottom.

At 160 feet he saw it, and his breath caught. It was exactly as Coven had described it—a ghost ship seeming to sail right up at him, enormous beyond imagining. And lying on the bottom beside the starboard bow, like a wounded behemoth staring blankly with its cyclopean eye, was the blunt face of a locomotive.

Fantastic!

He wanted to stop his descent long enough to unsnap the video camera from his belt, switch on its light and adjust its settings. But though he kicked hard, thrusting upward with his flipper blades, he felt himself continuing to sink. He was overweighted for this depth: His neoprene suit had compressed, lost its buoyancy, and he was too heavy, descending too fast. He pressed the button that shot air into his vest, and once again he was nearly neutral in the water. He checked his air gauge—1,800 pounds—and told himself to control his breathing.

Then he aimed his camera at the bow of the ship, pressed the trigger and let himself drift gradually downward.

It was alive, whatever this thing was, and slow and clumsy.

And it was coming.

The creature cocked its whips and fluttered its tail fins and, very slowly, began to move out of the shadows toward the prey.

Scott dropped down onto the bow of the ship. He was still breathing too fast, he could hear his heart, but he didn't care. This was incredible! The size of it!

He found something to wrap his legs around, to steady himself—it was a *toilet,* for God's sake, right here on the deck!—and he brought the camera's viewfinder up to his mask, trying somehow to get it all in frame.

His world became a tiny square with a green light in one corner and some numbers on the bottom.

He felt a change in the rhythm of the water around him, but he didn't turn to look: It had to be a blip in the current, or perhaps Susie arriving nearby.

He saw a vague, shadowy movement at the farthest left edge of the frame, but he assumed it was an illusion caused by the dappled light.

Something touched him. He jerked, turned, but all he could see was a blur of purple.

And then the something had him around the chest and was squeezing.

He dropped the camera, twisted around, but the something kept squeezing. Now there were stabbing things in it, like knives. He heard a crack—his ribs, breaking like sticks of kindling.

The last thing he saw, in his mask, was a bubble of blood.

Susie could see nothing above, nothing below. She was fighting to stay in control, not to panic. Why hadn't Scott waited for her? They were supposed to go down together. Lucas had insisted; they had agreed. But no, Scott had gone off on his own. Impatient, selfish. As usual.

She checked her air gauge—1,500 pounds—and her depth gauge—110 feet. She'd never make it. She was gasping, and she could envision air disappearing with every breath. She felt surrounded, compressed, imprisoned. She couldn't even make it to the surface. She was going to die!

Stop it! she told herself. Everything's fine. *You're* fine.

She clung to the anchor line and closed her eyes, willing herself to take slow, deep breaths. Oxygen nourished her, her brain cleared, panic subsided.

She opened her eyes and looked at her air gauge again: 1,450 pounds.

She decided to drop down the line another fifty feet. Maybe she could at least see the shipwreck from there. Then she'd start up.

Still clutching the rope, she let herself fall. A hundred and twenty feet, 130, 140, then . . . what was that? Something was moving below. Something was coming up at her.

It had to be Scott. He had seen the wreck and taken his pictures and was already on the way back.

She'd never get to see it. She'd have to settle for Scott's description—endlessly repeated, inevitably embellished. She'd have to endure his sly asides about this being a "man's dive, too tough for the girls."

Too bad, but . . .

This moving thing, this purplish thing, it wasn't Scott

rising at her. It was huge, so huge it couldn't possibly be alive. But what was it? What could it—

Her last sensation was surprise.

Lucas looked at his watch: 10:59. They'd better be on their way up in the next sixty seconds. If not, he'd have to get on the radio and find out where the nearest decompression chamber was. Because these two were gonna be bent up like corkscrews.

That is, unless they never got there at all, chickened out, maybe hung at 150 feet or so, from where they could just see the shipwreck. It was common enough: Big ships underwater freak a lot of people.

That was it, had to be. They'd gotten halfway down and decided this was out of their league after all. They were at 125, 150. They could stay another five minutes. 11:02.

He lay on the bow and shaded his eyes and stared hard down the anchor line, looking for even a glimmer of one of those snazzy wetsuits.

He heard a noise down aft. Je*sus*! Stupid bastards had come up away from the anchor line, probably run out of air and shot for the surface. Be lucky if one of them didn't have an embolism.

Or maybe they'd been decompressing at ten or twenty feet, then come up under the boat. Sure. Made sense.

But why hadn't he seen them? The water was clear as gin.

He stood up and started aft. The noise was still going on, a weird noise, a wet, sucking kind of noise.

Now he smelled something.

Ammonia. *Ammonia?* Here?

As he edged along the side of the cabin, the boat suddenly heaved sharply to starboard.

Christ! What was that?

He heard wood crack and splinter.

The boat was listing badly now, he had to struggle to keep his footing. He jumped down into the cockpit. The gin pole was gone, snapped off three feet above the deck.

He looked over the transom, and what he saw froze him and drove the breath from him. It was an eye, an eye as big as the moon, bigger even, in a field of quivering slime the color of arterial blood.

He shouted—not words, just noise—and snapped upright, to flee the eye. He lurched to the right, took a step, but the boat heaved again, and he was thrown backward. His knees struck the transom, his arms flailed out and he tumbled overboard.

# 13

MARCUS SHARP CHECKED his fuel gauges and saw that in another fifteen or twenty minutes he'd have to turn back to the base.

He had been aloft for a couple of hours, ostensibly on a routine training patrol, in fact trying to spot shipwrecks. He had circled the island, flown low over the reefs in the north and northwest, looking for ballast piles. He had spotted the known wrecks, the *Cristóbal Colón* and the *Caraquet,* but nothing new.

He had hoped to find a virgin wreck for Whip, preferably a late-sixteenth-century Spanish ship laden with ingots and gold chains and perhaps some uncut emeralds. But he'd settle for anything old and untouched, to replenish Whip's rapidly depleting reserves of enthusiasm, hope and money.

Sharp was feeling guilty, because he'd all but promised Whip he could keep that raft, and he'd heard that the police had confiscated it, on the orders of that self-important little shit, St. John.

And it *was* Sharp's fault, at least partly, because—as Captain Wallingford had pointed out in his most patronizing way—Sharp had had no authority to deputize Whip Darling to do anything, let alone to give Darling what amounted to evidence. The logic of Sharp's defense had failed to move Wallingford, who had subjected him to a half-hour lecture on the proper behavior for American servicemen stationed in foreign countries.

Now Sharp was cruising along the South Shore, off Elbow Beach. He could see scores of people frolicking in the surf, and a few snorkelers offshore exploring the wreck of the *Pollockshields*.

Shark bait, Sharp thought . . . if there are any sharks left.

The *Pollockshields* had been a menace for generations. An iron steamer loaded with World War I ammunition, she had sunk on the shallow reefs in 1915. Though much of the ammunition was still live, that wasn't the problem. The iron was. Snorkelers came out from Elbow Beach and poked around the wreck and got caught in the waves that broke over it, and sometimes they were slammed up against the sharp shards of iron. They'd be cut and bleeding and forced to swim hundreds of yards back to shore, through the calm, murky shallows that were the hunting grounds of reef sharks— or, rather, had been.

At five hundred feet, Sharp made a slow circle over the snorkelers, reassuring himself that no dark shadows were lurking nearby, and then he banked off to the west.

Whip had said a friend of a friend had been poring

through the Archives of the Indies in Seville, looking for details of a Spanish fleet that had sunk off Dominica in 1567, when he had seen a reference—almost a parenthe-sis—about one of the ships being separated from the others early in the voyage and running up on the south side of Bermuda.

Looking for that lost lamb was a shot in the dark, but what the hell . . . he had nothing better to do.

Sharp's co-pilot, a lieutenant junior grade named Forester, finished the copy of *People* he'd been reading and said, "I gotta take a fearsome leak."

"Almost home," Sharp said.

He was about to give up, to gain altitude and turn back to the northeast, when his radio came alive.

"Huey One . . . Kindley . . ."

"Go ahead, Kindley. . . ."

"Feel like a little flake patrol, Lieutenant?"

"If it doesn't take more'n ten minutes. Otherwise Forester busts a gut and we all swim home. What's up?"

"A woman called the cops, said she saw a boat go to pieces a mile south of Sou'west Breaker."

"Go to pieces? What did she mean, blow up?"

"No, that's the strange part. She said she was looking through her telescope for humpback whales—some-times she can see 'em from her house—and she saw this fishing boat, thirty-five or forty feet she says, just . . . go to pieces. No flame, no smoke, no nothing. It came apart."

"Sure . . . fat chance. Okay, I'll have a look," Sharp said. "It's on the way home anyway."

He pressed his stick to the left, and the helicopter banked off to the south.

Forester said, "Make it fast, or I'm gonna pee in my pants."

"Grab it and strangle it," Sharp said. "That's an order."

Sharp left Southwest Breaker to his right, so that the sun was almost directly overhead and slightly behind him, and there was no glare on the water. He could see perfectly.

But there was nothing to see.

He flew south for two minutes, then turned southeast. Nothing. Nothing floated, nothing bobbed, nothing broke the endless roll of the blue swells.

"Kindley . . . Huey One . . ." Sharp said into his radio. "I gotta break off. Nothing down there."

"Come on home, Huey One. Probably nothing to it."

Sharp turned east.

"Hey!" Forester said, and he tapped the Plexiglas beside him and pointed downward.

Sharp banked to the left and looked. He saw two white rubber fenders, then some planks, then, half-submerged, looking like a white blanket covered with blue haze, the entire roof of a boat's cabin.

"Can't stop now," Sharp said, "or we'll be down there with it." He set his course at 040, straight for the base.

He had crossed the reef line and was about to be over land when he looked to his right and saw the *Privateer* chugging slowly westward along the shore.

Go home, he told himself, don't do this. You don't need to give Wallingford an excuse to chew your ass a second time.

Then he thought, Screw Wallingford. Sharp had been chewed out by some of the greats, and Wallingford was decidedly junior varsity. What else could they do to him, bring him up for a Captain's Mast? So what? He was formulating new priorities, and the navy was slipping down the list fast.

He pressed the "talk" button on his microphone and said, "*Privateer* . . . *Privateer* . . . *Privateer* . . . This is Huey One. . . ."

* * *

Darling was in the wheelhouse, drinking a cup of tea and wondering how much he could get if he sold his Masonic bottle—it was a good bottle, rare, 170 years old—when the call came over Channel 16.

He picked up the microphone from its hook. "*Privateer* . . . go to twenty-seven, Marcus."

"Going to twenty-seven . . ."

"More bullshit?" Mike said.

"Wasn't his fault about the raft," said Darling. "He tried to do us a good turn."

"*Privateer* . . . Huey One . . ." said Sharp. "Whip, there's a boat wrecked about two miles dead ahead of you, call it two-three-zero from where you are. Mile and a half off the beach."

"Wrecked how?"

"Don't know. There's wreckage on and under the surface. I haven't got fuel left to look for survivors. Police boat's probably on the way, but you're closest."

"Roger that, Marcus. I'll go check it out." Darling started to hang up, but then a kindness occurred to him, and he pushed the button again and said, "Hey, Marcus . . . probably be going out this weekend, if you're interested."

There was relief in Sharp's voice as he replied, "*I'll say* . . . that is, if they don't have me swabbing latrines."

Darling replaced the microphone on its hook, dialed the radio back to Channel 16 and said to Mike, "See? Do a good turn for a friend and they give you a reaming. Hell of a note." He pushed his throttle forward and watched the tachometer needle rise from 1,500 rpms to 2,000.

"Why'd the navy get on Marcus's case?" asked Mike.

"Why d'you think? 'Cause the earl of fucking St. John got on theirs."

Darling was finding himself so angry so often these days that he was beginning to wonder about himself. He'd have to be careful not to let himself slip over the edge into paranoia.

He and Mike had returned the damaged gear to the aquarium and had explained what little they knew about what had happened to it. Darling had begun to outline how he thought new gear might be improved, when the deputy director—a slight, nervous black man whose Vandyke beard, Darling had always believed, was a disguise for his mousy personality—had said, "I'm afraid not."

"Afraid not what?"

"We'll be . . . ah . . . terminating our agreement with you."

"*What? Why?*"

"Well, this was . . . ah . . ." He wouldn't look at Darling. "Expensive equipment . . . after all."

"Sharks are big animals . . . *after all.* . . . Jesus, Milton, if you want me to hang the gear at ten feet, sure, nothing'll touch it. But you want me to hang it down where the action is, maybe actually catch something interesting, there are risks. That's the whole point."

"Yes, but . . . I'm afraid that's that."

"Who's gonna catch your critters for you?"

"Well . . . that's yet to be decided."

Darling had taken a deep breath and closed his eyes, trying to suppress the rage—and the fear, he had to admit—at the thought of eight hundred dollars a month vanishing into the ether.

"It's St. John, isn't it? . . ."

Milton had looked away, at the telephone, as if praying for it to ring. "I don't—"

"Wildlife management. He's decided wildlife management takes in the aquarium, too . . . right?"

"You're jumping to—"

"He's gonna take *my* eight hundred a month and go out with a dip net and a case of Budweiser, and when he doesn't come back with shit, he can blame it on the oil spills off California." Darling was right, he knew it.

Milton was sweating; his eyes darted from side to side. "For heaven's sake, Whip . . ."

"You're right, Milton, I'm overreacting." He had walked to the door and opened it. He could see Mike outside, talking to a tortoise so old it was said to have been a gift to Bermuda from Queen Victoria. "But you know what? I feel sorrier for you. I may not make much of a living, but at least I don't have to earn my pay by kissing the ass of that Irish lizard."

Darling was convinced that St. John saw him as a threat to his power, a rebel against the construction of his little empire. St. John was determined to bring Darling to heel . . . or to destroy him.

And what rankled Darling, what ate away at his guts, was the fact—more evident day by day—that St. John was succeeding. He had all the weapons.

"There," said Mike, pointing to some floating wood. It was about three by five feet, with a patch of indoor-outdoor carpeting nailed to it and two short lengths of chain dangling from it.

"Swim step," Darling said. "Bring it aboard."

Mike went outside, grabbed the boat hook and went aft, while Darling climbed the ladder to the flying bridge.

From up here, twelve feet above the surface, he could see debris everywhere, some a foot underwater, some bobbing on the surface. There were fenders, planks, cushions, life jackets.

The water was patched with rainbow slicks: oil that had leaked from the engine as the boat sank.

"Sling it all aboard," he called down to Mike.

For an hour he cruised among the debris, as Mike grabbed piece after piece of flotsam and tossed it into the cockpit.

"Want that too?" Mike said, pointing to a white wooden rectangle, twelve feet wide by fifteen feet long, that hung a foot or two beneath the surface.

"No, that's his roof," Darling said from the flying bridge. Then something came to him, and he said, "Hang on," and he put the boat in neutral, letting it drift, and went down the ladder. He picked up a four-pronged grapnel attached to twenty feet of rope, and he tossed the hook at the wood. He let it drop till it caught the far edge, then he hauled back on it, dragging the corner of the roof out of water. He had a glimpse of pea-soup green on the underside of the roof.

"It's Lucas Coven's boat," he said, letting the wood fall back, coiling the rope as he brought the hook aboard.

"How d'you know that?"

"I saw him painting the boat last spring. He was doing the whole inside of the house in baby-shit green. Said he'd got the paint on sale."

"What the hell was he doing out here?"

"You know Lucas," Darling said. "Probably had some half-ass scheme to make two dollars in a hurry."

They had known Lucas Coven for more than twenty years and always thought of him as suffering from a case of the "almosts": everything Coven did he could almost make a living at, almost but not quite. He couldn't afford enough fish traps to cover his boat expenses, and when traps were outlawed he had no other trade. He'd do anything for a few bucks—haul water, paint houses, build docks—but he never stuck with anything long enough to make a steady go of it.

"How do you make two dollars out here? Nothing here."

"No," Darling agreed. "Nothing but the *Durham*."

"Nobody dives on the *Durham* . . . nobody with sense."

"Right again. Let's have a look." Darling picked up a rubber fender. There were no marks on it, no scratches, no scars, no burns.

"He had a GM in her, didn't he?" Mike said.

"Yeah. Six-seventy-one."

"So that didn't blow him up. Propane stove?"

"Maybe. But Christ, they'd've heard that bang all the way in St. George's." Darling picked up a section of planking with a brass screw-cap countersunk in it.

"So what blew him up? He carry explosives?"

Darling said, "Nothing blew him up. Look here. No char, no smoke, no disintegration like you'd see in an explosion." He put his nose to the wood. "No stink. You'd smell it if there'd been heat to it." He tossed the wood onto the deck. "He was busted up . . . somehow."

"By what? Nothing out here for him to hit."

"I don't know. Killer whales? This was a wooden boat. Killer whales could splinter a wooden boat."

"Killer whales!? In hailing distance of the beach?"

"*You* come up with something, then." Darling felt anger welling up again. Mike always wanted answers, and it seemed he had fewer and fewer of those. "What else? UFOs? Martians? The frigging Tooth Fairy?" He dropped the wood onto the deck.

"Hey, Whip . . ." Mike said.

Annoyed now with himself, Darling said, "Shit!" and kicked a life jacket, which rose off the deck and would have gone overboard if Mike hadn't caught it.

Mike was about to toss it aside when he noticed something. "What's this?"

Darling looked. The orange cloth covering the kapok had been shredded, and the buoyant material beneath was exposed. There were two marks in it, circles, about six inches in diameter. The rim of each circle was ragged, as if it had been cut by a rasp, and in the center was a deep slash.

"For God's sake," Darling said. "Looks like a scuttle."

"Sure." Mike thought Darling was joking. An octopus? "Moby-bleeding-scuttle," he said. "Besides, you ever seen a scuttle with teeth in its suckers?"

"No." Mike was right. The suckers on an octopus's arms were soft, pliable. A man could unwrap them from around his arm as easily as removing a bandage.

But what was it, then? It was an animal, for certain. This boat hadn't blown up, hadn't hit anything, hadn't been struck by lightning, hadn't magically disintegrated. It had come up against something and been destroyed.

Darling tossed the life jacket onto the deck and kicked some pieces of wood aside to clear his way forward. One of the planks struck the steel bulwark, and as it fell back to the deck something dropped out of it and landed with a click.

It was a claw, like the other one, crescent-shaped, two inches long and sharp as a razor.

He looked overboard, at the still water. But the water wasn't really still, it was alive, and, as if to remind Darling, it sent a gentle swell at him that heaved the boat upward.

As the boat settled again, something floated out from underneath it: rubber, blue with a yellow chevron on either side.

A wetsuit hood.

Darling picked up the boat hook and dipped it overboard and scooped up the hood. It came up like a cup, full of water, and in the water were two little black-and-yellow-striped fish: sergeant majors. They were feeding on something.

Darling held the hood in his hand. A smell rose from it, sharp and acrid. Like ammonia.

His body was shadowing the hood, so he turned into the sun and let light fall into the dark pocket.

What the fish were feeding on looked like a big marble.

Mike came up behind Darling and looked over his shoulder. "What've you— Holy sweet Jesus!" Mike gasped. "Is that human?"

"It is," said Darling, and he stood aside to let Mike retch into the sea.

# 14

THE WOMAN WATCHED through her telescope until her head ached and her vision began to blur. She had seen the navy helicopter come and go, and seen Whip Darling show up in that ramshackle *Privateer*. But where were the police? She had done her civic duty by reporting what she saw; the least the police could do was follow up.

Now it looked as if someone were throwing up over the side. Probably hung over. Fishermen were all the same: fish all day and drink the night away.

If the police weren't going to respond, perhaps she should call the newspaper. Sometimes reporters were more diligent than the police. The only reason she hadn't called the paper earlier was that she was worried that one of her humpbacks might have wrecked the

boat—by accident, of course—and an ignorant reporter
might be tempted to say bad things about whales. But
she had looked and looked, and seen no sign of whales,
no spouting, no flukes, so it was probably safe by now
to call the paper.

The reporter stared at the flashing light on his telephone as he hurried to pull a notepad from his desk
drawer, and blessed his luck. He had been trying to find
this woman for an hour, ever since he had heard the first
reports on the newsroom's police-band radio, but Harbour Radio had refused to give him her name.

This story could be his ticket out of the trenches, his
passport to the big time. He had spent the past three
years writing on numbing topics like the fish-trap con-
troversy and the rise in import duties, and he had begun
to despair that he'd never get off this godforsaken rock.
The problem with Bermuda was that nothing ever happened here, at least nothing of interest to the wire ser-
vices or the news magazines or the television networks.

But this was different. Deaths at sea, especially deaths
under mysterious circumstances, were dynamite. If he
could play up the mystery, maybe impose a Bermuda
Triangle slant on it, he might catch the eye of the AP or
the Cleveland *Plain Dealer* or, dream of dreams, *The
New York Times*.

He had about given up on the woman and was on his
way out the door to go to Somerset, to wait for Whip
Darling, when the switchboard operator had relayed the
call.

He pushed the flashing button and said, "Brendan
Eve, Mrs. Outerbridge. Thank you for calling."

He listened for a few minutes, then said, "You're sure
it didn't explode?"

Again she talked, and again he listened. Lord, but the
woman could talk! By the time she had finished, he saw

that he had scribbled four pages of notes. He could write a treatise on the history of humpback whales.

But there had been nuggets of value in the woman's monologue. He noticed that there was one phrase he had written down several times, and he underlined it: "sea monster."

# PART
# TWO

# 15

DOCTOR HERBERT TALLEY hunched his shoulders and shielded his face against the wind, a roaring northeaster that drove salt water off the ocean and blended it with rain, creating a brackish spray that burned leaves brown. He stepped in a puddle and felt icy water slop over his shoe tops and seep between his toes.

It might as well be winter. The only difference between summer and winter in Nova Scotia was that by winter all the leaves had been blown away.

He crossed the quadrangle, stopped at Commons to pick up his mail and climbed the stairs to his tiny office. He was winded by the exertion, which annoyed, but didn't surprise, him. He wasn't getting enough exercise. He wasn't getting *any* exercise. The weather had been so vile for so long that he hadn't been able to swim or jog. He had taken pride in being a young fifty, but he was beginning to feel like an old fifty-one.

He vowed to start exercising tomorrow, even in a whole gale. He had to. To go to flab would be to admit defeat, to accept the loss of his dreams, to resign himself to whiling away his days as a teacher. Some might say that academia was the graveyard of science, but Herbert Talley wasn't ready to be buried just yet.

Days like today didn't help. A grand total of six students had showed up for his lecture on cephalopods:

six stuporous summer-school students, misfits who had been denied their diplomas until they passed their science requirement. He had done his best to infuse them with his enthusiasm. He was among the world's leading experts on cephalopods, and he found it incredible that they couldn't share his appreciation of the wondrous head-foots. Perhaps the fault lay in him. He was an impatient teacher, who preferred showing to instructing, doing to telling. On field trips and expeditions he was a wizard. But there weren't any more expeditions, not with the economy of the Western world about to implode.

Talley's office had room for a desk and a desk chair, a lounge chair and reading lamp, a bookcase and a table for his radio. One wall was taken up with a *National Geographic* map of the world, which Talley had dotted with pushpins representing events in malacology: expeditions of which he was keeping track, sightings of rare species, depredations by pollution and cyclical calamities like red tides and toxic algae blooms, which could be natural or man-made. The other walls contained his framed degrees, awards, citations and photographs of the celebrities of his field: octopus and squid and oysters and clams and conchs and cowries and chambered nautiluses.

Talley hung his hat and raincoat on the back of the door, turned on the radio, plugged in the electric kettle for water for tea and sat with his airmail copy of *The Boston Globe,* the only newspaper he had access to that recognized the existence of issues other than fishing and petty crime.

There was no news, really, at least nothing to excite an aging malacologist stuck in the wilds of Nova Scotia. Everything was more of the same.

Lulled by Bruno Walter's soothing rendition of Beethoven's Sixth Symphony and by the patter of rain and the whisper of wind, warmed by his tea, Talley struggled to stay awake.

Suddenly his eyes snapped open. A phrase—one phrase out of all the thousands of words on the enormous page in his lap—had infiltrated his doziness and imprinted itself on his mind. It had awoken him like an alarm.

Sea monster.

What about it? What sea monster?

He scanned the page, couldn't find it, ran down each column top to bottom, and then . . . there it was, a tiny item on the bottom of the page, a filler, what was called boilerplate.

### THREE DIE AT SEA

*Bermuda* (AP)—Three persons died yesterday when their boat sank from unknown causes off the shore of this island colony in the Atlantic Ocean. The victims included the two children of media magnate Osborn Manning.

There was no evidence of explosion or fire, and some local residents speculated that the boat had been struck by lightning, though no electrical storms had been reported in the area.

Others, recalling the mysteries of the Bermuda Triangle, blamed the incident on a sea monster. The only clues noted by police were strange marks on wooden planks and an odor of ammonia in some of the debris.

Talley held his breath. He read the item again, and again. He rose from his chair and went to the wall map. His pushpins were color-coded, and he searched for red ones. There were only two, both off Newfoundland, both marked with reference dates from the early 1960s. Off Bermuda there was nothing.

Until now.

Obviously, the reporter hadn't known what he was writing about. He had gathered facts and lumped them together, not realizing that he was inadvertently including the key to the puzzle.

Ammonia. Ammonia was the key. Talley felt a thrill of discovery, as if he had suddenly stumbled upon a new species.

This species wasn't new, however; it was Talley's old nemesis, his quarry, a creature he had spent a large part of his professional life seeking, a creature he had written books about.

He tore the item from the paper and read it again. "Can it be?" he said aloud. "Merciful God, please let it be. After all these years. And, it's time."

It was true, it had to be. There was nothing else it could be. And it was only a thousand miles away, a couple of hours away by air, waiting for him.

But as quickly as he had become elated, he was overcome by gloom. He had to get to Bermuda, but how? He must mount a search, a proper scientific search, but how would he pay for it? The university was funding nothing these days; grant money had vanished. He had no cash of his own, and no family to borrow from.

He had a vision of himself as a mountain climber, with the summit of his aspirations suddenly appearing through a break in the clouds. He would have to struggle to reach it, but struggle he would.

He *had* to. If he missed this chance, he would be acknowledging that he was the most contemptible of academic frauds, a reciter of other people's data, an amalgamator of other people's theories.

The solution was simple enough: money, the world was full of money. How could he get some of it?

From the radio came the strains of music he knew but couldn't name, a lilting melody, a song, haunting and sad but somehow hopeful too. What was it? The blank in his memory annoyed him, so he pushed from his mind all thoughts of money and concentrated on identifying the piece.

The song ended, there was a brief pause, and then another song began—equally haunting, equally hopeful—and Talley knew what it was: Mahler's *Kindertotenlieder*, the song cycle about the death of children. A nice irony, Talley thought, that from the most ghastly of tragedies could come a wondrous masterpiece. It would take a spiritual giant to create beauty out of the death of children.

Children . . .

He stopped breathing.

There it was. His answer.

He took the newspaper clipping from his pocket and smoothed it on the desk before him. Manning, he read . . . "media magnate Osborn Manning."

He picked up the telephone and asked the operator for Directory Assistance for New York City.

Osborn Manning sat in his office and tried to focus on a report from one of his vice presidents. The news was good. With the economy heading for the dumper, people weren't willing to pay seven dollars for a movie or fifty for the theater, weren't taking Sunday drives or visiting amusement parks. They were opting for cheap entertainment, his entertainment, cable television. Subscriptions were up across the country, and his people had been able to buy half a dozen new franchises at distress prices, from operators who couldn't keep up with their bank debt. Manning had no bank debt. He had seen the troubles coming, and had concluded that in the nineties, cash would be king. He had sold off most of his marginal companies in late '88, at the top of the market, and now he had more cash than many emerging nations.

So what? Would cash bring back his kids? Would cash make his wife whole? He hadn't known how much his family mattered to him, until he lost it. Could cash restore a family?

Cash couldn't even buy him revenge, and revenge was one thing he craved, as if it could help expiate his sin of being a distant, almost an absentee, father. In his private, unspoken yearnings, he wished his children had been murdered by some hophead. Then he could have killed the hophead himself, or hired someone to do it.

But he didn't even have the luxury of imagining revenge, for he had no idea what had killed his children. No one knew. Freak accident. Terribly sorry. Pain gnawed at his stomach, a spasm flashed from just below his rib cage down into his bowels. Maybe he was getting an ulcer. Good, he thought. He deserved it.

He tossed the report aside, leaned back in his chair and looked out the window at the sprawl of Central Park. The late-day sun was glittering gold off the windows on Fifth Avenue. It was a view he loved, or, used to love. He didn't care anymore.

The intercom buzzed on his desk. He spun around and punched a button and said, "Dammit, Helen, I told you I—"

"Mr. Manning . . . it's about the children."

"What about them?" And then, to see what the words felt like in his mouth, he added, "They're dead."

There was a pause, and in his mind's eye Manning saw his secretary swallow.

"Yes, sir," she said. "But there's this Canadian scientist on the phone."

"Who?"

"A man who says he knows what killed the children."

Manning suddenly felt cold. He couldn't speak.

"Mr. Manning . . . ?"

He reached for the phone, and he saw that his hand was shaking.

# 16

THEY HAD RESTED, mother and calf, on the surface of the sea with the others in the small pod, since the sun had lowered into the western sky and the moon had appeared as a pale wafer in the east.

It was a daily gathering, fulfilling a need for socialization. No matter where they were, no matter how dispersed during the day, as night began to fall the pod came together, not to feed, not to breed, but to experience the comfort of community.

In times past, long ago but still within the memory of the eldest of the pod, there had been many more of them. There was no questioning, for these whales with the largest brains on earth did not question, they accepted. They accepted their smaller numbers, would accept the inevitable further shrinkage, would accept even when the pod was perhaps reduced to two or three.

But these sophisticated brains, unique among animals, did recognize loss, did know sadness, did, in their way, feel. And accept though they might, they also lamented.

Now, as darkness fell, the pod disbanded. In ones and twos and threes they moved slowly apart and drew breaths through the tops of their heads, a chorus of hollow sighs; they filled their enormous lungs and dove into the darkness. Instinct drove them north, and north they would go, until months from now the planet's rhythms shifted and sent them south again.

Mother and calf dove as one; only a few months ago, this would have been impossible. When the calf was younger, its lungs were still developing, and they had lacked the capacity to sustain an hour-long dive into the deep. But now the calf was two years old, had grown to twenty-five feet long and more than twenty tons of weight. The teeth in its lower jaw had erupted into pointed cones efficient for gripping and scooping. The calf had ceased to nurse and now it fed on live prey.

As they dove in the black water, propelling themselves with powerful sweeps of their horizontal tails, from their blunt foreheads they emitted the pings and clicks of sonar impulses that, on return, would identify prey.

The creature hung in the dark, doing nothing, anticipating nothing, fearing nothing, letting itself be carried by the current. Its arms and whips floated loose, undulating like snakes; its fins barely moved, yet kept it stable.

Suddenly it was struck a blow, and another, and what passed for hearing in the creature registered a sharp and penetrating ping. Its arms withdrew, its whips coiled and cocked.

Its enemy was coming.

The sonar return was unmistakable: prey. The mother thrust downward with her tail, accelerating, pulling away from her calf as she drove herself ever deeper.

The calf strove to keep up, and with its striving—

though as yet it had no sense of this, felt no urgency—it was consuming oxygen too fast.

Though the prey was already located and had made no effort to escape, the mother's brain fired sonar missiles again and again, for it had determined that this was to be the calf's first mature kill. The prey was large and must be stunned by sonar hammers before the calf could set upon it.

Besieged, the creature recoiled. Chemical triggers fired, nourishing the flesh, galvanizing it and streaking it with luminescence. As if in contradiction of the color display, other reflexes voided a sac within the body cavity, flushing a cloud of black ink into the black water.

Blows struck it again and again, pounding the flesh, confusing the small brain.

Defense impulse changed to attack impulse. It turned to fight.

As the mother closed in on the prey, she slowed, permitting the calf to draw even, then to pass her. She unleashed a final burst of sonar blows, then swerved and began to circle the prey.

The calf plunged downward, excited by the prospect of the kill, impelled by a million years of imprinting.

It opened its mouth.

The creature felt the pressure wave, was driven backward by it. The enemy was upon it.

It lashed out with its whips. They flailed blindly, then found flesh, hard and slick. Automatically they surrounded it and their circles fastened to it and their hooks dug in.

The muscles in the whips tightened, drawing the

enemy to the creature and the creature to the enemy, like two boxers in a clinch.

The calf closed its mouth on . . . nothing. It was perplexed. Something was wrong. It felt pressure behind its head, confining it, slowing its movement.

It struggled, pumping with its tail, corkscrewing, frantic to rid itself of whatever was holding it down.

Now its lungs began to send out signals of need.

The mother circled, alarmed, sensing danger to her calf but incapable of helping it. She knew aggression, she knew defense, but in the programming of her brain there was no code for response to a threat to another, even to her own offspring. She made noises—high-pitched, desperate and futile.

The creature held on, anchored to its enemy. The enemy thrashed, and from its motion the creature sensed a change in the balance of the battle: No longer was its enemy the aggressor; it was trying to escape.

Though here in the absence of light there were no colors, the chemicals in the body of the beast changed their composition from defense to attack.

The more its enemy struggled to rise, the more the creature drew water into its body and expelled it through the funnel beneath its belly, forcing itself and its enemy down into the abyss.

The calf was drowning. Deprived of oxygen, the musculature in its tissue shut down bit by bit. An unknown agony coursed through its lungs. Its brain began to die.

It stopped struggling.

The creature felt its enemy stop struggling and begin to sink. Though it still clutched the flesh, gradually the creature released the tension and let itself fall with its kill, slowly spiraling.

The whips tore away a chunk of blubber and fed it to the arms, which passed it back to the snapping protuberant beak.

The mother, circlıng, followed her calf with sonar pings. She sent clicks and whistles of distress, a bleat of helpless despair.

At last her lungs, too, were exhausted, and, with a final sonic burst, she thrust up toward the life-giving air above.

# 17

MARCUS SHARP SAT on the beach and wished he were somewhere else. He couldn't remember the last time he had gone to a beach, probably not since the times with Karen. He didn't like beaches much; he didn't like sitting on sand and watching water while his skin fried in the tropical sun. A misguided impulse, born of desperate frustration, had led him to jump on his motorbike and drive the fifteen miles from the base to Horseshoe Bay.

It was a Saturday; he was off duty and had hoped to go diving with Whip Darling. But when he had called at eight that morning, Darling had told him that he and Mike intended to chip paint all day. Sharp had offered to help, but Darling had said no, they'd be working in a tight hold in the stern of the boat, nowhere near big enough for three people.

Sharp had read for an hour and then, at eleven o'clock, had found himself scanning the titles in the video store. He had looked at his watch and realized, with a feeling of depression bordering on nausea, that in order to get through the rest of Saturday he would have to rent not one, not two, but at least three movies.

This is your life? he had said to himself. Deciding between *National Lampoon's Christmas Vacation* and *Look Who's Talking*? Is all that's left to you a choice between spending your time with an infantile adult or a smart-ass infant? What would Karen say? She'd say, Live, Marcus. Go rob a bank, fly a plane, trim your toenails, *any*thing. Just do *some*thing!

He had walked out of the video store and tried to find a tennis game, but all the tennis players he knew were playing soccer, and he didn't like the game: It was all technique with little result; he liked high-scoring games. He had called a couple of dive-tour operators; the boats had all left for the day. He had volunteered to take a helicopter up; none was available.

So he had gone to the beach, impelled, he guessed, by some vague hope that he might meet a girl worth talking to, having lunch with, maybe even making a date with to go dancing. Not that he knew how to dance, but anything was better than sitting around the Bachelor Officers Quarters watching reruns of *Cagney & Lacey*.

It had been a mistake. As he sat on the beach and watched children frolic in the wave wash and couples stroll along and families picnic under palm trees, he had felt more and more lonely, more and more hopeless. He wondered if there were any singles clubs on the island. Maybe he should become a lush and join Alcoholics Anonymous, just for the company.

He had seen two girls with potential, American tour-

ists, pretty and vivacious, wearing bikinis brief enough
to stir interest but not so brief as to announce that they
were on the prowl. They had even stopped and spoken
to him. Why, he wasn't certain; possibly because he
looked safe: thirtyish, and obviously not a self-styled
stud, what with his workingman's tan—all white except
for his arms and face. One had fair skin and red hair, the
other was deeply tanned and raven-haired.

He had wanted to talk to them; his mind had flooded
with conversational gambits—the navy, helicopters,
shipwrecks, diving, Bermuda. But he was out of practice
in the dating game, and after he had answered their
questions about moderately priced restaurants in
Hamilton, he had let them get away. Within five minutes, of course, he had thought of several stratagems
that might have intrigued them, and he cursed himself
as a dim-witted fool.

Perhaps they'd go in the water, and he'd have a second chance. He'd go in nearby and, as the locals would
say, have a go at chatting them up.

Then he thought: Why bother? What would it accomplish? He didn't feel driven by his glands. He didn't feel
driven by anything.

And that, brother, he had concluded, is your problem.

Sharp looked at the water and saw, a hundred yards
offshore, a wind-surfer trying valiantly to catch a puff of
breeze and sail a few feet. But there was no breeze, so he
kept toppling over backward and dragging the sail
down on top of him.

Sharp wondered how deep the water was out where
the guy was wind-surfing. Whatever had destroyed that
boat and killed the divers was in deep water.

Sharp found it interesting that there had been no
panic, especially after the paper had quoted that dippy
woman word for word and included all her idiotic

claims about a sea monster. People were still swimming, still sailing, still wind-surfing. He had been in his teens when *Jaws* had swept the States, and he had vivid memories of parents refusing to let their children get their feet wet, of beaches being closed and of otherwise rational adults declining to swim in water over their heads . . . in lakes.

Perhaps the current lack of panic could be attributed to lack of knowledge. No one knew what kind of thing might be out there, but it wasn't a shark and it wasn't a whale, so there wasn't even credible speculation. Sharp suspected that Whip would have an idea, but Whip wasn't a man to make guesses. Guesses, Whip would say, were a waste of time and energy.

Sharp was hungry, and so he got to his feet and started toward the concession stand. He was about to turn into the trees when he saw the two American girls. They were tying their hair back with rubber bands. They saw him watching them, and they waved at him, ran into the water and began to swim.

Okay, he thought, what the hell. . . . He'd wait till they stopped swimming, then he'd go in and swim out to them and try to think of something clever to say.

When they were thirty or forty yards offshore, the girls stopped and treaded water. Their heads were three or four feet apart, and they were talking and laughing.

Sharp walked down to the water's edge. He saw one of the girls wave, and he waved back.

The girl waved again, with both hands, and then she disappeared underwater, and now the other one was waving, too, and shouting. No, not shouting, Sharp realized. Screaming.

"Omigod," he said, and he took a couple of running steps and dove into waist-deep water and swam, sprinting. He churned the water, breathing only every third or fourth stroke.

He looked up to get his bearings; he was almost there. He saw the redheaded girl flailing and shrieking, and every time she raised her arms out of the water she'd sink. The other girl was trying to get to her, to get under her windmilling arms, to grab her and stop her hysterics.

Sharp swam up behind the redhead and pinned her arms to her sides and wrapped his arms around her and leaned back, kicking to keep himself afloat and her head out of water. He looked for the shark, the barracuda, the man-o'-war. He looked for blood.

"I've got you," he said. "You're okay. Calm down, it's okay."

The girl's shrieks were subsiding now into sobs.

"Are you hurt? What happened?"

The other girl said, "She just all of a sudden started screaming and waving her arms."

Sharp felt the girl relax, and he released his grip and put a hand under her back to keep her afloat.

"Something . . ." she said.

"Bit you?" Sharp asked.

". . . horrible and slimy and gross . . ."

"What, stung you?"

"No, it . . ." She rolled over and clung to Sharp, weeping and almost sinking him.

Sharp said, "Let's get you to shore." He took one of her arms, and gestured for the other girl to take the other arm. Together they sidestroked toward shore, holding the girl between them. Soon they could touch bottom.

The girl said, "I'm okay. I just . . . it was . . ." She looked at Sharp and, trying to smile, said, "Thanks."

"Back in a minute," Sharp said, and he turned toward deep water and swam an easy breaststroke. When he gauged that he had reached the spot where the girls had been, he stopped swimming and spun in a slow circle, searching the water. He didn't know what he was looking for. Box jellyfish didn't exist in Bermuda; there were no sea wasps. Besides, the girl was unhurt, just scared. There were Portuguese men-o'-war, but they were unmistakable: Their purple bladders floated on the surface. He supposed there were big, harmless jellyfish that hung under the surface, but she'd have seen them, parts of them would have stuck to her.

He started for the shore, slowly, breaststroking, and then his hand touched something; he jerked upward, backpedaled. He looked at the water where his hand had been. There, a foot underwater, was something creamy white and roundish, about the size of a watermelon. Gingerly, he reached forward and touched it. It was slimy, ragged, pulpy. It felt like rotten meat. He put his hand under it. The underside was hard and slick. He brought it to the surface, and as soon as the air touched it, his nostrils were assailed by a vile smell of putrefaction that made his eyes water.

It wasn't meat, it was fat. Blubber. Pinkish white and shredded.

He rolled it over. The skin side was blue-black and newly scarred, near the middle, with a circle, five or six inches across, of what looked like cuts. In the center of the circle was a single deep gash that went all the way through the skin and into the blubber. On one of the edges was half of another circle.

"Sweet Jesus . . ." Sharp said.

Pushing the thing ahead of him, he swam to shore.

On the beach, the children were gathered around something that had washed up. They were prodding it with a stick and pushing one another toward it and saying "Yuk!" and "Gross!"

Sharp looked at it and realized that it was another piece of blubber, smaller, with two half-circles, one on either end.

As he turned away, a parent came up to the children and saw what they had and said, "Holy shit!" and then called, "Hey, Nelson, come looka this!"

Sharp held the thing as far away from his face as he could. The girls were sitting together, the redhead wrapped in a towel, the other's arm around her shoulder.

"She's okay," said the dark-haired girl, smiling and adding, "We want to thank you. Can we—" The breeze carried the stench of Sharp's prize to her. "What's *that*?"

"Gotta go," Sharp said. He scooped up his towel, wrapped the blubber in it, put on his sunglasses and walked up to the lot where he had left his motorbike.

# 18

DARLING AND MIKE were on their knees in the after hold of the *Privateer*, sanding away the rough edges around the paint they had chipped. They wore surgical masks to keep the paint dust out of their lungs, and goggles to protect their eyes.

Darling had owned the boat for six years, and the hull had held up well. There weren't any significant leaks, even around the stuffing box, but the hold trapped humidity, and humidity and salt air eventually ate through everything.

He was in a foul mood. He hated chipping paint, would much prefer to have let the yard do it when the boat was hauled out for bottom-painting in the fall. But the yard was charging forty dollars per man-hour, and Darling was beginning to wonder if he'd even be able to afford to have the boat pulled up on the slip so *he* could paint the bottom.

He felt the boat dip slightly as a weight came aboard, heard footsteps on the deck above. He looked up and saw Sharp standing by the open hatch. "Hey, Marcus . . ."

"Sorry to interrupt."

"Don't be. I'd welcome Lucifer himself to get me away from this godforsaken work."

"Could you look at something for me?"

"You bet." Darling removed his mask and goggles and started up the ladder.

Mike kept sanding until Darling said, "Come look, Michael boy. Don't miss a chance for a breather."

Sharp had set the bundle on a cutting table amidships and was standing away from it, to avoid the smell.

As Darling approached, the stench hit him, and he said, "Christ, lad! What you brung me, something dead?"

"Very," Sharp said, and he told Darling what had happened at Horseshoe Bay.

Darling held an end of the towel while Mike unrolled it. Flies materialized from nowhere, and two gulls that had been sitting on the water rose up and began to circle over the boat.

"Whale," Mike said.

Darling nodded. "Young, too."

"What tells you that?" Sharp asked.

"The blubber's thin; he hasn't got his full ration yet. See how it goes to pink after a few inches?"

Mike said, "Sperm whale?"

"I warrant."

"Prop got him?"

"No," Sharp said. "Turn it over."

Darling used a knife blade to flip the blubber. In the direct sunlight, the circle of marks shone like a necklace, and putrid flesh was oozing out of the slash in the center.

Mike and Darling looked at each other, then Darling said softly, "Son of a bitch . . ." He walked into the cabin, reached up on a shelf for something, then came back holding an amber-colored crescent claw. He slid the claw into the slash in the blue-black skin. It fit perfectly.

"Son of a bitch . . ." he said again.

Sharp said, "What is it, Whip? What did this?"

"I hope it isn't what I think it is," Darling said.

"What?"

Darling pointed to the blubber and said to Mike, "Drop that mess over the side, let the breams have a feed." Then he turned to Sharp. "Come on."

"Where to?"

"Need to consult a book or two."

As Darling led the way up the path to his house, he noticed his daughter's car in the driveway. "Dana's here," he said. "Wonder what about."

Sharp had never been inside Darling's house before, and he looked quickly around. It was a classic eighteenth-century Bermuda house, built like an upside-down ship. Sturdy wooden knees supported the ceilings; twelve-by-twelve beams braced the walls. The chests, cabinets, tables and floors were all of wide-board Bermuda cedar, relics of the days before the blight that killed all the cedar trees. The rooms were cool and dark and redolent of the rich spiciness of cedar.

The two women sitting in the dining room jumped when they saw Darling in the doorway.

The younger woman—tanned and sharp-featured,

with sun-bleached hair—quickly shuffled the papers on the table before her, covering some with others.

Darling didn't seem to notice. He said, "Hey, Lizard," and went to her and kissed her on the cheek. "What brings you up here?"

"Plotting and planning," she said. "What else?"

"That's the way, keep the bastards at bay. You know Marcus Sharp? Marcus, this is Dana."

"Know *of* you," said Dana, and she smiled and shook Sharp's hand.

"Nice to meet you," Sharp said. He thought Dana looked uneasy, awkward. She kept her back to the table, blocking the pile of papers.

Darling led Sharp through the living room to a small room beyond, lined with bookcases and furnished only with a huge cedar desk and two chairs.

"I should be ashamed," Darling said as he turned on a light.

"Why?"

"Putting my faith in science. The only thing scientists admit is what they know. What they don't know—what might be, all the stuff in the realm of the possible but unproven—they dismiss as myth."

Sharp let his eyes scan the titles on the shelves. It seemed that every book ever written about the sea was here, from Rachel Carson to Jacques Cousteau, Samuel Eliot Morison to Mendel Peterson, Peter Freuchen to Peter Matthiessen. And not only books about the sea, but books on coins, ceramics, glassware, shipwrecks, treasure, weaponry.

"Now let's see." Darling pulled a large cased volume from a shelf, and read the title aloud: *"Mysteries of the Sea."* He removed the case, and opened the book.

"About ten years ago," he said as he leafed through the pages, "I was on a boat in the Sea of Cortez with some aquarium people from California, helping them gather strange critters. One night, we saw some Mexicans fishing with lights, and we cruised over to have a look. They were jigging for big squid. Humboldt squid, four or five feet long, fifty or sixty pounds. I'd never seen the big ones before, so I decided to get in the water with them. As soon as my mask cleared, one of the bastards made a run at me. I swatted at him, and faster than I could believe, one of his whips shot out and grabbed my wrist. I thought a hundred needles were stabbing me. I punched him in the eye, and he let go, and I started up, figuring this wasn't a healthy place to be. Then all of a sudden I felt myself being dragged down. *Three* of the goddam things had me, and they were yanking me down into the gloom. I tell you, the Lord must have a special place in His heart for stupid Bermudians, 'cause everything they grabbed broke away: one of my flippers, my depth gauge, a collecting bag. I took off for the surface. For some reason, they didn't chase me, and I got back on the boat. But I had nightmares for a month."

"Jesus," Sharp said.

Darling turned a page, then said, "There," and pushed the book toward Sharp.

"What's *that*?" Sharp asked as he stared at the picture on the page. It was a nineteenth-century woodcut of a hideous creature, a prehistoric-looking beast with a huge bulbous body that ended in a tail shaped like an arrowhead. It had eight writhing arms, two whips twice the length of the body and two gigantic eyes. In the picture, the beast was rising up out of the sea and destroying a sailing ship. Bodies were flying from the wreckage, and a woman, her eyes wide with terror, was hanging from the creature's beak.

"That," Whip said, "is the granddaddy of the critter that grabbed me. It's *Architeuthis dux,* the oceanic giant squid."

"Talk about nightmares. It can't be real . . . can it?"

"It's real, all right, rare but real." Darling paused. "In fact, Marcus, it's more than real. It's out there now. It's here."

Sharp looked at Darling. "Come on, Whip. . . ." he said.

"You don't believe me?" Darling said. "Okay. Maybe you'll believe Herman Melville." He reached up and pulled out a copy of *Moby-Dick,* and flipped through the pages until he found the one he wanted. Then he read aloud: " '. . . we now gazed at the most wondrous phenomenon which the secret seas have hitherto revealed to mankind. A vast pulpy mass, furlongs in length and breadth, of a glancing cream-color, lay floating on the water, innumerable long arms radiating from its centre, and curling and twisting like a nest of anacondas, as if blindly to clutch at any object within reach.' "

As Darling closed the book, Sharp said, "Whip, *Moby-Dick* is fiction."

"Not altogether. The whale is fact, based on a real incident that happened to a ship called the *Essex*."

"Still . . ."

"You want facts? Okay, we'll find you facts." Darling pulled out another book, and squinted as he read the faded lettering on the spine. *"The Last Dragon,"* he said, "by Herbert Talley, Ph.D. This should do it." Years before, he had turned pages down as marks, and he opened the book to the first mark. "Giant squid have been written about since the sixteenth century, maybe even earlier. You've heard the word *kraken*? It's Swedish for 'uprooted tree.' That's what people thought the monsters looked like, with all those tentacles snaking around like roots. Nowadays, scientists like the word *cephalopod,* which is a pretty good description."

"Why?" asked Sharp. "What's it mean?"

" 'Head-footed.' It's 'cause their arms, what people thought were their feet, spring right out from their head." He turned to another mark. "Here, Marcus," he said. "One of the buggers came up in the Indian Ocean and dragged down a schooner called the *Pearl,* just like in that woodcut. Killed everybody. There were more than a hundred witnesses." Darling slapped the book. "Damn," he said. "I can't believe I didn't figure this out sooner. It's so obvious. There's *nothing* else that could have torn up our gear like that. Nothing else. No shark that's ever swum is big enough and mean enough to break a thirty-eight-foot boat into splinters." He paused. "And nothing else is so all-out, bone-deep evil."

"But, Whip. Look at the date." Sharp pointed at the book. "Eighteen seventy-four. That's not today."

"Marcus, those marks on the whale skin, you saw for yourself." Darling took one of the claws from his pocket and held it up. "What kind of beast has knives like that?" Darling felt a growing sense of urgency. Suppose he was right. Suppose what was out there was a giant squid. What could they possibly do? Catch it? Hardly. Kill it? How? But if they didn't kill it, what could they do—what could anybody do—to get rid of it?

He pulled more books down from the shelf, handed a few to Sharp, then sat on the couch and opened one. "Read," he said. "We better learn everything we can about this beast."

They pored through Darling's books about the sea. The references to giant squid were sketchy and often contradictory, some experts claiming that the animals grew no bigger than fifty or sixty feet long, others insisting that hundred-footers, or bigger, swam in all the oceans of the world. Some said that the sucker disks of giant squid contained teeth and hooks; some said they contained one or the other; some said neither. Some said that they had photophores in their flesh, which made them glow with bioluminescence; some said they didn't.

"Nobody can agree about anything," Sharp said after he had read for a while. "That's the bad news. The good news is that all the recorded attacks on people took place in the last century."

"No," said Darling, and he passed the Talley book to Sharp. "With this beast, it looks like there is no good news."

Sharp glanced at the open page. "Shit," he said. "Nineteen forty-one?"

"And not far from here, either. Twelve torpedoed sailors in a lifeboat. It was overloaded, and a couple of them had to hang overboard. The first night, in pitch-darkness, there was a scream, and one of the men was gone. Second night, same thing. So now they all crowded into the boat. The third night, they heard a scratching noise on the gunwale, and they smelled something. Well, it seems that the giant squid that had been following them—staying down during the day and coming up at night—was feeling around with one of his whips. It touched one of the men, snapped around him fast as lightning and hauled him overboard. Now they knew what it was, and the next night they were ready for it, so when the whip came up and started hunting, they jumped on it and cut it off, but not before one of the men got beat up pretty bad. The squid went away, never came back. The guy who got beat up, they found he'd had pieces of flesh torn away the size of an American quarter. They figure the animal was . . . what?"

Sharp ran his finger down the page. "Twenty-three feet," he said. "The size of a big station wagon."

Darling thought for a moment, then said, "How big would you say those marks on that whale skin were?"

"Five inches?"

"Judas Priest." Darling stood up. "This goddam squid may be as big as a blue whale."

"A blue whale!" Sharp said. "For crissakes, Whip, that's twice as big as your boat. It's bigger than a goddam dinosaur. A blue whale's the biggest animal that's ever been."

"In body mass, yes, but maybe not in length. And sure as hell not in nastiness."

As they headed back outside, they passed the dining room, and Charlotte looked up and said, "Whip, what's this about a giant squid?"

"Giant squid? What are you, some kind of psychic?"

"It was on the radio just now. Somebody found something on a beach, and one of the scientists at the aquarium said—"

"Yes, Charlie," Darling said. "It looks like we've got ourselves a giant squid."

"They're having a big meeting about it tomorrow night. Down at the lodge hall. Fishermen, divers, sailboat types. The whole island's in an uproar."

"I don't wonder."

"How big is a thing like that?"

"Big."

"William," Charlotte said, and she rose from the table and came over and took Darling's arm. "Promise me."

"Come on, Charlie. Nobody but a horse's ass would make a run at a beast like that."

"Like Liam St. John, for instance."

"What do you mean?"

"St. John said on the radio that he's going to catch it. To save Bermuda. He says he and what he called his 'people' know how to do it."

"Fat bloody chance," Darling said. "Dr. St. John's gonna end up in the belly of the beast, and good riddance." He leaned over and kissed her and looked beyond at the pile of papers on the table. "What are you girls doing, taking over General Motors?"

"Nothing," Charlotte said, and she kissed him back. "Go away." She started toward the table, stopped and said, "You had a call."

"Who from? What'd they want?"

"They didn't say. Foreigners. The one I talked to sounded Canadian. They just wanted to know if you were available."

"Available for what?" Darling said. "Never mind, I can guess. If they call again, you can tell 'em I *was* available, until about ten minutes ago. Now, all of a sudden, I think I've retired."

# 19

WHAT A JOKE, Darling thought as he left the lodge hall. They had called it an island forum, but it had really been nothing but a charade, a vehicle for the premier, Solomon Tucker, to show the citizenry that he was concerned, without ever having to do anything. Not that there was anything anybody could do; but the premier hadn't gone so far as to admit that: Like most politicians, he'd retreated from here to Christmas, without actually surrendering.

Everybody had been allowed to blow off steam and offer cockamamy suggestions for dealing with a monster that few people had ever heard of and nobody had ever seen. Now, if things calmed down and returned to normal, old Solly could credit "democracy in action"; if things got worse, he could lay off at least half the blame on the people, who had been asked to participate but hadn't had any solutions. He was a winner either way.

Darling took a deep breath of night air and decided to walk home. It was only a couple of miles, and he needed the exercise after sitting for two hours. He figured the meeting would go on for at least another hour, with people squabbling over how to phrase the warnings that would have to be issued.

It was probably too late to worry. Thanks to Liam St. John and his everlasting crusade for personal publicity, this morning's paper had carried the headline MONSTER IS GIANT SQUID, ST. JOHN CONFIRMS. By now, that news would be burning up the wires all around the world.

Some people had voiced the hope that the Newport-to-Bermuda race, which was already under way, wouldn't be affected, but the part of it that benefited Bermuda already had been. Hotel reservations were down; caterers were finding themselves with no affairs to cater; taxi drivers were sitting idle, playing cribbage on the hoods of their cabs.

Even Darling himself had managed to lose a pile of money he didn't have. Halfway through the meeting, Ernest Chambers, the diver who had offered Darling charter work during the race layover, had jumped to his feet and announced that two-thirds of his dive trips had been canceled, and what was the government going to do about it.

Predictably, Liam St. John had waited till things seemed at an impasse before he rose from his seat in the row of cabinet ministers and, after a vain attempt to make himself appear taller than his five feet four by fluffing up his helmet of pumpkin-colored curls, asked for public support for his plan of action.

Since nobody knew enough about the monster to pass judgment on St. John's plan, a clamor had gone up to get Darling to say what he thought about it. After all, somebody had pointed out, "Whip's caught at least one of everything God ever put in the ocean around here."

And Darling had told them what he'd read, and his conclusions: that the appearance of a giant squid around Bermuda was probably a fluke, a natural accident; that since boats and human beings weren't its normal food, in all likelihood it would eventually go away; and that to set out to catch or destroy it was pointless, because in his opinion no one could do it, Dr. St. John's ambitious plan notwithstanding. In sum, Darling had said, leave it alone for a while and wait.

St. John had termed Darling's approach "do-nothing defeatism," and that had set off a new round of circular arguing.

As Darling had left, elbowing through the crowd of standees, he had heard someone mention issuing a formal Notice to Mariners, someone else suggest a press release pointing out that more people were killed every year by bee stings than by all sea creatures put together, and the premier announce the formation of a committee to explore options—to be chaired by Dr. St. John.

Darling walked along the road to Somerset, and thought about what to do. Part of the problem with all those people, he decided, was modern times. Back in the old days, they would have accepted the advent of something like *Architeuthis* without question. The unexplainable and unpreventable were part of life, and people learned to live with them. Not anymore. People were spoiled; they couldn't accept a situation that demanded patience and offered no easy solutions.

As he came to a narrow part of the road, buttressed on both sides by high limestone walls, a car approached from behind. He stepped off the pavement and backed against the wall to let the car pass, but as it passed him, it slowed and stopped just ahead.

Now what? he thought. He looked at the trunk of the car and saw a BMW insignia. Somebody rich . . . and foolish: In a country with a speed limit of 20 mph, a BMW wasn't transportation, it was a trophy.

A man got out of the passenger's side and started back toward him. "Captain Darling?" he said.

Darling saw a tweed jacket and tan-colored pants and low-topped walking boots, but he couldn't see the man's face. "Do I know you?" he said.

"My name is Dr. Herbert Talley, Captain."

Talley, Darling thought. Talley. There was something familiar about that name, but he couldn't place it. "Doctor of what?"

"Malac— . . . well, squid, Captain. Doctor of squid, you could say."

"You don't have to talk down to me. I know the word 'malacology.' "

"Sorry. Of course. Could we give you a lift home?"

"I'm happy to walk," Darling said, and he started around the car, but then he remembered, and he stopped and said, "Talley. Dr. Talley. You wrote that book, right? *The Last Dragon*."

Talley smiled and said, "Yes. I did."

"Good book. Full of facts. At least, I took 'em for facts."

"Thank you. Ah . . . Captain . . . we'd like to talk to you. Could you spare us a few minutes?"

"Talk about what?"

"About *Architeuthis*."

An alarm bell rang in the back of Darling's brain: This must be the man who had telephoned. Charlotte had said he sounded Canadian, and Talley's pronunciation of the word 'about,' as if it were 'a boat,' was a dead giveaway. He said, "I've said all I have to say."

"Perhaps you could listen, then, just for a few minutes . . . a drink?"

"Who's 'we'?"

Talley gestured toward the car. "Mr. Osborn Manning." When Darling said nothing, seeming not to register, Talley said, "Manning . . . the father of the—"

"Oh yeah. Sorry."

"We . . . he . . . we would appreciate a word with you."

Darling hesitated, wishing Charlotte were with him. He wasn't good at fencing with slick people. On the other hand, he didn't want to be rude, not to a man who had just lost both his children. What would *he* feel like if Dana were eaten by some . . . thing? He couldn't imagine and didn't want to try. Finally, he said, "No harm, I guess."

"Fine," Talley said, holding open the back door of the car. "There's a nice hotel around the—"

Darling shook his head. "Go up the road a hundred yards, pull in under a sign that says 'Shilly's.' I'll meet you there."

"We'll drive you."

"I'll walk." Darling stepped around the car.

"But—"

"Shilly's," Darling said, and kept walking.

Shilly's had once been a one-pump gas station; then, in succession, a discotheque, a boutique and a video-rental store. Now it was a one-room restaurant, owned by a retired shark fisherman. It advertised itself as "the home of Bermuda's famous conch fritters," which was a local joke since Bermuda's conchs had been fished out years ago. If pressured, Shilly would serve a patron something he called fried fish, but he made his living purveying cheap booze. The skeleton of the old gas pump still stood in the parking lot, painted purple.

Darling could have let them take him up to the hotel;

he had nothing against hotels. But they would have
been comfortable there, and he didn't want them to feel
comfortable. He wanted them to be on edge, and to
make the conversation short and to the point.

As he turned into the parking lot, he saw that the
BMW was parked between two battered vans.

He walked into Shilly's and stood for a moment,
letting his eyes adjust to the darkness. He smelled stale
beer and cigarette smoke and the spicy, sweet aroma of
marijuana. A dozen men crowded around the snooker
table, shouting and placing bets. A few others argued
over an ancient pinball machine. They were hard men,
all of them, with short fuses. Every one was black.

There were several empty tables near the door, but
Talley and Manning were standing together in a corner,
as if they had been sent there as punishment by a
teacher.

An enormous man, black as a Haitian and broad as
a linebacker, slid off a barstool and ambled over to
Darling. "Whip . . ." he said.

"Shilly . . ."

"They with you?" Shilly tipped his head toward the
corner.

"They are."

"Good enough." Shilly lumbered to the corner and
let his face crack into a grin. "Gentlemen," he said,
"please be seated." He pulled a chair out from the nearest table and held it for Manning.

When they were seated, Shilly said, "What's your
pleasure?"

Manning said, "I'd like a Stolichnaya on the—"

"Rum or beer."

"Make it three Dark and Stormys, Shilly," Darling
said.

"You got it," Shilly said, and turned back to the bar.

Darling looked at Osborn Manning, who appeared to

be in his early fifties. He was impeccably tended: His nails were polished, his hair perfectly shaped. His blue suit looked as if it had been pressed while he waited to be seated. His white shirt was starched and spotless, his blue silk tie held in place by a gold pin.

But it was Manning's eyes that Darling couldn't stop looking at. In the best of times they would have seemed sunken: His forehead stopped in a shelf of bone over his eyes, and his brows were thick and dark. But now they looked like two black tunnels, as if the eyes themselves had disappeared.

Maybe it's just dark in here, Darling thought. Or maybe that's what grief does to a man.

Manning noticed Darling staring at him, and he said, "Thank you for coming."

Darling nodded and tried to think of something civil to say, but couldn't come up with anything better than, "No problem."

"Do you live nearby?" Talley asked, making conversation.

"Close enough." Darling nodded at the north wall. "Across Mangrove Bay."

Shilly brought the drinks, and Talley took a gulp and said, "Splendid." Darling watched Manning's reaction as he took a sip: He winced but suppressed a grimace. To a mouth used to vodka and ice, Darling thought, rum and ginger beer must taste like anchovies with peanut butter.

There was an awkward silence then, as if Talley and Manning didn't know how to begin. Darling had a fair notion of what they wanted of him, and he had to force himself to resist the temptation to tell them to cut to the chase, get to the bottom line. But he didn't want to seem eager; over the years, he had made quite a few dollars by keeping his mouth shut and listening. At the very least, he always learned something.

Manning sat stiffly, his suit coat buttoned, his hands folded in front of him, and stared at the light of the single candle on the table.

What the hell, Darling thought, no harm in being polite. He said to Manning, "Sorry about your youngsters."

"Yes," was all Manning said.

"I can't imagine what . . . we have a daughter . . . it must be . . . ." He didn't know what else to say, so he shut up.

Manning looked away from the candle and raised his head toward them. His eyes still seemed hidden back in their caves.

"No you can't, Captain. You can't imagine. Not till it happens to you." Manning shifted in his seat. "You know the worst feeling I ever had up to then? It was when they were applying to college. It was the first time my children were ever threatened by something I couldn't protect them from. Their lives, their futures, were in the hands of strangers I had no control over. I've never felt so frustrated in my life. One day I found I was losing the sight in one eye. I went to doctors, had all manner of tests, nothing was wrong. But I *was* losing the sight in that eye. Then I was playing squash with a friend, and I told him about it—an excuse, I suppose, for why I was losing so badly—and he said that when his kids had applied to college, he had developed ulcerative colitis. What I had was hysterical blindness. As soon as they were accepted into schools, it went away. I swore then that nothing like that would ever happen again." He squeezed his hands together and shook his head. "You want to know what the feeling is like? I feel like I'm dead."

Talley took another gulp of his drink and said, "Captain Darling, we liked what you said at the meeting."

"You were there? Why?"

"In the back of the room. We wanted to see how people are reacting to all this."

"That's easy," Darling said. "They're scared to death. One step short of panic. They see their world being threatened by something they can't even understand, much less do anything about."

"But you're not . . . scared, I mean."

"You heard what I said back there. It's like anything else big and awful in nature. You leave it alone, it'll leave you alone." He thought of Manning's children, and added, "Generally . . . as a rule."

"That doctor back there. St. John . . . he's a fool."

"That's one way to put it."

"But there is something I disagree with you on. What's happening here is not an accident."

"What is it, then?"

Darling saw Talley glance at Manning, then Talley said, "Tell me, Captain, what do you know about *Architeuthis*?"

"What I read, what you wrote, other stuff. Not a whole lot."

"What do you *think* about it?"

Darling paused. "Whenever I hear talk about monsters," he said, "I think about *Jaws*. People forget *Jaws* was fiction, which is another word for . . . well, you know, B.S. As soon as that picture came out, every boat captain from here to Long Island and down to South Australia started fantasizing about thirty- and forty- and fifty-foot white sharks. My rule is, when someone tells me about a critter as big as a tractor-trailer truck, I right away cut a third or a half off what he says."

"Sound," said Talley, "very sound. But—"

"But," Darling said, "with this beast, seems to me when you hear stories about him, the smart thing to do is not cut anything off. The smart thing to do is double 'em."

"Exactly!" Talley said. His eyes were bright, and he leaned toward Darling, as if pleased to have discovered a kindred spirit. "I told you I'm a malacologist, but my specialty is teuthology . . . squid . . . specifically *Architeuthis*. I've spent my life studying them. I've used computers, made graphs, dissected tissue, smelled it, tasted it—"

"*Tasted* it? What's it taste like?"

"Ammonia."

"Ever seen a live one?"

"No. Have you?"

"Never," Darling said. "And I'd like to keep it that way."

"The more I studied, the more I realized how little anybody knows about the giant squid. Nobody knows how big they grow, how old they get, why they strand sometimes and wash up dead . . . not even how many species there are: People say three, some say nineteen. It's a classic example of the old saw The more you know, the more you realize how little you really know." Talley stopped, looking embarrassed, and said, "Sorry. I get carried away. I can cut this short if you—"

"Go on," said Manning. "Captain Darling has to know."

They're setting me up, Darling thought: They're trolling for me, teasing me like I was a hungry marlin.

"I have a theory," Talley said, "as good as most and better than some. Up to the middle of the last century, nobody quite believed in the existence of *Architeuthis,* or of *any* giant squid. The few sightings were dismissed as the rantings of sailors gone mad. All of a sudden in the 1870s there was a rash of sightings and strandings and even attacks on boats, and—"

"I read about them," Darling said.

"The point is, there were so many witnesses that for the first time people believed them. Then it all stopped again, until the early 1900s, when, for no reason, there were more sightings and strandings. I wondered if there was a pattern, so I collected reports of every sighting and every stranding, and I fed them into the computer with all the data on major weather events, current shifts and so forth, and I told the computer to find some rhyme or reason to it.

"The computer's answer was that the pattern of sightings and strandings coincided with cyclical fluctuations in branches of the Labrador Current, the big cold-water funnel that sweeps up the whole Atlantic coast. For most of the cycle, *Architeuthis* is never seen, alive or dead. But in the first few years of the change, for whatever reason—water temperature, food supply, I don't pretend to know—the beast shows up."

"How long are the cycles?" Darling asked.

"Thirty years."

"And the last one began in . . ." He knew the answer before the words were out of his mouth.

"Nineteen sixty . . . ran through sixty-two."

"I see."

"Yes," Talley said. "You do see. It's here because it's time." Talley leaned forward, his hands on the table. "But the truth is, I can give you a volume of facts, and document them for you, and not for a second can I tell you *why* they're so. Some people think *Architeuthis* may get trapped in warm-water currents and suffocate for lack of oxygen and die and wash ashore. Other people think it could be *cold* water that gets him, water less than, say, minus ten degrees centigrade. Nobody knows."

This man, Darling thought, is in love with giant squid. "Doc," he said, "this is all very interesting, but it doesn't say a lick about why the beast is suddenly eating people."

"But it does!" Talley said, and he leaned farther forward. "*Architeuthis* is what we call an adventitious feeder. He feeds by accident, he eats whatever's there. His normal diet—I've looked in their stomachs—is sharks, rays, big fish. But he'll eat *any*thing. Let's say that cyclical currents are bringing him up from the two-, three-thousand-foot level where he usually stays. And let's say he's finding that his usual food sources are gone. You'd know about this, Captain. From what I hear, Bermuda's almost fished out. And let's say all he's finding to eat is—"

There was a sharp *snap!* that sounded like a rifle shot, and something flew past Darling's face.

Osborn Manning had been clutching his plastic swizzle stick so hard that it shattered. "Sorry," he said. "Excuse me."

"No," said Talley. "*I'm* sorry. Lord . . ."

"Doc," Darling said after a pause, "there's one thing you haven't talked about—Nature's number one rule, balance. When there get to be too many sea lions, up jump the white sharks to keep 'em down. When there get to be too many people, up jumps some plague like the Black Death. Seems to me, this critter being around here is saying nature's out of whack. Why?"

"I have a theory," Talley said. "Nature's not out of whack, people have *put* nature out of whack. There's only one animal that preys on *Architeuthis,* and that's the sperm whale. Man has been killing off the sperm whales—they could already be practically extinct. So it's possible that more and more giant squid are surviving, and now they're showing up. Here."

"You mean you think there's more than *one*?"

"I don't know. My guess is not, because there's not enough food to support more than one. But I could be wrong."

More questions crowded into Darling's mind, more theories swam around and tried to coalesce. Suddenly he realized that he was taking the bait, and he forced himself to back off, to prevent Talley from setting a hook in him.

He made a show of looking at his watch, then pushed his chair back from the table. "It's late," he said, "and I get up early."

"Ah . . . Captain . . . ," Talley said, ". . . the thing is, this animal can be caught."

Darling shook his head. "No one ever has."

"Well, no, not a true *Architeuthis*. Not alive."

"What makes you think you can?"

"I know we can."

"Why in God's name do you want to?"

Talley started. "*Why?* Why *not*? It's unique. It's—"

Manning interrupted. "Captain Darling," he said, "this . . . this creature, this beast . . . it killed my children. My only children. It has destroyed my life . . . our lives. My wife has been sedated since . . . she tried to—"

"Mr. Manning," Darling said. "This beast is just an animal. It—"

"It is a sentient being. Dr. Talley has told me . . . and I believe . . . that it knows a form of rage, it knows vengeance. Well, so do I. Believe me. So do I."

"It's still just an animal. You can't take revenge on an animal."

"Yes I can."

"But why? What good will it—"

"It's something I can do. Would you have me sit back and blame fate and say, 'That's the way it goes'? I will not. I will kill this beast."

"No you won't. All you'll succeed in doing is—"

Talley said, "Captain, we can. It *can* be caught."

"If you say so, Doctor. But leave me out of it."

Manning said, "How much do you charge for a day's charter?"

"I don't—"

"How much?"

Here we go, Darling thought. I never should have come here. "A thousand dollars," he said.

"I'll give you five thousand dollars a day, plus expenses."

When, after a moment, Darling hadn't replied, Talley said, "This isn't only personal, Captain. This animal *must* be caught."

"Why? Why not just let it go away?"

"Because you were wrong about another thing back at the meeting: It won't stop. It will go on killing people."

"Five minutes ago that was a theory, Doc. Now it's a fact, is it?"

"A probability," Talley acknowledged. "If it's found a food source, I see no reason why it will move on. And I don't believe there's a living thing out there that can stop it."

"Well, neither can I. Get someone else."

"There *is* no one else," Manning said. "Except that jackass St. John . . ."

". . . with his master plan," Talley broke in. "Does that man truly think he can catch *Architeuthis* by throwing explosives in the ocean? It's ridiculous . . . a game of blindman's bluff!"

Darling shrugged. "He'll get his name in the papers. Look, Mr. Manning, you've got all that money, you can hire yourself some big-time experts, bring in a ship."

"Don't think I didn't try. You think I want to work with you . . . with locals? I know islanders, Captain, I know Bermudians." Manning put his elbows on the table and leaned toward Darling. His voice was low, but its tone had an intensity that made it seem like a shout. "I've had a house here for years. I know all about small islands and small minds; I know how you people strut around and bray about your independence; I know what you think about foreigners. As far as you're concerned, I'm just another rich Yankee asshole.''

Talley looked stricken. Darling leaned back, smiled and said to Manning, "You do have a way with words."

"I'm tired of this crap, Captain. Here's the way it is: I could have chartered a boat, there were people up and down the coast dying to come. But your pigheaded government has so many rules and regulations, so many permits and licenses, so many fees and duties, that it would have taken months to set it up. So I have to use locals, and that means using you. You're the best. As I see it, we've got only one problem, you and I, and that's money. I haven't come up with the right figure yet. Tell me, then. Tell me your price."

Darling looked at him for a long moment, then he said, "Let me tell you how *I* see it, Mr. Manning. You are rich and you are a Yankee, but I don't hold those against you. What makes you an asshole is that you think money will bring your children back. You think killing the beast will. Well, it won't. You can't buy yourself peace."

"I have to try, Captain."

"Okay," Darling said. "You've laid down your cards; here are mine. I've got two hundred and fifty thousand dollars wrapped up in my boat, and, no question, I could use your money. But the only other asset I've got is wrapped up in these clothes, and if I lose that asset, my personal worth is zero." He stood up. "So thanks but no thanks." He nodded at Talley, and walked out.

"Think about it, Captain," Manning called after him.

When Darling had gone, Talley finished his drink, sighed and said, "I must say, Osborn, you were—"

"Don't tell me how to do business," Manning said. "Charm wouldn't have worked any better. We understand one another, Darling and I. We may not like one another, but we understand one another." He signaled to Shilly for the check.

Talley was furious. This couldn't be happening. Everything had gone so well. He had a blank check from Manning, had meshed his own obsession with Manning's and had created a common purpose. He could buy anything he wanted, and had: the best equipment, the newest, the most sophisticated.

Best of all, he had a plan.

But now the final thing he needed, the last cog in his elaborate machine, was not available.

He had to hide his discouragement from Manning, in case it might become contagious. If Manning canceled his check, thirty years of research, of hopes, of dreams, would vanish like steam.

They did not speak again until they were in the parking lot, and then Manning said, "How much do we know about Darling?"

"Just reputation. He's the best around."

"No . . . about *him* . . . personally."

"Nothing."

"Nose around, see what you can learn. There's not a man alive who doesn't have enemies. Find one. Throw money at him. Tell him you want to know everything there is to know: dirt, gossip, lies, rumors. Start with the fishermen. Small community, no work, no money . . . I'll bet they're worse than actors—they'll sell their own mothers for the chance to ruin a competitor."

"You want to destroy the man? Why?"

"No. I want to control him, but I can't until I know what there is to know. Old truism, Talley: Knowledge is power. I'll go downtown in the morning, talk to some people, cash a few chips."

"Talk about what?"

"Weaknesses . . . liabilities. Another old truism:

Every man has his price. All we have to do is find Darling's, and then he's ours."

Charlotte was waiting in the kitchen when Darling arrived home. When he had finished telling her about the evening, she kissed him and said, "I'm proud of you."

"Five thousand a day." Darling shook his head. "I could've gotten ten days' work out of it, maybe more."

"Yes, but then . . . ?"

Darling put an arm around her. "You could've thrown me a hell of a funeral."

Charlotte didn't smile. She looked up at him and said, "Just remember your promise, William. Don't get involved with people who've got nothing to lose."

# 20

THE WHEEL WAS huge, and it took both hands and all her concentration to control it. It was a circle of stainless steel, four feet across, and it seemed to have a life of its own, wanting to yank away from her and let the boat fall off the wind and wallow. It reminded her of an unruly horse. The answer was to show it who was boss; then it would behave.

Katherine wasn't about to make a mistake now, not after waiting for three days and nights for the chance to take the helm, listening to her father and Timmy and David and the others talk about how tough the boat was to steer in a quartering sea, how it took a man's strength to control the boat, how they should wait for the wind to die down and the conditions to be just right . . . blah, blah, blah.

She sat up straight and braced her knees against the wheel post and gripped the wheel so tightly that her fingers began to cramp. The muscles in her arms already ached, and soon, she knew, they would begin to sting.

Timmy lounged on the cushions beside her. Up forward, David and Peter were sprawled on the deck, working on their tans. They had nothing to do now, on a broad reach, except wait until it was time for the next watch to take over.

"Come off a bit," said Timmy.

"Why?"

" 'Cause there's a flutter of luff in the main." Timmy pointed to the top of the mainsail. "Jeez . . . why do you think?"

She looked up, squinting at the brilliance of the white sail against the blue sky. Timmy was right, which annoyed her; it was something she should have seen herself. Or heard. Noticed, anyway. But the luff was so tiny, so insignificant, that she couldn't believe it would make a difference.

She heaved on the wheel, turning it to the right, until she saw the trailing edge of the sail stop quivering. The boat heeled to starboard, and she had to brace herself with her feet.

"That's got it," Timmy said.

"Thank heavens. I'm sure glad you saw that. Now we'll win for sure."

"Hey, Kathy . . . it's a *race*."

"Could've fooled me."

There wasn't another boat in sight. How many had started? Fifty? A hundred? She had no idea. Enough so that the starting line had looked like a riot, with boats zigzagging back and forth and people yelling at each other and horns blowing. But as the hours had passed, the numbers had seemed to shrink: fewer and fewer boats nearby, then fewer and fewer in sight, as if one by one they were being swallowed up by the sea. She knew that all that was happening was that each captain was trying his own strategy, going off on his own tacks, using computers and experience and guesswork and, for all she knew, voodoo to find the perfect combination of wind and tide and current that would give him an edge.

Still, it was eerie to be alone on the ocean like this. The boat was almost fifty feet long, and down below it seemed as big as a house, but up here—with the waves on either side and the horizon stretching forever and the sky completely empty—it felt as tiny as a bug on a carpet.

Her father stuck his head up through the hatch. "How's it going, Muffin?"

She had begged him to call her Katherine. Just for this trip. Or Kathy. Anything but Muffin.

"Fine, Daddy."

"How's she doing, Tim?"

Be nice, she prayed. Don't be a typical shithead brother.

"Pretty good . . ." Tim said.

*Thank you . . .*

". . . only a little absentminded now and then."

*Shithead!*

"We just raised Bermuda on the radar . . . edge of the fifty-mile ring."

"Great!" Katherine said, hoping that was the right thing to say.

"Sure is. Means we can cruise right along all night, and if we're lucky hit the channel just after daybreak. We don't want to try it in the dark."

"God, no," said Tim. "Remember last year?"

"Don't remind me."

Of course, Katherine thought. Last year. When I wasn't there. That's when the excitement always happens: when I'm not there.

Her father started to pull his head back, then stopped and said, "Funny thing . . . Bermuda Harbour Radio's broadcasting a Notice to Mariners about some animal that's attacking boats."

"A whale?" Katherine said. "Maybe it's sick."

"I don't know, I think they're just trying to juice up tourism, play on the Bermuda Triangle thing. Anyway, no point taking chances. Put your lifeline on whenever you move around."

"Daddy, it's not even rough."

"I know, Muffin, but better safe than sorry." He smiled. "I promised your mother I'd take extra-special care of you." He gestured to Tim, then backed down into the cabin.

Tim sat up, reached over to Katherine's life jacket, unwrapped her jury-rigged lifeline and snapped it into the steel ring on the wheel post.

"What about yours?" she said. "You're not even wearing a life jacket."

"I've done this race three times," Tim said. "I think I know how to walk around a boat."

"So do I!"

"Argue with Dad, then, not me. I'm just following orders." Tim smiled at her and lay back on the cushions.

She flexed her fingers to quell the cramps, and shifted her weight to try to ease the strain on her arms and shoulders. She wasn't wearing a watch, had no idea how much longer she had to wrestle with this stupid wheel. Not too much longer, she hoped, or she'd have to ask Tim to take over for her, and he'd make some crack that would put her down—nothing mean, really, just some dumb macho remark.

She wasn't a quitter. She had pleaded to come on this trip, and she was determined to do her share, including standing watches. She knew that her brothers had argued against her coming along, and that if her mother hadn't sat her father down and had a heart-to-heart talk with him about fairness and equality and all the rest, she'd be back in Far Hills teaching tennis to ten-year-olds. She owed it to her mother, and to herself, to prove that she could be an asset, not a liability.

But she couldn't wait for it to be over, to get to Bermuda and spend a couple of days lying on the beach and tooling around on a motorbike, while her father and the others talked sailing over drinks at the Yacht Club—no, the *Dinghy* Club, they called it here. Cute.

Then she'd fly home, that had been the deal. Thank God.

She couldn't fathom the mystique of big-boat sailing, although she feigned enthusiasm and tried her best to master obscure terms like "klew cringle" and "running backstay."

She enjoyed day sailing in small boats at the shore. It was fun to spend a couple of hours on the water, racing against friends, yahooing around, sometimes even capsizing—but then going home to a hot shower and decent food and a good night's sleep.

But this: This was a marathon of boredom, discomfort and fatigue. Nobody slept more than four or five hours a day. Nobody bathed. She had tried to take a shower once, but had fallen down twice and cut her head on the soap dish, so had resigned herself to sponging off whatever she could reach whenever she could. Everything felt soggy. Everything stank of salt and mold. The entire belowdecks smelled like a giant wet sneaker. You needed a graduate degree in engineering to operate the toilets. Both of them clogged at least once a day, and blame inevitably fell on Katherine and the only other female on board, David's stuck-up girlfriend Evan . . . as if girls somehow conspired against marine plumbing. Katherine had been appointed "assistant chief cook and bottle washer," which turned out to be a bad joke because how can you cook anything decent when the whole boat is always tilted at an angle so you can barely stand up? All she had been able to do was keep hot coffee and soup available day and night, and sandwich makings in a Tupperware bowl in the sink for whoever wanted something more.

She wouldn't have minded any of the bad stuff if there had been enough good stuff to compensate, but as far as she could tell, ocean racing—in good weather, at least— consisted of a lot of talk, a lot of sitting around, and about half an hour a day of frantic action, during which her contribution was to stay out of the way.

Katherine had concluded that it must all have something to do with male bonding, and while she was glad to have seen it firsthand, she would be perfectly happy henceforth to hear about it and to smile politely at her brothers' tales of heroics on the high seas.

Her arms and shoulders were shrieking now; she had no choice; she'd have to turn the wheel over to Tim.

But then suddenly—blessedly—the watch changed. Her father and her uncle Lou came up through the hatch to relieve her and Tim, and Lou's two boys went forward to replace David and Peter.

"Good job, sweetheart," her father said as he slid behind the wheel. "Right on course."

"You have any idea how we're doing?" Tim asked.

"Hard to tell. I think we've got a shot at second or third in our class. Lot of boats on the radar, but I can't tell what they are."

Katherine unsnapped her lifeline from the steel ring and went below. She took off her life jacket and tossed it on her bunk. Tim squeezed by her and went forward into the fo'c'sle and flung himself on one of the bunks. Didn't even take his shoes off. No wonder the place smelled like a gym.

Katherine decided to have a cup of soup and read for a while, until she fell asleep. Nothing else to do.

She heard her father shout, "Ready about!" Footsteps hammered on the fiberglass overhead. She gripped the railing of the top bunk, where Evan was asleep and snoring like a chain saw, and braced herself.

"Hard alee!" called her father, and the boat righted itself and hung there for a second and then, as the boom came around and the sail caught the wind with a *whump!,* it heeled to port. There was a clatter of crockery in the sink, as dirty cups shifted and tumbled over one another.

She should wash the cups. That was her job. But it was Evan's job, too, and Evan hadn't bothered, she'd just gone to sleep. To heck with it; she'd wash them later. She rinsed one cup and poured some soup for herself and drank it down.

On her way back to her bunk, she stopped and looked at the radar screen. It glowed like a green video game. A yellow line swept clockwise in a circle, flashing golden blips that she knew were other boats. At the top of the screen was a ragged smear.

Hello, Bermuda, she thought. Save some sun for me. And maybe, while you're at it, a good-looking lifeguard. One who hates sailboats.

She was glad she had looked—it made her feel less alone.

She lay down in her bunk and turned on the little reading light over her head and picked up her copy of Anne Rice's *The Mummy*—her mother's choice for her, and perfect for a trip like this: romantic, scary, long enough to last several days and easy to pick up and put down without losing the plot. She found her place.

Ramses had brought Cleopatra back to life, and Cleopatra was making out with every man she met and then killing him, and . . .

She had to go to the john. She sighed and got up and walked aft, past the chart table, and opened the door to the head. The smell assaulted her, worse than the public johns in Penn Station. She didn't have to look, but she did, and sure enough, it was clogged. She stepped on the flush pedal and gave the pump handle one try, but the sound—a strangled gurgle—warned her against trying again.

She went forward to the other head. There was a piece of masking tape on the door, with OUT OF ORDER on it in marking pen.

Swell.

She went back to her bunk and opened the drawer beneath it and fetched her emergency john: an empty quart mayonnaise jar.

Then she returned to the after head and held her breath as she peed in the jar, thinking only: Please let tomorrow come, let me go to sleep and not wake up till we're at the dock.

When she had finished, she screwed the top tight and started up through the hatch.

"Life jacket," her father said.

"I'm just . . ." She showed him the jar.

"*Both* now?"

"Uh-huh. Again."

"Lord . . . well, we'll fix 'em when we get in."

Uncle Lou said, with a little snicker, "Ladies . . ."

"Uncle Lou . . ." Katherine said. "I wasn't great at biology, but I think men go to the john, too . . . sometimes."

"I stand corrected," Uncle Lou said, smiling.

"Here," said her father, and he held his hand out to take the jar.

"I'll do it," she said.

"Muffin . . ."

"I'll *do* it."

"Then put your life jacket on."

"Daddy . . . Oh, all right." She backed down the ladder and went to her bunk and got her life jacket. She was angry, embarrassed, annoyed. Nobody else was wearing a life jacket, and they were running around the deck like monkeys. She wanted to take three steps to empty a jar overboard, and he was making her dress up like an astronaut.

She put the life jacket on and thought, Who's being dumb now? Why don't you let him throw it over for you? Because. Because what? Because it's . . . private. Stupid. He used to change your diapers. Never mind, too late now.

She went up through the hatch and stepped around the wheel and started forward on the leeward side of the boat. The sun was low in the western sky, low enough so that the ocean swells blocked it, and here, further shaded by the big sail, the light was as dim as evening.

"Snap in," her father said.

"Yes, sir." She snapped the lifeline onto the quarter-inch cable connecting two stanchions.

"I know you find this hard to believe, but I'm not being a pain just to amuse myself."

"No, sir." She knew she sounded petulant, but she couldn't help it.

She unscrewed the cap of the jar and, her knees braced against a stanchion, leaned out to empty the jar. The jar was big for her hand, and as she upended it, it slipped. Reflexively, she reached for it with her other hand, and she dropped the cap, and she lunged to grab that, too, and then suddenly there was a little stutter in the wind, a puff that pushed the boat farther over. And then suddenly there was nothing supporting her legs, and because most of her weight was overboard she lost her balance and fell, somersaulting.

In that split second, she knew that the lifeline would stop her and swing her back into the boat, and she tensed and raised her hands to her head. There was a jolt as the lifeline caught. She heard herself screaming, and something else, a weird tearing noise, and then, when she should have felt herself slamming against the side of the boat, she felt . . . water.

She was underwater, upside down, and then the life jacket righted her and she bobbed to the surface. She couldn't see—her hair was in her eyes. She wiped it away, and still she couldn't see anything but water, great undulating swells of blue-black water.

This couldn't be! What had happened? She looked down at her life jacket, and there was a jagged hole where the lifeline had torn away.

She could hear her father shouting, and other people too, a jumble of words, so she used her hands to turn herself around, and there, silhouetted against the setting sun, was the top of the mast, heading away from her, the sail flapping, the voices growing fainter.

A swell rose beneath her and carried her high on its crest, and now she could see all of the mast and even the top of the cabin. She screamed, but she felt—no, she *knew*—that the wind was snatching her words away and flinging them eastward into the night.

The swell passed her, and she slid into the trough, and now she saw none of the boat, not even the top of the mast.

She felt something in the water that encased her, a pulsing, very faint, but definite.

The engine. They'd turned on the engine. Good. Now they could maneuver, and find her fast. Fast. Before night fell.

Another swell came, and from its crest she saw the

mast again, looking farther away, and all the lights were on it—masthead light, running lights, anchor lights—so she would be able to see it.

She screamed again and waved her arms, but they couldn't hear her now. Of course they couldn't, not with the engine on.

Why did they keep moving away from her? Why didn't they turn around?

Then the boat did turn, its bow slewing to the right; it began to circle back to her. Good. They'd find her now.

The swell dropped her into a trough, where she could see nothing but water.

If she couldn't see them, how could they see her? They stuck up fifty feet. How far did she stick up? Two feet?

Save your strength, she thought. Don't scream, don't flail around till you're on the top of a wave, where they can see you.

A swell raised her up, and she saw the boat, almost all of it . . . but it was moving away from her, in a different direction! She screamed.

As that swell dropped her down again, she turned her head to the west. The sun was gone, leaving only an orange glow on the horizon, and pink-rimmed clouds against the darkening sky. Overhead she could see stars.

It would be dark soon. They had to find her . . . *had* to . . . or . . .

Don't even think about it.

God, it was cold! How could she be so cold so soon? She'd only been in the water a few minutes, but her arms and legs were trembling, and her throat and jaw were quivering so badly that she had trouble breathing.

It floated in the cool middle layer of the ocean water, unthreatened, unperturbed, drifting.

It had fed recently, gorging itself, so for now it felt no urgency to hunt.

It was existing, merely existing.

And then, from somewhere far away, it felt the thrum of a pulse, faint waves that coursed through the water and tapped at its flesh.

Curious rather than concerned, it fluttered its tail fins and slowly rose.

Had it encountered warmer water, it would have stopped, for comfort was its only imperative. But the cool layer continued, and so it allowed itself to rise.

It sensed light now, and the pulse was nearer, and there was something else, something apart from the pulse, disturbing the water above.

Something alive.


A swell lifted Katherine, and when she reached the crest she saw the boat, the whole boat—nearby!—a dark shape against the twilight sky, with the white and red and green lights shining from the mast.

She screamed and waved her arms, then slid off the crest and back into the trough again.

They hadn't seen her, hadn't heard her. *Why?* They were so close! She had heard *them,* had heard the engine and even maybe a voice.

She was downwind, that was why. Sound was carrying from them to her but not from her to them.

Dark. It was dark, almost night. And cold. And deep. How deep? Forever deep.

Now, at last, terror struck her, a true gut primal fear that flooded through her veins and tore at every nerve ending.

Her father had talked of monsters, and now she knew they were going to get her. Nightmare images flashed into her mind, images she hadn't had in years, since she was six or eight, all the beasts that had lived under her bed and in the closet and in the rustling trees outside her window. Always her mother had come into her room and comforted her, told her everything was fine, the monsters were make-believe.

But nobody rushed to comfort her now. Make-believe was real.

She felt so alone, a loneliness she had never known existed, as if she were the only living thing on the planet.

Thoughts tumbled over one another in her head: Why had she insisted on coming on this trip? Why hadn't she let her father empty the jar for her? Why, why, why?

She tried to pray, but all she could think of was, Now I lay me down to sleep. . . .

She was going to die.

No!

She screamed again—not on purpose, not to be noticed, but the scream of a living being protesting death.

She was carried to the top of another crest, and saw that the boat was there, even closer, but something was different. It wasn't moving; it had stopped. She could hear no engine noise.

As she slid into the trough, she heard a voice: her father, talking through a loud-hailer.

"Katherine, can you hear me? We can't see you, but we've turned off the engine, turned off everything, so we'll be able to hear you. If you can hear me, as soon as I stop, you scream, honey, scream for all you're worth, okay? . . . Now scream!"

She thought: He called me Katherine.

She screamed.

It was one hundred feet below the surface. It hovered, letting its senses gather information.

The pulse from above had stopped, but there was disturbance on the surface, and something small, moving.

The living thing.

Slowly, it rose.


"I hear you, Katherine! Again! Again!"

She screamed again, her voice scratchy, not as loud, but she summoned all her strength and forced herself to scream again, and again.

A swell caught her, and from its crest she saw a searchlight swinging toward her. She prayed she wouldn't drop away until it had found her, but she was dropping, dropping. She waved her arms. It was going to miss her!

At the last instant, the light caught her upraised hands—she saw the beam illuminate her grasping fingers—and stopped swinging, and she heard the voice on the loud-hailer cry, "Got you!"

Then she heard the engine start again.


The pulse had begun again . . . closer, more distinct, moving toward the small living thing.

Excited now, it rose, and its color changed. It was excited not by hunger, not by a sense of an impending battle or an imminent threat, but by a desire to kill.

It began to feel the swells, for it was near the surface.


When Katherine reached the top of a swell, the light hit her face and blinded her. But the boat was there, she could feel the beat of the engine, she could smell the exhaust.

Something splashed beside her, something big, and she felt an arm around her waist and heard a voice say, "I've got you . . . it's okay . . . it's okay."

Timmy. She wrapped her arms around him, and then she felt herself being pulled, and her hand touched the hard side of the boat.

* * *

It was there, the living thing, directly above, thrashing.

A wounded animal.

Prey.

More than prey.

Food.

The creature drew a mass of water into the caverns of its body and expelled it through the funnel in its belly, and it shot upward.

Hands grabbed Katherine and pulled so hard she thought her arms might come out of their sockets, but then she was in her father's embrace, and he was crushing her against him and saying, "Oh, sweetheart . . . oh baby . . . oh Muffin . . ."

Other hands pulled Timmy aboard, and he fell onto the deck, coughing.

Then someone said, "What's that smell?"

She heard the clunk of the engine's gears engaging, and she felt the boat begin to move.

Then, as her father carried her to the after hatch, voices:

"Hey, look!"

"What?"

"Back there."

"Where?"

"Something in the water."

"I don't see anything."

"There! Right there!"

"What? What is it?"

"I don't know. Something."

"Probably just our wake."

"No, I don't think so."

"It's nothing. We've got her back. Forget it."

\* \* \*

The pulse was fading again, the living thing was gone.

The creature wallowed in the swells and scanned the water with one of its mammoth yellow-white eyes. It raised its whips and swept them across the surface, searching. But it found nothing, and so it sank back into the deep.

Wrapped in blankets, Katherine lay in her bunk, and let her father feed her soup. He was laughing and crying at the same time, and his hand shook so that finally she took the soup from him and fed herself.

Evan had taken her clothes off for her—not so stuck-up anymore, in fact rather nice—and washed her off with hot water and given her one of her own sweat suits.

Timmy stopped by on his way to the shower and didn't say anything, just bent down and kissed her forehead.

David and Peter and Uncle Lou, everybody, came in one at a time and said something, and there wasn't a condescending remark among them.

She felt like a celebrity, and she liked it. For once, she had a story she could tell, when everybody else was boasting. For once, the excitement had included her.

Her eyes drooped. She thought she'd like to sleep all the way to Bermuda.

# 21

AS WHIP DARLING took a breath, he realized that the air was coming slowly, reluctantly, as if he were sucking on an empty soda bottle. His tank was almost out. He might get one more breath, two at most, before he'd have to surface.

Never mind, he was only five feet down. If he drew a vacuum, he'd spit out the mouthpiece and exhale and go up.

But he didn't want to have to go up now and change tanks and come back down, just to finish this stupid, cussed job that should have taken twenty minutes and was already into its second hour. Replacing the government buoys was easy; anyone who could master a pair of pliers could do it; he'd done it a hundred times. All you had to do was unshackle the buoy from the chain, put a temporary float on the chain, haul the buoy aboard, drop the replacement buoy overboard, shackle it on the chain and retrieve your float. Piece of cake.

Not this time. First, Mike had given him the wrong size shackle for the chain, then the wrong size pin for the shackle. Then Darling had dropped the correct pin and had had to go up to find another one, because Mike was so rattled about Darling being down there alone that he couldn't find his ass with both hands. Then, while Darling was aboard looking for the pin, Mike had dropped the boat hook with which he was holding the buoy, so the buoy had drifted away on the tide and they'd had to haul the anchor and chase it, because no one man was going to dive in and drag a three-hundred-pound steel buoy that wanted to travel.

It should have been Mike down here anyway, and Darling passing him the proper equipment piece by piece—and it *would* have been Mike if Darling hadn't decided that Mike was so obviously panicked about being chewed on by some great villain that he might forget to breathe and have an embolism and die. And so Darling had decided to do the job himself.

He held his breath and set the pin to the shackle and whacked it with the hammer. In the water, the hammer moved in slow motion, and most of its force was spent before it struck, so he had to hit the pin again. His vision was distorted by the water and the mask and the bouncing around of the buoy, so he hit the pin awry, and it skipped off the shackle and tumbled away, down into the blue.

Darling shouted "Shit!" into his mouthpiece as he watched it fall. He took his final breath from the tank, sucking in every last atom of air, and pulled the spare pin from the waistband of his bathing suit. He struck it with the hammer, and it slid in like a sharp knife into fresh fish. He spun it tight with pliers, then looked around below, to make sure nothing was cruising in the gloom that might make a run at him as he surfaced. He spat out his mouthpiece and exhaled and kicked upward into the sun.

Mike was waiting on the dive step. "Done?" he asked as he took Darling's tank and weight belt and hauled them up onto the deck.

Darling nodded and pulled himself up onto the dive step and lay facedown, catching his breath.

"What are we doing out here, Michael?" he said when finally he could speak. "We should be sitting in a condo in Vero Beach, drinking Pink Ladies and watching the sunset, instead of casting ourselves into the sea and damn near drowning, all for a measly five-dollar bill."

"It pays the fuel."

"Barely," Darling said, and thought to add something nice to make Mike feel better about not doing the diving himself. "Only thanks to you."

Mike had determined that with some minor fiddling with the engine, he could make it run fine on a mixture of diesel oil and kerosene, which brought the cost of fuel down by more than a third. And that meant that they could actually make a couple of dollars from crappy jobs like this.

Darling hadn't had to work on the government's buoys in years, had hoped he'd never have to again. But when he had heard that the government wanted to change one of the major channel buoys and was letting the job out for bids, he had gotten into the bidding and, to his amazement—embarrassment, almost—found himself the low bidder.

Now they were doing the job, for $500, and because they were running on cheaper fuel they might actually clear $250 on the day—not exactly ransom money, but better than sitting around the yard counting the hairs on the neighbor's cat.

There was no other work, at least not work Darling would do. The aquarium retainer was gone, and the race layover had passed without a single dive charter for anybody, because as soon as the racers had hit shore and seen that article in *Newsweek,* with the picture of the giant squid from the Museum of Natural History in New York, they had concluded that diving was out . . . even on the shallow reefs, where the worst thing likely to happen was a coral cut on the knee. It had been nearly two weeks since anybody had seen a sign of the squid, and still not a single diver had gone into the water.

It made no sense, but then, Darling thought, lots of things didn't. Soon enough, there'd be reports of people refusing to take showers for fear that a giant squid would come out of the shower head or up the drain and eat them.

Other people were getting work, though. One of the glass-bottom boats had painted a new name on its transom, SQUID HUNTER, and was taking tourists out to the edge of the reefs and letting them peer into a hundred feet of water, while the captain, dressed up like Indiana Jones, scared the bejesus out of them with bullshit broadcasts over his P.A. system in his best Vincent Price voice.

It was nonsense, but Darling didn't fault the man; he'd had to do something. Some of the boats that took out snorkelers might as well have been in dry dock. Visitors were afraid to get near the water, and they weren't about to pay thirty dollars to ride around and be told what they should be seeing.

An enterprising gift-shop owner was already selling a line of squid-theme jewelry, junk made from seashells and silver wire. And there was talk that one of the fishermen was making a fortune catching little school squid and freezing them and casting them into blocks of Lucite and selling them as Genuine Miniature Bermuda Triangle Monsters.

Representatives of the far-out environmental groups had arrived, and were going door to door raising money for their Save the Squid campaign. Darling had been asked to be a local spokesman for the campaign, but he had refused, on the grounds that *Architeuthis* was doing a fine job of saving itself without any help from him or anyone else.

The Save-the-Squidders hadn't been in Bermuda for

forty-eight hours before they got into a fight with the opposition, some big-time sport fishermen who were sending their Rybovitches and Hatterases and Merritts down from all points westward to go monster fishing. A couple of them had gotten impatient waiting for their boats and had tried to charter Darling, but he'd turned them down, same as he'd turned down Manning and Dr. what's-his-name . . . Talley.

Sometimes he regretted turning down Talley, especially days like today, when his mouth ached from biting on a regulator mouthpiece, when he was frozen like a Popsicle and whipped to the point of coma . . . all for a couple of hundred bucks that he'd have to split with Mike.

But, as the saying went, Talley and Manning were folks to feed with a long spoon. Charlotte had pointed out that each in his own way was the most dangerous kind of person to get mixed up with: A person who has nothing to lose. Darling had never stopped to think exactly what *was* worth risking his life for, outside of Charlotte and Dana, but he knew for sure it wasn't some creature that ate people for breakfast and boats for lunch.

Besides, he wasn't totally out of hope. A restaurant down in town needed its dock repaired, and if he landed the job it could be a week's work at a thousand a day. He'd heard that the telephone company might be wanting a cable laid . . . scut work, pumping mud to dig a trench to lay the cable in, but honest work that paid some bills without destroying anything.

That was all he wanted . . . work. He didn't know how Charlotte was keeping food on the table and the lights turned on and the insurance paid up, but she was, somehow.

Darling washed the salt off in the shower, and put on a pair of shorts, while Mike stowed the dive gear and

fried a mackerel from the cold box. They'd been meaning to use the mackerel as bait, but since there wasn't
anything around to catch, they figured they might as
well eat it.

After lunch, they cruised southwest along the outer
edge of the reefs, meandering toward home. Darling
intended to stop at the town dock on the way and
submit his bill to Marine & Ports. He had a friend there
who had promised to pay him in cash.

"Look there," Mike said, pointing down from the
flying bridge. Two snappers were floating belly-up, and
the boat passed between them.

A moment later, they saw two more, then a porgy and
an angelfish and four or five sergeant majors. All dead,
all bloated.

"What the hell's going on?" Darling said.

They heard a noise then, in the distance, a deep,
resonant *ka-WHUMP,* and they felt a thud through the
steel at their feet, as if someone were hammering on the
hull with a maul.

Then, half a mile ahead and to the right, in deep
water, they could see a boat, and in front of the boat a
torrent of spray descending onto what looked like a
hump of ocean water. As they watched, the hump withdrew, absorbed by the sea, and the spray became a white
smear on the surface.

Mike picked up the binoculars and focused on the
boat. "It's the aquarium's boat," he said.

"Christamighty," said Darling. "Liam's gone and got
himself a permit to bomb the beast."

Herbert Talley licked the salt spray off his sunglasses
and wiped them on his shirttail. He found the little gray
fish that had been blown out of the water and had struck
him in the back of the head, and he tossed it overboard
where the others—the dozens, the scores, that had been

killed by the concussion—were bobbing to the surface, their white bellies turned to the sun.

"That was close," he said, and he restrained himself from using the other words he wanted to say, words like "fool" and "idiot."

"Not really, Doctor," said St. John, whose curls, water-soaked and blast-blown, hung like jungle weeds down the sides of his head. "I've made a study of explosives. We were quite safe."

St. John looked over the side, shading his eyes to see down beneath the layer of dead fish. He straightened up, took a step forward and shouted to his men in the bow, "Rig another one! And set this one for a hundred fathoms."

The helmsman, a muscle-bound graduate student who looked like the star of a sex-and-surfers movie, stuck his head out of the cabin and said, "How far do we go to find a hundred fathoms?"

"Use the fathometer, for God's sake. You know how, don't you? . . . Or do I have to do everything?"

"We just blew it out."

"Go that way, then!" St. John said, and he waved his arm in the general direction of darker water.

When he turned back to Talley, he said, "You agree that when we kill the animal, it will float."

"If," Talley said. "If you kill the animal. Yes." Agree? Talley had told St. John, who hadn't known the first thing about the biology of *Architeuthis*.

"Even when we blow it to shreds?"

"Yes." Talley saw no point in qualifying his assertion, since St. John seemed to have about as much chance of killing *Architeuthis* as a ten-year-old had of hitting a sparrow with a slingshot.

"It'll come to the surface even from a hundred fathoms . . . six hundred feet?"

"From anywhere. As I told you, the ammonia content of the flesh makes it lighter than seawater. It will float, just like oil, just like—"

"I know, I know," St. John said, and he turned away toward the bow.

Talley swallowed bile, and tried to think how to escape from this diminutive bully who was treating him like an apprentice. He should never have accepted St. John's invitation to come along.

On the phone, however, St. John had been polite, receptive, even eager to have Talley observe his attempt to kill the giant squid. He had welcomed Talley aboard the thirty-five-foot aquarium boat, had introduced him to his crew of four—including the young man in charge of explosives, who looked nauseated, either from nervousness or anticipatory seasickness—and then proceeded to lecture Talley about the subject that Talley had made his life's work, a lecture laced with pseudofacts gleaned, Talley imagined, from comic books, horror movies and supermarket tabloids.

When Talley had contradicted one of St. John's putative facts—not rudely, not didactically, he had simply stated that there was no conclusive evidence to affirm St. John's assertion that there were only three species of *Architeuthis,* that many scientists believed there could in fact be as many as nineteen species, all with subtly different characteristics—St. John's response had been a curt "Ridiculous!" and he had changed the subject, convincing Talley that he had no interest in learning anything, and that he expected Talley only to approve and applaud whatever he did.

The amazing thing was that St. John was so ignorant of how ignorant he was; he truly believed the nonsense he purveyed. It was as if his brain gathered data from all sources—the reliable, the marginal and the fantastic—and selected that which it liked and discarded all the rest and molded its own gospel truth.

St. John had stayed away from Talley for most of the voyage, had instructed Talley to stay aft—"where it's safe"—while he lectured his crew about giant squid and underwater explosives. The only reason he had bothered to say anything else to Talley—and it hadn't been phrased as a question but as a speculative musing about the flotation of certain kinds of flesh—was that one of his crew had wondered how they would know if they had killed the monster because if it didn't have a swim bladder it would probably sink to the bottom . . . wouldn't it?

St. John had looked stricken until Talley had volunteered that *Architeuthis* flesh had positive buoyancy, information that St. John had then passed along as if it had sprung whole from the cornucopia of his mind.

Talley didn't mind feeding St. John data. By now, all he wanted to do was to get off this boat, before St. John pulled some boner that blew them all to bits.

If only he and Manning had been able to charter a boat of their own. They had tried, but there was nothing of suitable size available except an old ferry that needed a complete overhaul. There were a few medium-size government boats, but as they inquired about each, they encountered bureaucratic confusions, all concocted, Talley was becoming convinced, by St. John, who wanted the creature to himself.

Manning had made another attempt to arrange for a boat from the States, but traveling time and clearances and inspections and duties threatened to keep them landlocked for most of the year.

Meanwhile, Talley knew, his one chance, perhaps the only chance he would ever have, to see and study and film the animal that had obsessed him for thirty years, was fading with every passing day. Seasonal changes in currents and water temperature and the flow of the Gulf Stream might encourage *Architeuthis* to move on.

Their only hope, clearly, was Whip Darling. From what they had heard about him and learned from their conversation with him, they knew that he was the perfect man for the job: expert, ingenious, sensible, tough and determined. His boat was perfect, too. Talley and Manning had rented a punt and rowed across Mangrove Bay one evening, after seeing Darling and his wife leave their home in a taxi. They had boarded the boat in the long shadows of twilight, had studied its broad stern, which was obviously capable of holding huge reels of cable, its engine and the shelves of spare parts, had approved of the lifting gear and the hauling gear, even the rake of the bow and the cast of the bottom, which spoke of the boat's ruggedness and stability.

They had debated trying to buy the boat from Darling, but from a few artificially casual conversations with the staff at Cambridge Beaches, and with workers at the boatyard, Talley had learned that boat and man were inseparable. Buying the boat was the same thing as buying the man, and the man had made it clear he was not for sale.

They had yet to discover a weakness in Darling that they could exploit, but Manning wasn't about to give up. He insisted that, given enough time, he could find an Achilles' heel in a saint. He still had a few more acquaintances to talk to, a few more favors to call in.

Talley, on the other hand, could think of no one else to question, nothing else to try. He had one other person to meet, this evening, but he assumed that the conversation would produce nothing but a request for money in exchange for a promise of juicy gossip about Darling. There had been a few of those, but Talley had declined to pay until he heard the information, and in no instance had the dirt been worth a dime.

Then he had gotten a phone call last night from someone who said his name was Carl Frith, and that he was a fisherman. He said he had heard that Talley was nosing around about Whip Darling, and maybe he could help. The only reason Talley hadn't refused the meeting outright was that Frith had begun by saying he didn't want any money. All he wanted was justice . . . whatever that meant.

"Set!" called a voice from the bow.

St. John said to the helmsman, "Are we in position?"

"Yes, sir."

"How far are we from the charge?"

"About a hundred yards."

"Get closer. I want to be sure the signal reaches."

"But—"

"Get closer, damn it! You want it to work, don't you? . . . Or don't you?"

"Yes, sir." As the helmsman put the boat in gear and gave it power, Talley moved as far aft as he could. He tapped the fiberglass and wondered if it had any flotation built into it.

Then St. John shouted, "Fire!" and the crewman turned the switch on the firing box.

For a moment nothing happened, there was only silence, and then there was a sound of rumbling and a sensation as if a giant hand had grabbed the boat and was trying to lift it into the sky. And then the water erupted around them.

Finally the boat fell back, and the spray dissipated, and St. John came aft and leaned over the side. Little fish—pink and red and gray and brown—floated to the surface.

"Deeper," he said. "He must be down deeper. We'll have to try to go deeper."

The helmsman stepped out of the cabin and said, "Doctor. Ned says we've sprung a leak."

"A leak? Where?"

"The glass cracked. In the viewing ports down below."

"Why did you get us so close?"

"What? You told me—"

"The safety of this vessel is your responsibility. If you thought it was dangerous to get so close, you had an obligation to refuse."

The helmsman just stared at him.

"Idiot!" St. John said, and he started forward. "How serious is the leak?"

"Maybe we should start home, just in case."

"Nonsense. Fix it with epoxy," St. John said, and he disappeared inside the cabin.

Talley thought, Great, now we're going to sink, and I'll probably drown out here in the middle of nowhere. He looked around in the cockpit, searching for something that might float. He saw a wooden hatch cover, and unhooked it so it would float free if the stern went underwater. He looked toward shore, estimating how far it was. . . . Three miles? Four? He couldn't tell, but it seemed a long, long way.

Then, as he turned back, he saw a boat in the near distance. It wasn't doing anything, it was just there, its bow pointed this way. It was a big boat.

Be thankful, he thought. At least maybe someone will come to save you.

He heard their engine drop into gear and felt the boat labor into a turn and begin to head for shore.

St. John came out of the cabin, sweating, and his face had a purplish tinge to it, either from exertion or rage.

"There's a boat over there," Talley said. "Perhaps we should—"

"I see it." St. John banged on the cabin bulkhead and shouted, "Hey!"

The helmsman stuck his head out the door. "Yes, sir?"

"You see that boat over there? Call them on the radio and tell them to follow us in."

"*Tell* them, Doctor?"

"Yes, Rumsey . . . *tell* them. Tell them who we are and tell them to follow us in, in case we need help. They'll do it. You can bet on it."

"Yes, sir." As the helmsman backed into the cabin, St. John said, "Do you recognize them?"

"Yes, sir."

"Who is it?"

"*Privateer* . . . it's Whip Darling."

"Oh," St. John said, and he hesitated for a second before adding, "forget it."

"Sir?"

"Forget it. Don't call them. Just get us home."

The helmsman frowned, then shrugged and went inside.

"Look how she's riding," Mike said.

"*Low* . . ." Darling said. "She's holed herself."

"Want to follow 'em in?"

"They want help, they can call us," Darling said. "I'd like that, but I don't think Liam would."

He put the wheel hard over, pushed the throttle forward and headed for the marker that signaled Western Blue Cut. He stayed in deep water, and for several minutes the bow of the boat shed the corpses of small fish.

Mike said, "He sure blowed everything to ratshit."

"It's a shame being dumb isn't a crime," Darling said, "or we could lock that man up for life."

"What was he using?"

Darling shrugged. "I don't imagine *he* knew. Long as it went *bang,* that's all he cared. Water gel . . . C-4 . . . maybe plain old dynamite."

"You don't just buy that stuff at the grocery store."

"Sure you do. Look at all the powder we've got. All

you have to say is you need to blast for a dock or a foundation. The permit man never takes into account the asshole factor."

"Still, makes you wonder. . . . Hey!" Mike had been looking to the north, and he was pointing at something shiny floating between two swells.

Darling swung the wheel, and the boat rocked as it took the waves on its port quarter.

"Be damned," Darling said as they neared the floating thing. "More of that spawn . . . if that's what it is."

It was another of the gelatinous doughnuts, an oblong measuring six or eight feet by two or three feet, undulating, with a hole in its center.

Darling put the boat in neutral and leaned on the railing of the flying bridge and looked down.

"I'd say it was whale spew," he said. "You know . . . ambergris . . . that is, if there were any whales left around."

"It's not dark enough," Mike said. "And it doesn't stink."

"No . . . gotta be spawn, but spawn of what I'm damned if I know." Darling paused. "We should take some back for that Dr. Talley to have a look at."

"Want me to dip it up?"

"Why not?"

Mike went down the ladder, found the long-handled dip net and went aft, where the boat's combing was low and he could reach the water easily.

Darling turned the boat in a tight circle and maneuvered it so that the mass of jelly slid close down its side.

Mike leaned overboard and scooped with the net. As he touched the jelly, it fragmented.

"Damn," he said. "She come apart."

"Get any of it?"

"Lemme try again."

Darling backed down, and Mike held the handle of the net and stretched his arm out.

As the net touched water, something grabbed it, and pulled. Mike's shins struck the low bulwark, and because too much of his weight was outboard, he started to fall.

"Hey!" he yelled, flailing with his free hand but finding only air.

"Let it go!" shouted Darling, but Mike didn't. As if his hand were welded to it, he clutched the aluminum handle of the dip net, and was pulled overboard. His body turned half a somersault and he landed in the water on his back. Only then did he let go of the net.

Darling ran to the back of the flying bridge and half jumped, half slid down the ladder and hurried aft. The boat was already out of gear, so Mike was in no danger from the propeller, but Darling was worried he might panic and swallow water and drown himself.

And panicked Mike was. He forgot how to swim. He screamed incoherently and windmilled with his arms . . . not five feet from the stern of the boat.

Darling grabbed a rope, cleated one end and held up the other. "Michael!" he shouted.

But Mike didn't hear him, he just kept thrashing and screaming.

Darling coiled the loose rope and aimed it at Mike's head and threw it. It hit him in the face, but Mike ignored it, until his hands found it and, in reflex, fastened on. Then Darling pulled him to the dive step at the stern of the boat, bent down and grabbed him by the collar and hauled him up onto the step.

Mike lay there, whimpering and spitting water. Then he coughed and gasped and rose to his knees and said, "Fuck this."

"Why, Michael," Darling said, smiling. "It was just a

big old turtle, that's all. I saw him . . . must've decided to fight you for the spawn."

"Fuck him. Fuck you. Fuck everything. Forever."

Darling laughed. "You okay?"

"I'm gonna go be a taxi driver."

When Mike had wrung out his clothes and wrapped a towel around himself, Darling returned to the wheel and circled around to where the dip net was floating on the surface. He put the boat in neutral and let its momentum carry it over to the net. He snagged it with the boat hook and brought it aboard.

The turtle had torn a hole in the netting, but a few globs of jelly clung to some of it. Darling held one of the globs to the sunlight and looked closely. There were little things inside, too small to make out. He debated scraping it off the netting and storing it in a jar, but there probably wasn't enough of it to be worthwhile. So he washed the jelly away in the water, dropped the net on the deck and went up to the flying bridge.

A few minutes later, when Darling had turned into the mouth of Western Blue Cut, Mike appeared on the flying bridge with two cups of tea.

"I don't like this," Mike said, handing Darling one of the cups.

"Falling overboard can mess up your day."

"No, I mean everything. Everything's making me go apeshit. I've been overboard before and I've never gone apeshit."

"Don't let it get to you. Everybody has a bad day."

"Everybody doesn't go apeshit, though. Friggin' critter's got me spooked. I half wish Liam *would* blow the bugger up. Who'd have thought a fuckin' squid could make me mental?"

"Stop it, or you *will* make yourself mental . . . talk yourself right into it."

"Can't do what's already done."

Darling looked at Mike, huddled in a towel, his hands shaking, and he thought: This thing has opened a dark door inside this young man. It's weird how things we don't understand can arouse demons we don't even know we have.

They were well up in the shallows, with the fortress of Dockyard looming to the left and the pink cottages of Cambridge Beaches peeking through the casuarinas to the right, when Mike, who was leaning on the railing and facing aft, said, "Never seen that fella before."

Darling looked back. To the north, at least three miles away, approaching the entrance to the deep North Channel, was a small ship, no more than 120 to 150 feet long, with a white hull and a single black stack.

"He's not local," said Mike.

"Not hardly."

"Not navy neither. It looks like one of those private research vessels."

Darling picked up the binoculars, braced his elbows on the railing and focused on the ship. He could see a lifeboat suspended from davits on the starboard side, and, aft of the cabin, a huge steel crane. On a cradle beneath the crane was something oval, something with portholes in it.

"I'll be damned, Michael," Darling said. "Whoever he is, he's got a submersible, one of those little submarines, mounted on his stern."

# PART THREE

# 22

CAPTAIN WALLINGFORD WAS hunched over his desk, signing requisition forms, when Marcus Sharp arrived, rapped twice on the doorjamb and said, "Captain?"

"Sharp. What is it?" Wallingford spoke without looking up. "No, wait, don't tell me. You've heard the scuttlebutt that there's a research vessel here, loaded with space-age search gear, including a state-of-the-art, two-million-dollar submersible, and they've come to look for the giant squid. You've heard that we're going to put a navy man on that ship and in the submersible when they go down, and you've come to volunteer. You think you're the best man for the job." Wallingford looked up and smiled. "Well?"

"I . . . yes. Sir." Sharp stepped into the office and stood before the captain's desk.

"Why you, Sharp? You're a chopper jockey, not a submariner. And why should I send an officer, why not just a seaman? All I need down there is a pair of eyes, somebody to make sure these turkeys don't poke around where they shouldn't, or screw up one of the navy's acoustical cables by accident."

"I'm a diver, sir," Sharp said. "I know what the underwater looks like. I know what all that sensitive equipment of ours looks like down there. I might be able to see things other people wouldn't." He paused. "I've had UDT training."

"UDT training?" said Wallingford. "Christ, Sharp, these people aren't here to blow anything up. They're magazine hotshots who want to be the first to take pictures of a live giant squid . . . a squid that, from what I hear, is probably a thousand miles away from here by now."

"What's the deal with the Bermuda government? I'd've thought the last thing Bermuda wanted was any more publicity."

"Money. What else? Bermuda's hurting. Tourism is in the dumper. Hotels are in trouble, restaurants are in trouble, sport fishing has pretty well stopped. The diving business is *out* of business. When these people from *Voyager*—"

"*Voyager?*"

"It's the magazine. It's new, started by some guy in the ball-bearing business with a ton of money. They had their brand-new Finnish submersible down in the Cayman Islands, taking pictures of weird things in deep water, and when they heard about the squid up here, they saw it as a chance for a coup—a scoop that might catapult 'em into the league with *National Geographic.* The *Geographic* doesn't have a submersible. Nobody does, no Americans anyway, except the navy, and we only have one that's worth a damn. At any rate, Bermuda said to itself, Hey, why not let them in? If they find the squid, fine, maybe they can figure out a way to kill it. If not, let them spend their time and money looking around, and when they don't find the squid, we can publicize the hell out of the fact that the thing is gone, and tell the world Bermuda's safe again."

"Where does the navy fit in? I mean, these are Bermuda waters, this seems—"

"Where do we *fit*? Sharp, come on. . . . Bermuda *has*

no waters. These are NATO waters by law. But the fact is, they're American. Every drop. Do you really think the Bermudians put down all those sonar trackers? Do you think the Bermudians laid all those cables, the ones that keep track of Soviet subs? This is America out here, Sharp. And when the Pentagon heard about this deal, about that ship with all the high-tech gear, they were all over me like sweat, to make sure I got a U.S. Navy man on the ship and on the submersible. Nobody, I don't care if they're American citizens or Munchkins, nobody is gonna poke around our deep-water assets without our being right beside him, looking over his shoulder.''

Wallingford leaned back in his chair. "So there it is, Sharp," he said. "Now, as for you, why would you want to go down in that thing? You think you'll spot some shipwrecks for your pal Whip Darling?''

"No, sir," Sharp said quickly, embarrassed. It had never occurred to him that Wallingford knew about his using helicopter time to cruise above the reefs and look for wrecks. He should have realized it, however, since he was never alone on the chopper, there was always at least one person with him, and the navy base was a tiny community full of people with plenty of time to gossip. "What would be the point?" he added. "Even if I saw something at five hundred or a thousand feet, there'd be no way to recover it.''

"What is it, then?" said Wallingford. "What makes you want to go half a mile down into the ocean, with people you don't know, in a little steel coffin, to look for something that probably isn't there and might kill you if it is?''

"Because . . ." Sharp hesitated, knowing that most people would have trouble understanding his reasoning. "It's something I've never done before. I want to see what it's like.''

"You've never been to the moon before, either. Would you go to the moon if somebody asked you?"

"Yes, sir. Yes, I surely would."

"God almighty, Sharp," Wallingford said, shaking his head. "Okay, you've got it. Be at Dockyard at sixteen hundred. They're gonna go out and anchor tonight, and put the sub down first thing tomorrow."

"Thank you, sir," said Sharp. "How official is this? Should I wear a uniform?"

"No. But take a sweater and some warm socks. I hear it's cold three thousand feet down there in the dark."

"Yes, sir." Sharp saluted and turned to go.

"Sharp," Wallingford said, stopping him at the door.

"Sir?"

"I was gonna send you, even if you hadn't volunteered." Wallingford grinned. "I just wanted to hear you make your case."

Back in his quarters, Sharp packed an overnight bag, and threw in a Walkman, a few tapes and a book. By the time he had taken a shower and put on a pair of jeans and a denim shirt, it was nearly 1500. Dockyard was at the other end of Bermuda, an hour away by motorbike, so he picked up his bag and started out of the room. At the door he remembered that he had been scheduled to go diving the next day with Darling, and so he went back inside and picked up the phone.

Darling's wife answered, and before Sharp could leave a message she said Whip was down on the boat and she'd go fetch him. While he waited, Sharp wondered whether he should tell Darling where he was going. Knowing the navy's passion for secrecy, he assumed that this trip was classified, even though it involved a national magazine that planned to document it on film. But the navy liked to classify everything, from the number of potatoes bought for the mess to the price paid for enlisted men's socks.

Screw secrecy, he decided. The odds were good that Darling knew all about it anyway.

"Glad you called, Marcus," Darling said when he picked up the phone. "I was gonna call you. How about a rain check for tomorrow's diving? There's a bunch of people here from some magazine who want to put a submarine down to take pictures of the squid. They've hired me as escort."

"You're going? What do you mean, escort?"

"They don't know where to look for the thing. They don't know where the drop-off is, or where the bottom shelves off, or where the deep begins. They've got a fathometer and a side-scan sonar, and if they took the time they could find out for themselves. But that boat must cost ten thousand a day to run, so they see using me as a shortcut."

"And you agreed to go? I thought—"

"Marcus. It's a thousand dollars a day. But all I'll do is show 'em where to go, tell 'em where to aim their cameras and float around over their submarine in case it has to surface away from the ship." Darling laughed. "You can be damn sure I'm not going down in that sub."

"Whip," Sharp said, and he paused, feeling his enthusiasm begin to ebb. "I'm supposed to go with them."

"You? What for?"

"The navy's worried that they'll snoop around our sonar gear, maybe decide to justify their expenses by doing a story on how much money we're wasting monitoring Soviet submarines that don't exist."

"What makes Wallingford so sure they won't find the squid?"

"The navy thinks it's gone away," Sharp said. "So do

the people from the Oceanographic Administration and Scripps."

"Well, I don't. Neither does Talley, or he would have gone back to Canada. No, it's likely that the critter is down there, Marcus. I'm pretty sure he's down there somewhere." For a moment there was silence on the line, then Darling said, "You said you were going with them. You don't mean you're going down in that submarine."

"Sure," Sharp said. "That's the whole point."

"Don't."

"I have to, Whip."

"No you don't, Marcus." Darling paused, then said, "There's one thing we both have to remember: There's a big difference between being brave and being foolish."

# 23

THE ROYAL NAVY Dockyard had been built in the nineteenth century by convicts—called "transports," for they had been transported out from England and housed in prison hulks grounded on the muddy bottom of Grassy Bay. Its stone walls were more than ten feet thick, its cobbled streets had been paved by hand. It occupied the entire northern end of Ireland Island, and had once been a civilization unto itself. There had been barracks for hundreds of soldiers, cook houses, jail cells, sail lofts, chandleries, rope lockers and armories.

Now, as Sharp walked along the quay toward the little ship tied to the dock, a dock that still occasionally sheltered British and American ships-of-the-line, he passed boutiques, cafés, souvenir shops, a museum.

Lettering on the transom identified the ship as the *Ellis Explorer,* from Fort Lauderdale. Measuring his paces, Sharp walked along the dock beside the ship. She was 150 feet long, more or less, and most of her was open stern. About halfway between the fantail and the cabin, the submersible rested on its cradle, covered by a tarpaulin. Clearly, the ship was brand-new, built, he guessed after appraising its sleek lines, in Holland or Germany, and it was meticulously tended. There wasn't a speck of rust on the hull, not a chip or a scuff mark on the paint. Ropes on the deck were perfectly coiled, and the steel-and-aluminum superstructure gleamed in the afternoon sun. Whoever owns this vessel, he thought, isn't worried about money.

A woman stood in the bow, tossing pieces of bread to a school of little fish.

"Hello," Sharp said.

She turned to him and said, "Hi." She was in her late twenties, tall and lithe and deeply tanned. She wore cutoff jeans, a man's Oxford shirt with its tails tied at her waist and a Rolex diver's watch. Her sun-bleached brown hair was cut short and swept back from her face. A pair of sunglasses hung from a cord around her neck.

"I'm Marcus Sharp. . . . Lieutenant Sharp."

"Oh," she said. "Right. Come on aboard."

Sharp walked up the gangway and stepped onto the deck.

"I'm Stephanie Carr," the woman said, smiling and holding out her hand. "I take pictures." She led him aft, into the cabin.

The cabin was large and comfortably furnished. There were two folding tables on gimbals, two vinyl-covered sofas bolted to the deck, a stack of plastic chairs, racks of paperback books and, on a shelf, a television set and VCR. Steps led up to the bridge forward and down to the galley and the staterooms aft.

A short, wiry man with a crew cut, who might have been anywhere between thirty and forty-five, sat on the deck and watched a tape of a James Bond movie.

"That's Eddie," Stephanie said. "He drives the sub. Eddie, this is Marcus."

Eddie gestured distractedly and said, "Hey."

Sharp noticed that one of the tables was littered with cameras, strobes, light meters and boxes of film. "Do you have a writer with you?" he asked Stephanie.

"No," she said. "I do it all. Besides, if we get pictures of this monster, no one's going to care about words." She pointed to the staircase aft. "There are a couple of empty cabins below. You can put your stuff wherever you want."

Sharp tossed his bag onto a chair. "Who's Ellis?" he said. "The name—*Ellis Explorer*."

"Barnaby Ellis . . . Ellis Bearings . . . the Ellis Foundation . . . Ellis Publications. The bearings funded the foundation, the foundation owns the boat. When one of the publications needs the boat, they borrow it from the foundation."

"You work for him?"

"No, I'm free lance. I work for the *Geographic,* for *Traveler,* for whoever wants to pay me."

"Hey, navy man," a voice called down from the bridge.

"Come meet Hector," Stephanie said, and she led the way up onto the bridge.

Hector appeared to be in his mid-forties. He was dark-skinned and beefy, and he wore a starched white shirt with captain's shoulder boards, creased black trousers and spit-shined black shoes. He was working with a pencil and a ruler on a chart of the waters around Bermuda. "This Darling," he said, "he tells me to go anchor out here"—he tapped a spot on the chart—"but out here there's no bottom."

"Did he talk you through it?" Sharp asked.

"Every step. Around the point here, north from here to the buoy, then northwest to here. But the chart says there's no bottom till five hundred fathoms. I can't anchor in five hundred fathoms."

"Do what he says," said Sharp. "If he says there's a bottom there, there's a bottom there. It may be a sea mount, it may be a ledge. It may be part of the shelf."

"But the chart—"

"Captain," Sharp said, "in Bermuda, if I had to choose between some mapmaker from Coast and Geodetic Survey and Whip Darling, I'd go with Whip Darling every time."

It was after five when they left the point at Dockyard behind and headed north toward the channel markers. Sharp and Stephanie stood on the observation deck atop the cabin and watched the little puffs of cumulus cloud change color as the lowering sun struck them from different angles.

"Where do you live?" Sharp asked.

"San Francisco, sort of. But nowhere, really. I keep a tiny apartment there, just to have a place to come back to, but I'm away ten or eleven months a year."

"So you're not married."

"Hardly," she said, smiling. "Who'd have me? He'd never see me. When I got started in this business—fresh out of college, I was working for a little paper in Kansas, and I moonlighted wildlife pictures—I knew I'd have to make a choice. I knew I couldn't have it both ways. A lot of my friends are photographers who specialize in what I do—sports, adventure, animals—and

of the ones who get married, ninety percent get di-
vorced."

"Is it worth it?"

"It has been. I've been everywhere in the world, my
passport's as thick as the phone book. I've met a lot of
people, done a lot of crazy things, photographed everything from tigers to army ants. But I'm beginning to get
tired of it. Now and then, I think about settling down.
But every time I do, the phone rings, and I'm off to
somewhere new." She waved her hand at the sea, and
said, "Like now."

"How much do you know about giant squid?"

"Nothing. Well, almost nothing. I read a couple of
articles on the way over. I gather that nobody's ever
gotten a picture of one, and that's enough for me; it isn't
often one of us gets to do something that's never been
done before."

"There's a reason, you know. They're rare, and
they're dangerous."

"Well," she said, "that's the fun of it, right? Look at
it this way, Marcus. We're getting paid to do what other
people couldn't do if they had all the money in the
world: take chances and make discoveries. It's called
living."

As Sharp looked at her, he suddenly felt a stab of pain
that he hadn't felt in many months, the pain of remem-
bering Karen.


"I tell you," Hector said, pointing at the fathometer,
"there's no bottom here." A faint orange light whirled
on a circular screen, blipping brighter as it passed the
mark for 480 fathoms.

"Are you sure you're in the right place?" Sharp
asked.

"The SatNav says I'm on the money, right where he
said."

Sharp looked out the window. There was nothing in the color of the water that suggested a shallow spot; the sea was a uniform gray, like burnished steel. "Drop the anchor," he said.

"Easy for you to say, navy man," said Hector. "It's not your two grand worth of anchor and chain."

"Drop it. If you lose it, I'll dive it up for you myself." Sharp smiled.

Hector looked at him, then said, "Shit," and pushed the button that released the anchor. They heard a splash, followed by the rattle of chain through the hawsehole in the bow. A crewman in a striped matelot shirt stood on the forepeak and watched the chain plummet.

"Mind if I turn on your side-scan?" Sharp asked.

"Go ahead."

Sharp turned the switch on the side-scan sonar and pressed his face to the rubber gasket. The gray screen brightened, and a white line appeared, created by reflected sonar impulses, showing the contour of the bottom more than half a mile away. Where is it? he wondered. Where's the secret shelf that'll snag the anchor before it disappears into the deep?

He heard Hector say, "I'll be damned," and just then a tiny white stroke appeared on the top left corner of the sonar screen, reflecting a little outcropping from the cliff. The rattle of the anchor chain stopped.

"Two hundred and ten feet," Hector said. "How the hell did Darling know that?"

"Twenty-five years at sea out here, that's how," Sharp said. "Whip knows every pimple on the ledge; and he knew how the tide would carry your anchor."

"Does he know where this giant squid is?"

"Nobody knows that," Sharp said, and he went down the steps into the cabin.

*   *   *

They had dinner in the cabin: microwaved hamburgers, steamed pasta and salad. When they had washed the dishes, Eddie and the two crewmen gathered around the TV and watched a tape of *The Hunt for Red October,* and Hector returned to the bridge.

Stephanie poured coffee for herself and Sharp, took a cigarette from one of her camera bags and led him outside onto the open stern. The moon was so bright that it extinguished the stars around it; the sea was as flat as glass.

"What about you?" she asked him. "Are you married?"

"No," Sharp said, and then—he wasn't sure why—he told her about Karen.

"That's rough," she said when he had finished. "I don't think I could deal with that kind of pain."

Before Sharp could say anything else, they heard Hector shout, "Hey, navy man!" from the bridge.

They walked forward along a passageway on the port side and up four steel steps to the outside door of the bridge.

"Come here," Hector said.

Sharp stepped inside the bridge. In darkness, it looked like an abandoned nightclub, for the only lights were the red and green and orange glows from the electronic gear.

"What do you make of that?" Hector said, and he gestured at the side-scan sonar.

"Of what?"

"We've been swinging at anchor. I think maybe we swung ourselves right overtop a shipwreck."

As he bent to the machine, Sharp thought what a nice irony it would be if they did discover an old wreck, unseen and untouched for hundreds of years. They had the submersible, so they could reach the wreck, photograph it, perhaps even recover something from it. Whip would be amazed.

Sharp closed his eyes, then opened them again and let them focus on the gray screen. He knew that side-scan sonar images could be remarkably accurate, if the object being drawn was in good shape, alone and on a flat bottom. He had seen a side-scan picture in *National Geographic* of a ship that had sunk in the Arctic. The ship sat upright on the bottom, its masts and superstructure clearly visible, looking as if it were about to sail away. But that ship had sunk at anchor in three hundred feet of water. If there was a ship here, it had tumbled for half a mile, probably breaking apart as it fell. It might be nothing more than a heap of scrap.

What he saw was a shapeless smear. He looked at the calibration numbers on the side of the screen: The smear seemed to be twenty or thirty meters long, possibly the right size for a shipwreck.

"It could be," he said.

"Have a look at it from the sub tomorrow," said Hector. "A lot of ships were lost around here during the war. Maybe it's one of them. Give me the loran numbers, will you?"

Sharp stepped away from the sonar screen and crossed the bridge to the loran. He read the numbers aloud to Hector, who scribbled them on a piece of paper.

None of them looked at the sonar screen again. If they had, they would have seen a change in the shapeless smear. They would have seen some lines fade, others appear, as the thing three thousand feet beneath them began to move.

# 24

KAREN'S ARMS WERE out, reaching for him; her eyes pleaded for help, and she was screaming, but in a language he couldn't understand. He tried to reach her, but his legs wouldn't work. He felt as if he were slogging through transparent mud or being held back by something that forced him to move in slow motion. The closer he got, the farther away she seemed. And then something was chasing her, something he couldn't see but that must be huge and terrifying, for her fear became panic and her screams grew louder. All of a sudden she disappeared, and the thing chasing her was gone, too, and all that was left was a loud, piercing buzz.

Sharp awoke, and for a moment he didn't know where he was. The bed was small, not his, and the light was dim. Only the buzz remained, an urgent summons from somewhere near his head. He rolled over and saw an intercom phone on the bulkhead. He picked up the phone and mumbled his name.

"Rise and shine, Marcus," said Stephanie. "Time to go."

As he hung up, Sharp felt a rush of adrenaline. He had volunteered for this, but what yesterday had seemed exciting was fast becoming frightening. He had never ridden in a submarine, let alone a submarine a third the size of a subway car. He didn't like crowded elevators—who did?—and he felt uneasy in interior cabins on ships.

He suddenly wondered if he would discover he was a closet claustrophobe.

Well, he thought, you'll soon find out.

As he shaved and dressed in jeans, a shirt, wool socks and a sweater, his apprehension gave way once again to excitement. At least this was action, a challenge. At least this was something new. As Stephanie would say, this was living.

The sun had barely cleared the horizon when Sharp arrived in the cabin and poured himself a cup of coffee. Through the windows in the rear of the cabin he saw Eddie and one of the crewmen removing the tarpaulin from the submersible. Stephanie was on the afterdeck, mounting a video camera in an underwater housing. Then, as his gaze wandered to the right, he saw that the *Privateer* was tied to the port side of the ship. He started out of the cabin, but stopped when he heard Darling's voice behind him, up on the bridge, talking to Hector.

"Morning, Marcus," Darling said when Sharp appeared on the bridge. "Are you sure you still want to go down there and freeze your buns off?"

"Yes," Sharp said. "I'm sure."

Darling turned to Hector and said, "I'll have my mate hang off a ways till you launch, then he'll track the sub on my gear."

Sharp said, "What are you gonna do, Whip?"

"Keep an eye on you, Marcus," Darling said, and he smiled. "You're too valuable to lose." He left the bridge and walked aft to talk to Mike on the *Privateer*.

Sharp carried his coffee down to the stern. At the top of a ladder he met Stephanie on her way up, and she gestured for him to follow her through a watertight door above the main cabin and aft of the bridge.

It was the control room for the submersible, and it was dark, lit only by a red bulb in the overhead and by four television monitors that were showing color bars.

One of the crewmen, whom Sharp remembered as
Andy, sat before a panel dotted with colored lights and
keyboard buttons, wearing a headset and a microphone.

"Andy keeps tabs on all our systems," Stephanie said.
"Your friend Whip will be in here with him—we can
talk to him anytime."

Sharp pointed at the TV monitors. "The submersible
is hard-wired to the surface?"

"Everything's videotaped, for the foundation. One
fiber-optic cable does it all. I've got video cameras inside
and outside the sub, plus my still cameras. Can I give
you a camera? We'll be at different portholes, we may
see different things."

"Sure," Sharp said, "if you've got a real idiot-proof
camera. What do you want pictures of? Gorgonian corals? Algae growth?"

"No way." Stephanie grinned. "Monsters. Nothing
but monsters. Great big ones."


At close range, the submersible looked to Sharp like
a giant antihistamine capsule, a Dristan with arms.
Each arm had steel pincers on the end, and mounted
between them was a video camera in a globular housing.

The sun was higher now, and there wasn't a breath of
breeze. Perspiration poured from Sharp as he lowered
himself through the round hatch in the top of the submersible. The crewman manning the crane gave him a
thumbs-up sign, and he smiled wanly in reply.

Stephanie was already inside, as was Eddie, wearing
a down vest and crouching forward to check his
switches and gauges.

The interior of the capsule was a tube, twelve feet
long, six feet wide and five feet high. There were three
small portholes, one in the bow for Eddie, one on either
side for Stephanie and Sharp. A square cushion sat on
the steel deck before Sharp's porthole, and he dropped

to his knees and crawled to the cushion. He found that he could sit with his legs curled beneath him, or kneel with his face pressed to the porthole, or lie with his feet raised. But there was no way he could straighten out.

What would happen if he got a cramp? How would he shake it out? Don't think about it, he told himself. Just *do* it.

"How long does it take to get to the bottom?" he asked.

"Half an hour," said Stephanie. "We drop at a hundred feet a minute."

Not too bad. He could survive for an hour, anyway. "And how long do we spend down there?"

"Up to four hours."

"Four hours!" Never, Sharp thought. Not a chance.

He heard the hatch slam above him, and a metallic hiss as it was dogged down.

Stephanie passed him a small 35-mm camera with a wide-angle lens, and said, "All loaded and ready to go. Just push the button."

Sharp tried to take the camera, but it slipped from his sweaty palms, and Stephanie caught it an inch above the steel deck. "You look like death," she said.

"No kidding." Sharp wiped his hands on his trousers and took the camera from her.

"What are you worried about? This is a state-of-the-art deep boat, and Eddie is a state-of-the-art pilot." She smiled. "Right, Eddie?"

"Fuckin' A," Eddie said. He mumbled something into the microphone suspended from his headset, and suddenly the capsule jerked and began to rise as the crane lifted it off its cradle and swung it out over the side of the ship. For a moment it yawed back and forth like an amusement-park ride, and Sharp had to brace himself to keep from being tossed across the deck. Then it dropped slowly until it thudded into the water, and its motion changed to a gentle rocking.

Sharp looked through the porthole and saw the sea lapping at the glass. From overhead came the metallic sound of the shackle being released from the submersible's lifting ring.

The capsule began to sink. Water now covered the portholes. Sharp pushed his cheek to the glass and rolled his eyes upward, straining for one last glance at sunlight. Refracted through the moving water, the blue of the sky and the white of the clouds and the gold of the sun danced together hypnotically.

Then the colors faded, replaced by a monochromatic blue mist. All noise ceased, except for the soft whirring of the electric motor aboard the submersible.

The world had been swallowed by the sea.

Sweat was quickly evaporating from Sharp's forehead and from under his arms and down his back, and he felt chilly. In less than a minute, the temperature had dropped something like thirty degrees. And yet he was still sweating, not from heat but from fear, and the creeping onset of claustrophobia.

He looked through the porthole and saw that the blue outside was fast deepening to violet. He dared his eyes to wander downward. Rays of sunlight seemed to struggle to light the water, but they were dispersed and consumed. Below, blue yielded to black, and all was night.

They fell slowly, seeing nothing, hearing nothing, feeling nothing. Then Sharp realized he was taking comfort in the nothingness, for he began to recall the tales Darling had told him about what lived down here in this night, this dark. And he shivered.

# 25

SHARP WAS FREEZING. His wool socks were soaked with the condensation on the inside of the steel capsule. Up on the surface, the wetness had felt cool and comfortable, but now, although the condensation had evaporated, his socks had not dried. His toes were numb, the soles of his feet itched. He put his hands beneath his sweater and tucked them under his arms, and leaned away from the porthole to look over Eddie's shoulder at his gauges. The outside temperature was 4 degrees centigrade, about 40 degrees Fahrenheit. Inside it wasn't much warmer, just above 50. They were at two thousand feet, and falling.

Into his microphone Eddie said, "Activating illumination," and he flicked a switch. Two 1,000-watt lamps on top of the submersible flashed on, casting a flood of yellow that penetrated fifteen or twenty feet before being swallowed by the blackness.

And then a universe of life exploded before Sharp's eyes. Tiny planktonic animals swirled in and out of the light, a living snowstorm of sea life. An infinitesimal shrimp adhered to his porthole and began to march purposefully across the glass. Something resembling a gray-and-red ribbon with yellow eyes and a pompadour of tiny spikes wriggled up to the porthole, fluttered before it for a moment, then darted away.

"Look," Eddie said, pointing out his porthole. Sharp

craned to see, but whatever it was, was gone. He returned to his own porthole, and a moment later he could see it—it appeared, serenely circling the capsule, a creation of some disturbed imagination.

It was an anglerfish: round, bulbous and brownish yellow, trailing short, mucous fins. Its eyes protruded like blue-green sores, it had fangs like needles of diamond, its flesh was crisscrossed with black veins. It looked like a cyst with teeth. Where its nose should have been was a white stalk, and atop the stalk, glowing like a beacon, was a light.

Sharp had seen pictures of anglerfish. They used their stalks as lures, dangling the lights before their gaping mouths to attract curious and unwary prey.

Because there was nothing in the background to compare it to, Sharp had no idea how far away the fish was, or how big.

"What do you think?" he asked Eddie, and he held his hands a couple of feet apart.

Eddie grinned, and held up his hand and spread his thumb and index finger: The fish was four inches long, at most.

Sharp heard the motor drive on Stephanie's camera firing frame after frame. She was holding the lens against her porthole, and rotating the f-stop ring, hoping by random shooting to get a good exposure.

"I thought you only wanted monsters," Sharp said.

"What do you think these are?" Stephanie pointed out her porthole. "Good God, look at that!"

Sharp saw a flicker of yellow pass Stephanie's porthole. He turned back and waited for the animal to make its way around the capsule.

This creature seemed to have no fins; it might have been a yellow arrow, save that its entire digestive system, gut and stomach, hung down from a pouch and trailed along, pulsing. Its lower jaw was studded with pinprick teeth, and its black, milk-white eyes stuck out of its head like round buttons.

Soon, other animals swarmed around the capsule, drawn by the light, inquisitive and unafraid. There were snakelike creatures that seemed to trail hairs along their backs; large-eyed eels with lumps on their heads that looked like tumors; translucent globes that seemed to be all mouth.

Sharp started as Darling's voice suddenly boomed over the speaker inside the capsule. "You've got yourself a bloody zoo down there, Marcus," he said. "If the aquarium ever comes to its senses, I know where to drop my traps next time."

"Wait'll they see these pictures, Whip," Sharp said. "They'll come back to you on their hands and knees."

Forgetting his fear, ignoring the cold, Sharp picked up the camera Stephanie had given him, and adjusted its focus. He knelt on the cushion, and waited for the next miniature mystery to swim by.

# 26

MIKE SLAPPED HIMSELF in the face, and the sting roused him for a moment. But as soon as his eyes returned to the screen of the fish-finder, he felt his lids begin to droop. He stood up, stretched, yawned and looked out the window. The ship was about a quarter of a mile away, and behind it he saw the gray lump of Bermuda. Otherwise, from horizon to horizon the sea was empty.

Whip had told him to keep his eyes glued to the fish-finder—he called it the poor man's side-scan sonar—and for more than an hour Mike had. But the image hadn't changed at all: There was the line that delineated the bottom, and just above it the little dot of the meandering submersible. Nothing else. Not a broken smear that would signal a school of fish, certainly not the solid mark of something big and dense, like a passing whale.

Normally, Mike wouldn't have liked being left alone on the boat, but this was different: There was a ship nearby, and Whip was on it, and all the action was half a mile away and didn't involve him. He had nothing to do but watch, and report in if he saw something. Best of all, he had no decisions to make.

He didn't just feel calm, he felt hypnotized, not only by the static screen but also because the sea rocked the *Privateer* with such subtle gentleness that before he knew what was happening, he had twice found himself lulled to sleep. He might not have woken up at all if his head hadn't banged against the bulkhead.

The radio crackled to life, and Mike heard Whip's voice: "*Privateer . . . Privateer . . . Privateer . . .* come back."

Mike picked up the microphone, pushed the "talk" button and said, "Go ahead, Whip."

"How you doing, Michael?"

" 'Bout to fall dead asleep. This is worse than watching paint dry."

"Nothing's going on—take a breather."

"I'll do that," Mike said. "Make some coffee, go out in the fresh air and fiddle with that whoreson pump."

"Leave the volume up and the door open, so you'll hear me if I call."

"Roger that, Whip. Standing by."

Mike replaced the microphone on its hook. He

looked at the fish-finder one more time, saw that the image hadn't changed and went below.

In the wheelhouse, the fish-finder continued to glow. For several moments, the image stayed as steady as if it were a still picture. Then, on the right side of the screen, about a third of the way up from the bottom, a new mark appeared. It was solid, a single mass, and slowly it began to move across the screen, toward the submersible.

# 27

THERE HAD BEEN a change in the creature. Until now, as it had grown and matured, it had lived adventitiously, drifting with the currents, eating whatever food came its way. But food was no longer plentiful; passivity could not guarantee survival.

Its instincts had not changed—they were genetically programmed, immutable—but its impulse for survival had altered. It had started to become more active in its responses to its environment.

It could no longer live as a scavenger; it had been forced to become a hunter.

Hovering now at the confluence of two currents that swept around the volcano, the creature grew agitated; something was intruding, disturbing the normal rhythms of the sea.

It sensed a change in its surroundings, as if energy had suddenly surged into its world. There was a faint but persistent pulsing in the water; small animals darted back and forth, flashing bioluminescence; larger ones traveled nearby, subtly altering the water pressure.

The small and relatively weak human eye could not have perceived any light at all, but the creature's enormous eyes were suffused with rod cells that gathered and registered even the smallest scintilla of light.

Now it perceived more than a scintilla. Somewhere in the distance below there was a great light, moving, emitting the pulsing sound, galvanizing other animals.

The creature had not eaten in days, and though it did not respond to time, it **was driven** by cycles of need.

It drew water in through its body cavity and expelled it through its funnel, aiming for the source of light.

It began to hunt.

# 28

YOU LOOK COLD, Marcus," Stephanie said.

Sharp nodded. "You got that right," he said. His arms were crossed over his chest, his hands tucked into his armpits, but still he couldn't stop shivering. "How come you're not?"

"I've got a layer of wool over a layer of silk over a layer of cotton." She turned to Eddie. "Where's the coffee?"

Eddie pointed and said, "In the box there."

Stephanie reached over, opened a plastic box and took out a thermos bottle. She poured the top full of coffee and passed it to Sharp.

The coffee was strong, sour-bitter, unsweetened and harsh, but as it pooled in his stomach, Sharp welcomed the warmth. "Thanks," he said.

He looked at his watch. They had been down for nearly three hours, drifting at twenty-five hundred feet, about five hundred feet over the bottom, and they had seen nothing but the small, strange creatures that gathered curiously around the capsule and then vanished into the darkness.

"What say I put her down on the bottom?" Eddie said into his microphone.

Darling's voice came over the speaker. "Might's well," he said. "Maybe you'll see a shark."

Eddie pushed the control stick forward, and the capsule began to drop.

The bottom was like pictures Sharp had seen of the surface of the moon: barren, dusty, undulating. The submersible pushed a slight pressure wave before it, and mud rose up and billowed away as the machine moved along.

Suddenly Eddie straightened up and said, "Christ!"

"What?" Sharp said. "What is it?"

Eddie pointed at Sharp's porthole, and so Sharp shaded his eyes and pressed his face to the glass.

Snakes, Sharp thought at first. A million snakes. All swarming on a dead body.

And then, as he watched, he thought: No, they can't be snakes, they're eels. But no, not eels either—they had fins. They were fish, some kind of weird fish, writhing and twisting and tearing at flesh. Bits of flesh broke loose and floated away, and were instantly mobbed and ingested and reduced to molecules by other, smaller scavengers.

One of the eely, snakelike things detached itself from its food and backed away and, confused or enraged by the lights, attacked the submersible. It thrust its face at

Sharp's porthole and thrashed, as if to suck the entire machine into its belly. The face became nothing but a mouth, and around its edges were rasping teeth and a probing tongue. The body twisted like a corkscrew, frantic to force the face to drill a hole in the prey.

A hagfish, Sharp realized, one of the nightmare demons that bored holes in larger animals and gnawed the life out of them.

Eddie swung the submersible over the gnarled ball of hagfish, pressed its bow among them, driving them away, and then Sharp could see what they had been feeding on.

"A sperm whale!" he said. "It's the lower jaw of a sperm whale. Do you see that, Whip?"

"Yes," Darling's voice said, sounding flat and distant.

"What the hell kills a sperm whale?"

Darling didn't answer, but in the silence, Sharp suddenly thought: *I* know. And he began to sweat. He strained his eyes to see beyond the perimeter of light. Fish darted back and forth, not fading from view but suddenly appearing and disappearing, phantoms that crossed the rim of light. He was comforted by them and by what they signaled: Whip had once said that as long as fish were around, you didn't have to worry about sharks, because, long before a man could, the fish read the electromagnetic impulses that warned of a shark's intention to attack. It was when the fish vanished that you worried.

On the other hand, Sharp reminded himself, *Architeuthis* isn't a shark. He raised his camera to the porthole.

# 29

THE CREATURE'S EYES gathered more and more light; its other senses recorded the increased vibrations in the water. Something was there, not far away, and it was moving.

Its olfactories detected no signs of life, no confirmation of prey. If it had been less hungry, the creature might have been more cautious, might have hung back in the darkness and waited. But its body's needs were impelling the brain to be reckless, so it continued to move toward the source of the light.

Soon it saw the lights, little pinpoints of brightness piercing the black, and throughout its body it felt the thrumming vibrations emanating from the thing.

Motion meant life; vibrations meant life. And so, although it had yet to perceive the scent of life, it determined that the thing was alive.

It attacked.

# 30

THE THING'S NOT down here," Eddie said. "We're going up." He pulled back on the control stick.

Sharp looked at the digital depth readout on the console in front of Eddie. It was calibrated in meters, and as Sharp watched, the numbers changed—ever so slowly, he thought, and he tried to will the numbers to flash faster—from 970 meters to 969. He sighed and massaged his toes, and wondered if they were frostbitten.

Suddenly the capsule jolted and yawed to one side. Sharp was knocked off his knees, and he grabbed for a handhold. The capsule righted itself and continued upward.

"What the hell was that?" Sharp said.

Eddie didn't answer. He was hunched forward, his shoulders tensed.

Stephanie's back was pressed against the bulkhead, her hands braced on the deck. "What was it, Eddie?" she said.

"I didn't see," Eddie said. "It felt like we hit an air pocket, or like a ship passed overhead."

"You mean a current?"

Over the speaker Darling's voice said, "Not a chance. There *are* no currents down there." He paused. "Something's out there."

As Darling's words registered with Sharp, he suddenly felt a weight like a sack of rocks in his stomach. Oh God, he thought. Here we go.

He saw that his camera had tumbled across the deck, and now, as he retrieved it and checked its settings and adjusted the focus, he found that his fingers weren't working very well. They were trembling, and each one seemed to be independent and to defy the messages from his brain. A drop of sweat fell from the tip of his nose onto the lens, and he wiped it away with the tail of his shirt.

He looked over at Stephanie. She had her back to him, and her camera lens was against the porthole. She pressed the release button, and the motor drive fired a dozen frames in a couple of seconds. "Take some pictures, Marcus," she said over her shoulder.

"Of what?" Sharp said. "I didn't see anything."

"The lens is wider than your eye. Maybe it'll see something."

Before Sharp could reply, the capsule was jolted again, hard, and it careened to the left. A shadow passed before the lights, dimming them, then disappeared.

"God dammit!" Eddie shouted, and he fought the stick, righting the capsule.

Sharp put his camera to the porthole and pressed the shutter release, advanced the film and shot again.

The capsule was rising again. Sharp looked at the readout: 960 meters, 959, 958 . . .

# 31

THE GIANT SQUID rushed through the darkness, seized by paroxysms of frustrated rage. Its whips lashed out, hooks erect, then recoiled and lashed out again, as if trying to flay the sea itself. Its colors flashed from gray to brown to maroon to red to pink, then back to an ashy white.

It had passed once over the lighted thing, appraising it; then it had tried to kill it, although the signs of life the thing emitted were vague and uncertain.

The thing had been hard, an impenetrable carapace, and it had fought back with vigorous movement and alien sounds.

Because its attack had created no encouraging spoor of blood or torn flesh, the squid had not pressed the attack. It had moved on in search of other nourishment.

But its cells were not accustomed to being denied; its digestive juices had begun to flow in anticipation. Now they were causing the creature pain, confusion and rage.

Seeking food, any food, it rushed through the water, moving slowly upward, far behind the retreating lighted thing, not pursuing it but following it nevertheless.

# 32

THAT WAS *SOME*THING," Stephanie said as she pulled herself up through the open hatch and sat on its rim. She grinned down at Darling and Hector, who stood below on the ship's deck.

Sharp squeezed through the hatch and sat beside her. He took a deep breath, savoring the fresh air. Savoring safety.

"Did you see it?" Hector asked.

"We saw about a million of the weirdest things in the world," said Stephanie. "Things I never even imagined, let alone photographed, before."

"No, I mean the thing that knocked you around down there? What rocked the boat?"

"I don't know, I didn't really see it." She looked at Sharp. "Did you?"

"No," Sharp said, looking at Darling. "Did you get anything on the video, Whip?"

"Just a shadow," Darling said, and he began to walk around the submersible, examining it, touching the paint here and there.

Eddie, who had exited the capsule first and was helping the two crewmen secure it to its cradle, said, "Whatever it was, it didn't want to tackle the sub. It had a look at us and kept on truckin'."

"Maybe," said Darling. He had stopped in his circuit of the capsule, and he was touching something.

Sharp leaned over the side and looked where Whip's fingers were rubbing the paint. He saw five ragged scratch marks, two or three feet long; something had slashed through the paint and exposed bare metal beneath. "It's the squid, isn't it," he said.

Darling nodded and said, "Looks like it to me."

"Well, if it was," Eddie said, "he gave us a once-over and took off."

"We'll be ready for him next time," said Stephanie. "I'm going to readjust the video cameras." She pulled her legs out of the hatch, slid down off the capsule and said to Eddie, "What's your turnaround time?"

"Four hours," Eddie replied, looking at his watch. "We should be ready to go down again at about three-thirty, four o'clock."

Not me, Sharp thought, I've had enough excitement for one day. "I'll stay topside," he said. "I can see plenty on the TV screens to keep the navy happy."

"You couldn't go even if you wanted to, navy man," said Hector. "You've already been bumped."

"By whom?"

When Hector didn't answer, Sharp looked at Darling and saw a look of disgust on his face. Then Darling turned away and spit over the side of the ship.

# 33

HERBERT TALLEY WATCHED the ramshackle pickup truck head off down the driveway, then he turned and went into the house. He crossed the living room, walked down a hallway and opened the door to Manning's bedroom. "Wake up, Osborn," he said. The room smelled of night breath and stale brandy, and Talley went to the far wall, opened the curtains and raised the window.

Manning groaned and said, "What time is it?"

"Nearly noon. Meet me on the terrace."

While Manning brushed his teeth and poured himself a cup of coffee, Talley stood on the terrace and gazed across Castle Harbour. At the airport a mile away a 747 lumbered in for a landing, and when the pilot reversed his engines, the shriek was so loud that the spoon trembled on Talley's saucer. What was it about Tucker's Town, Talley wondered, that enticed the rich and famous to buy and refurbish huge houses practically on top of one another for the privilege of enduring deafening noise twenty times a day? Exclusivity, he decided; the gate at the end of the lane and the sign that said PRIVATE.

Manning came out from the kitchen, carrying his coffee and wearing a bathrobe. "What's up?" he said.

"That fisherman, Frith. He was just here. He overheard some interesting radio chatter about half an hour ago, between a research vessel and the navy base. A Lieutenant Sharp was reporting in."

"And?" Manning was edgy and impatient, and his hangover didn't help. When he saw Talley pause and smile, he barked, "Dammit, Herbert, stop playing games. What's going on?"

"The ship is called the *Ellis Explorer*. It's got a submersible on board. It's here looking for *Architeuthis*. I think they found it, even though they don't know for sure."

"Ellis," Manning said. "Barnaby Ellis?"

"I don't know, I guess so. But the point is, Osborn, I think the squid is still here and still hungry. And there's a ship out there with the equipment and capability to take people down to it. On that sub we could see it, study it, film it, learn about it. And you could kill it, if . . ." Talley paused.

"If what?" Manning said.

"If we can get on board. You have power, Osborn. Now's the time to use it."

Manning hesitated, thought for a moment, then got up and went indoors. Talley heard him punching numbers into a telephone.

Talley walked to the edge of the terrace and looked down at the big oval swimming pool. A scuba tank lay beside the pool, rigged with backpack and regulator. Talley could see that it had been there for days, if not weeks, for it was covered with pine needles, and a salamander had made a home among its straps. He wondered if the tank had been used by one of Manning's children, and if Manning had left it there as a kind of bleak memorial.

Talley had begun to feel restless. Manning was spending his evenings with a brandy bottle, and Talley sensed that his passionate anger was being transformed by inaction and frustration into despair.

He heard Manning talking into the phone, and he thought, Good; maybe this will get things going again.

When Manning came back, he said, "It's all set. I talked to Barnaby himself. The ship is here for one of his magazines. He agreed to bump his people and give us a crack at it tomorrow."

"Tomorrow?" Talley said. "Why not today? Frith said they've got a dive scheduled for this afternoon."

"The sub is filled. The Bermuda government's got someone on it this afternoon. It seems they've got a plan to kill the squid."

"How?" Talley suddenly felt sick. "How do they think they're going to kill that beast?"

"I have no idea," Manning said, "but I wouldn't worry about it."

"How can you be so nonchalant? You've spent—"

"I'd say their chances are about one in a million."

"Why?"

"Because the chief squid hunter they're sending is your friend Liam St. John."

# 34

SHARP AND DARLING stood on the observation deck and watched St. John unload his gear from the aquarium boat. There were four aluminum cases, two boxes of fresh fish and a modified fish trap, about three feet square, made of chicken wire and steel reinforcing rod.

St. John consulted with Eddie and Stephanie. Then Eddie called the two crewmen over, and they hauled the cases to the submersible and began to fasten the wire cage to the top of the submersible, forward of the hatch.

Stephanie climbed the ladder to the observation deck. "This should be interesting," she said. "He's even got Hector jazzed, and that takes some doing." She pointed to the afterdeck, and they saw Hector following St. John around, asking questions.

Darling looked at Stephanie, and after a moment he said, "Sometimes there's a reason certain things haven't ever been done, and that's because they can't be done."

"I know," Stephanie said, "but this doesn't look to me like an impossibility. Just a long shot."

Sharp said, "So you think he's got a chance?"

"A chance, yes. And he's sure got enough bait. A hundred pounds of fresh tuna should attract anything that lives down there, and keep it busy long enough for us to do what we have to do."

"How does he think he's gonna kill it?" Darling asked.

"With two weapons," Stephanie said, gesturing at the mechanical arms of the submersible. "Both are attached to the sub's arms, and he can work them from inside the capsule. One's a spear gun loaded with a syringe of strychnine, enough to kill a dozen elephants. The other's like a diver's bang-stick—it fires a twelve-gauge shotgun shell, loaded with globs of mercury that disperse like poisonous shrapnel. I don't know that much about giant squid, but it seems to me he's got enough firepower to kill it two or three times over. Eddie thinks so, too."

"I can see how you think it all makes sense," Darling said, "but what you haven't calculated is that this beast doesn't know sense. It doesn't play by our rules. It *makes* the rules."

"He's taken that into account."

"How?"

"If the weapons don't kill it, he thinks the squid might wrap itself around the capsule, and then it can be brought to the surface on the cables, and killed up here."

"My God, girl," Darling said. "That's like trying to catch a tiger by sticking your arm in his mouth and shouting, 'I've got him!' Don't you know what kind of beast this is?"

"He can't crush the submersible," Stephanie said. "I think it sounds like a pretty good idea."

"Well, I think it sounds like damn foolishness," said Darling, and he left the deck.

"Don't go down," Sharp said to Stephanie when Darling had gone. "Let St. John try it alone. You can go the next time."

"You're nice to care, Marcus," she said, and she touched his cheek. "But I want to go. That's what I'm here to do."


Darling entered the bridge, asked Hector's permission to use the radio and called over to the *Privateer,* which by now had drifted a mile to the north.

It took Mike several moments to respond. Darling assumed he had been out on the stern, napping or working on his pump.

"Just checking in, Michael," he said. "You staying awake?"

"Barely. Okay with you if I put a line down, try to catch me some snappers?"

"Sure, but drive the boat over here first. Get within a couple hundred yards, then kill the engine and let her drift. That way you'll be in position to track the sub."

"Okay. When are they putting it down?"

"In about an hour. And, Michael, once it's down

there, try not to nod off. I want you wide awake and
firing on all cylinders, in case you're needed."

"Roger that, Whip," Mike said. "*Privateer* standing
by."

# 35

MIKE TOOK THE boat out of gear and let it settle.
He looked across the still water and tried to gauge his
distance from the ship. A hundred and fifty yards, he
guessed, maybe two hundred. Just about right. He
turned off the engine.

He took the binoculars off the shelf in front of the
wheel and focused them on the submersible. The hatch
was open, and people were still fooling with the sub's
mechanical arms. He had plenty of time.

He went aft and cut up the mackerel he'd put out in
the sun to thaw. He rigged two hooks on a line, put
half the mackerel on each, then tied a two-pound weight
to the end of the line and tossed the rig overboard. He
let the line run through his fingers until he judged that
the hooks were about a hundred feet down. Then he
stopped it and stood with his hip against the bulwark,
holding the line in his fingertips and jigging it every few
seconds, to create the illusion of a wounded fish.

He saw at his feet the bucket that the mackerel had
been in. It was half-full of bloody water, scales and bits
of flesh. He picked up the bucket, tossed its contents
overboard and watched a little slick of blood and oil
begin to spread behind the boat.

When after five minutes he hadn't had a nibble, it occurred to him that if there were any fish around, they might be far above or far below his bait. The fish-finder was still on; he might as well take advantage of it, see if it could give him any clues. He cleated the line off and went forward, into the wheelhouse.

The screen was a mess, he'd never seen a pattern like this before. If he hadn't known for a fact that he was in three thousand feet of water, he'd have sworn the boat was aground. It looked as if some of the impulses sent out by the fish-finder were bouncing off something right beneath the boat, while others were getting through but being deflected on their way into the deep. The pattern was shimmery and indistinct.

Maybe something had gotten caught in the through-hull fitting that held the machine's transponder. When they got to shore, he'd put on a scuba tank and go under the boat and have a look. Or maybe the machine itself had broken down. These days, with everything made of chips and circuit boards and invisible magic things that could only be understood by Japanese people with microscopes, there was no way a normal man could look at a piece of electronics and make a decent diagnosis.

He decided that when he'd finished fishing, when the sub was down, he'd pull the machine apart and see if the problem was something simple, like a loose wire.

He went back to the stern and uncleated his line, and right away could tell that something was wrong with it; it was too light. The weight was gone, and probably the hooks and bait as well.

He cursed and began to reel in the line.

# 36

THE CREATURE BLEW a volume of water from its funnel and propelled itself through the blue water, searching for the faint trail of food scent that it had found, then lost, then found, then lost again.

It was not comfortable this close to the surface, was not accustomed to warm water and would not have been up here if hunger had not driven it. It had found two bits of food and had consumed them, and then it had rested in the cool shadow of something above. But it had felt itself tapped by a barrage of annoying impulses from that thing above, and so after a moment it had moved again.

It plunged from blue water to violet, then rose once more onto the terrain of blue.

It found nothing.

The higher it went, however, the closer to the surface it rose, the more promising the water seemed. There was no substance, but there were hints that tantalized the squid, as if the water near the surface contained the residue of food.

It rose still higher, close to something dark above, and soared directly beneath it, pushing a vast mass of water before and above itself.

# 37

GODDAM PUPPY SHARKS, Mike thought as he examined the end of the monofilament line. Leave a line cleated for one minute, and they sneak up on you and bite it the hell off.

The boat rose beneath him, as if lifted by a sudden sea, and he raised his eyes from the line and looked at the flat water. It was weird how ground swells could appear like that, out of nowhere. In the distance, he saw the crane on the *Ellis Explorer* pick the submersible up from its cradle and swing it out over the side of the ship.

How long did they say it took the submersible to get to the bottom? Half an hour? He still had time to put another line down. But this time he wouldn't leave it, he'd keep it in his fingers, and if some puppy shark wanted to make a run at it, he'd get the surprise of his life.

Mike took a new wire leader off the midships hatch cover, leaned back against the bulwark and held the eye of the swivel on the end of the leader up to his face so he could see to thread the monofilament through it. He missed on his first try. Getting old, he thought, soon be needing granny glasses.

There was a vague noise behind him, a squishing kind of noise. Part of his mind registered the noise, but he was concentrating on threading the monofilament through the eye of the swivel.

The line slid through the hole. "Gotcha," Mike said.

He heard the squishing noise again, closer this time, and there was a sound of scratching. He started to turn toward it. There was a smell to it, too, a familiar smell, but he couldn't quite place it.

And then suddenly Mike's world went dark. Something had him around the chest and head, something tight and wet. Mike's hands grabbed at it, then slipped off, as the thing that had him began to squeeze. He felt a pain as if a thousand ice picks were piercing his flesh.

As his feet lifted off the deck and he felt himself dragged through the air, he realized what had happened.

# 38

ANDY SAT AT the console in the control room. Darling stood behind him, wearing a headset, and Sharp stood beside Darling.

Because only two television cameras were in use, two of the four monitors were blank. The third showed the inside of the capsule: Eddie holding the stick and looking out his porthole, St. John testing the manipulators of the arms, Stephanie adjusting the lens of one of her cameras. The fourth monitor showed the scene outside the capsule: the bright aura from the lamps, the shower of plankton, and evanescent swirls of red as the eddying currents swept fish blood from the wire cage. Now and then, a small fish flashed before the camera, frantic with frustration at being unable to squeeze through the wire mesh and get to the source of the tantalizing spoor.

"Twenty-eight hundred," Andy said. "They're nearly there."

Soon they saw the bottom rise up. The turbulence of the submersible's propeller stirred the mud and caused a cloud that dimmed the video camera's lens.

The capsule settled, and the cloud cleared.

Suddenly a shadow passed over the bottom, disappeared and passed again, going the other way.

"Shark," said Darling. "Liam didn't figure on sharks. It'll probably go for his bait."

The image on the monitor jiggled as the capsule shook.

"What's that?" they heard St. John say.

"A shark, Doctor," Andy said into his microphone. "Just a shark."

"Well, do something!" said St. John.

Darling laughed. "We're half a bloody mile away, Liam. What do you want us to do?"

Andy pushed a button, then grabbed a control lever. The monitor of the exterior camera seemed to track outward, then it turned and faced upward. Now they could see the wire cage.

"It's a six-gill shark," Darling said. "Rare enough."

It was chocolate brown, with a bright green eye and six rippling gill slits. It was small, less than twice the size of the cage, but tenacious. It bit down on the corner of the cage and rolled its body, first one way, then the other, trying to tear a hole in the wire. Smaller fish hovered in the background, like vultures waiting to claim their share of the prize.

"Why haven't the fish taken off?" Sharp asked. "I thought they stayed away from feeding sharks."

"He's focused," Darling said, "and not on them. They can tell. He's sending out electromagnetic signals they can read clear as day. If he gets pissed off and turns on 'em, or another one comes by and gets jealous, *then* watch 'em scatter."

On the other monitor they saw St. John crawl forward and take the handles that operated one of the mechanical arms. Recessed in the control panel was a four-inch black-and-white monitor showing the image seen by the outside camera. Consulting it like a surgeon performing an arthroscopy, St. John pulled one handle, and the arm flexed; he pushed the other handle, and the arm rose and turned, pointing its needle toward the wire cage.

"Uh-oh," Darling said. He pressed the "talk" button and spoke into his microphone. "Don't do it, Liam. Leave the bloody shark alone."

St. John's voice came over the speaker. "Why should I let the shark take all the bait?"

"Listen. He can't take your cage. A six-gill doesn't have big rippers for teeth. He'll worry it and bend it, but he can't wreck it."

"So *you* say."

Darling sighed, searched for another tack, then said, "Look, Liam, you want to kill yourself, that's your business, but you got two other people down there with you maybe not so eager to play harps."

They saw Stephanie move toward St. John, and heard her say, "Doctor, if we waste one of your weapons on a shark, we're cutting our odds in half."

"Don't worry, Miss Carr," St. John said. "We'll still have plenty left to do the job."

On one monitor they saw St. John push a button; on the other they saw a burst of bubbles as the dart fired from the spear gun and struck the shark just behind its gill slits.

For a few seconds, the shark seemed to take no notice of the sting. Then suddenly its body arched, its tail and pectoral fins stiffened and its mouth jerked away from the cage and gaped. Rigid and quivering, it hung suspended in the water and then, like a fighter plane peeling away from formation, it banked to the right, rolled over, bounced once on the side of the capsule and fell into the mud.

The smaller fish closed in then, curiously circling the corpse before they turned back to the food in the wire cage.

One of the video monitors showed Stephanie pressing her camera against the porthole and snapping pictures.

"Won't a dead shark just bring *more* sharks?" Sharp asked.

"No," said Darling. "Sharks are strange that way. They'll kill each other, but if one of their own dies, they stay away. It's like they can read their own death in it." Darling paused and looked at the monitor. "Some things can't deal with death," he said. "Others thrive on it."

# 39

THE SQUID HAD fed, but after so long a deprivation, the protein it had consumed had not satisfied its hunger but rather had tantalized it, spurring a craving for more. And so the beast continued to hunt.

Suddenly, its senses were assaulted by new, conflicting signals—signals of food: of live prey, dead prey, of light, movement, sound. And so it began to charge back and forth, confused, defensive, ravenous, aggressive.

It moved upward in the water, seeking the source of the conflict, but it found nothing. And so it drifted downward, perceiving the soft bottom beneath it.

The rods in its eyes detected twinkles of bioluminescence from small animals nearby; it ignored them. Then more light flooded in, and more. Agitated, sensing both opportunity and danger, it drew water into its body and expelled it, propelling itself across the bottom.

As the beast drew closer to the source of light, the light became harsh, repellent. Reflex told it to retreat into the darkness, but its olfactory sensors began to receive strong, overwhelming waves of food spoor: fresh kill, rich and nourishing.

Hunger drove it onward.

It rose off the bottom, above the light, and let itself be carried into the darkness behind the light. It settled there, where signals of threat had disappeared, and it could concentrate on the scent of prey below.

It descended.

# 40

SHARP YAWNED, STRETCHED and shook his head; he was having trouble staying awake. They had been watching for over an hour, and there had been no movement on either monitor. It was hypnotic, like watching test patterns.

In the submersible, Stephanie, St. John and Eddie had hardly spoken and barely moved. Stephanie had taken a few pictures of the strange animals that swarmed around her porthole, but now she just knelt and watched.

St. John looked up at the video camera in the submersible, and he said, "What's the time?"

"Ninety minutes gone," Andy said into his microphone.

St. John nodded and resumed staring out his porthole.

The exterior camera had been readjusted, and it showed the body of the dead shark, belly-up in the mud. Earlier, a hagfish had darted in and tried to bore a hole in the shark, but the skin was too tough, and the hagfish had given up and gone in search of easier prey.

The door to the control room opened, and Darling entered, carrying two cups of coffee. He passed one to Sharp and said, "I couldn't find any proper cream, so . . . holy shit!"

"What?" Sharp said, and he followed Darling's eyes to the monitors.

"The fish. They're gone."

As Darling put on a headset and fumbled for the "talk" button on the microphone, Sharp realized what he meant: No abyssal creatures were patrolling the edge of darkness, no small fish hovered over the dead shark, no tiny scavengers gulped the bits of tuna that floated down from the wire cage.

"Liam!" Darling shouted into the microphone. "Look out!"

St. John started at the sound of the voice, and he looked around, but saw nothing. "Look out for—?"

There was a hollow sound then, a scraping, a crunch almost like the sound of a ship running aground. Then the capsule was jerked up and tilted forward. The interior camera showed Stephanie and St. John being hurled into Eddie, and all of them tumbling over the control panel. The exterior camera showed nothing but mud.

Eddie cursed, St. John grabbed the handles for the mechanical arm and tried to work them. "The arm's stuck in the mud!" he yelled.

"Put power to her!" Darling said to Eddie. "That beast won't like the propeller."

They saw Eddie pull back on the stick and apply power, and they heard the submersible's motor whine, then shriek as it raced.

The capsule tilted up; the mechanical arm came free.

"The camera!" St. John said.

Eddie reached for the controls for the outside camera as St. John flexed and raised the mechnical arm, his finger poised over the firing button.

The monitor showed the camera tracking out and turning: Mud gave way to water, then to a blur on the side of the capsule, then to . . .

"What the hell is that?" Sharp said.

The camera showed a field of circles, pinkish gray, each quivering on its own stalk, each apparently rimmed with teeth and each containing an amber-colored claw.

"Bad news, is what that is," said Darling, and he shouted into his microphone, "Fire it, Liam!"

Then, as the camera was ripped from its mounts, the screen went blank.


The creature crushed the camera in its whip and cast it away.

Then it turned back to the shredded remains of the food, its eight short arms scratching and clawing as it searched for more to feed to the snapping beak. But there was no more.

The creature was confused, for the spoor of food was everywhere, permeating the water. All its senses told it there was food; its hunger demanded food. But where was it?

It perceived a large, hard carapace, and associated it with the scent of food. It encircled the thing with its whips and set about to destroy it.

"I can't see!" St. John shouted. "Where did it go?"

"Fire it, Liam!" Darling shouted. **"Fire the dart!** The bastard's so big you can't miss."

They saw St. John push the button to fire the dart. "It didn't fire!" he cried, and he pushed the button again, and again.

Stephanie yelled, "Look!" She was pointing out her porthole. "In the mud. The spear gun. The thing tore it *off.*"

The capsule shuddered then, and rolled from side to side. St. John skidded and fell on top of Stephanie; Eddie hung on to the controls. The images through the portholes flashed and changed like pieces of glass in a kaleidoscope: mud, water, light, darkness.

Again the capsule shuddered, and there were screeching sounds.

Watching the single television monitor, Sharp felt sick with helplessness. "We've got to *do* something!" he said.

"Like what?" Darling asked.

"Bring it up. Start the winch. Maybe the motion will scare it off."

"It'd **take ten minutes** to reel in the slack in the cable," **Darling said. "And** they don't have ten minutes. Whatever's **gonna happen** is gonna happen now."

The creature sought weakness. There was weakness somewhere. There was weakness in all prey.

The thing was less than half the creature's size, and although it was strong and dense, it did not struggle.

The creature lifted it easily in its two long whips and turned it, probing for a soft spot, a crack. Then it drew the thing in to its eight short arms and clutched it. It opened its beak and let its tongue search the skin. The tongue traveled slowly: licking, probing, rasping.

"What's that noise?" St. John hissed. It sounded as if a coarse file were scraping at the hull.

The capsule was upside down now, and the three of them knelt on the overhead and braced themselves with their hands.

"It's playing with you," Darling said over the mike. "Like a cat with a toy. With any luck, it'll get bored and leave you be."

St. John tilted his head, apparently listening for another sound. "Our motor's quit," he said.

"As soon as the critter lets you go, we'll winch you up. Won't be long now."

Sharp waited until Darling had released the "talk" button, then said, "You believe that?"

Darling paused before he said, "No. The sonofabitch is gonna find a way in."

The tongue snaked across the skin, examining texture, seeking difference. But the skin was all the same: hard, tasteless, dead. The tongue speeded up, impatient as it licked.

A signal flashed across its brain and vanished.

The tongue stopped, retreated, began to lick again, slower. There. The signal reappeared, steady.

The texture here was different: smoother, thinner. Weaker.

Stephanie must have heard a noise behind her, for they saw her turn and look at her porthole. What she saw made her scream and back away.

St. John looked, and gasped.

"What?" Darling said.

"I think . . ." St. John said. "A tongue."

Andy changed the angle of the camera in the submersible and focused on the porthole. Then they could see it, too: a tongue. It licked in circles, covering the glass with pink flesh. Then it withdrew and changed its shape into a cone and tapped at the glass. It made a sound like a hammer driving carpet tacks.

Then the tongue receded, and for a moment the porthole was blanketed in black. There was the sound of a deafening screech.

St. John grabbed a flashlight from a clip on the bulkhead and shined it on the porthole.

They could see only part of it, for it was bigger than the porthole, much bigger: a curved, scythelike beak, amber-colored, its sharply pointed end pressing on the glass.

Stephanie flattened herself against the opposite bulkhead, while St. John knelt mutely and held the flashlight pointed at the porthole. Eddie turned his face to the camera and said, "God damn!"

There was a cracking noise then, and in a fraction of a second, an explosion of water, a booming sound, and screams . . . and then silence, as the monitor went dead.

They all continued mutely to stare at the blank screen.

# 41

AS SOON AS Darling got into the taxi, he took off his tie and stuffed it into his jacket pocket. He felt as if he were suffocating. He rolled the window down and let the breeze wash over his face.

He hated funerals. Funerals and hospitals. It wasn't only because they were associated with sickness and death; they also represented the ultimate loss of control. They were evidence of the flaw inherent in the precept that guided his life: that a smart and careful man could survive by calculating his risks and never overstepping the line. Hospitals and funerals were proof that the line sometimes moved.

Besides, he believed that funerals didn't do a damn thing for the dead; they were for the living.

Mike had agreed with him. They had made a pact long ago that if one of them died, the other would bury him at sea with no ceremony whatsoever. Well, Mike had been buried at sea, all right, but not the way they had planned.

It had been a small funeral, just family and Darling, with a few words from a Portuguese preacher and a couple of songs. There had been no questions, no recriminations, no discussion of what had happened. On the contrary, in fact, Mike's widow and her two brothers and two sisters had made a special effort to comfort Darling.

Which, of course, had made him feel even worse.

He hadn't told them the truth about how Mike had died. He and Sharp were the only ones who knew the truth, and there was no way anyone would ever suspect different. They had seen no point in painting pictures for the family that would haunt their dreams for the rest of their lives. So Darling had said that Mike had fallen overboard and drowned; that he must have struck his head on the dive step as he fell and knocked himself out.

They had told that tale to the authorities, too, with no conscience about suppressing evidence. There was enough carnage visible on the videotapes to satisfy all the ghouls. One more victim wouldn't make any difference.

When Darling had gotten no answer to his calls to the *Privateer,* he had been ready to chew Mike's ass from here to Sunday for falling asleep on watch. He and Sharp had borrowed Hector's Zodiac and sped across the half-mile of open water to the drifting boat. Sharp had been still in shock; he had ridden in the boat like a zombie. But when they had found Mike missing, he had quickly come around.

For the first fifteen or twenty minutes, they were convinced that Mike *had* fallen overboard. They had noted the run of the tide and the drift of the boat, and had used the quick, maneuverable little Zodiac to search a mile or more of ocean. But then they had decided that they needed the distance and perspective that the height of the *Privateer*'s flying bridge would give them, and they had returned to the boat. As they approached along the starboard side, they had seen scratch marks in the paint.

And then, when they had climbed aboard and run their hands along the bulwark, they had felt a telltale slime, and smelled a telltale odor.

Darling hadn't been on the boat when the accident

happened, and there probably was nothing he could have done even if he *had* been there. But he heaped blame on himself. Even though he knew it was mostly irrational, he also knew there was a kernel of justification to it. Mike had never been one to make decisions on his own; he had relied on Whip to tell him the right thing to do; he had never liked being alone on the boat, and Whip had known it.

Stop it, Darling told himself. There's no point to this.

The taxi driver had the radio on, and the midafternoon newscast began, with more gloomy news about the Bermuda economy. In the week since the submersible disaster, tourism had dropped almost fifty percent.

People were pressuring the government to do something to get rid of the beast, but nobody had any concrete suggestions, and the government continued to consult with scientists from California and Newfoundland, who couldn't reach a consensus. Eventually, they all predicted hopefully, the giant squid would just go away.

Nobody wanted to tangle with the beast anymore—nobody, that is, except that Dr. Talley and Osborn Manning. They had written to Darling, tried to call, sent him wires, every damn thing. They had even tried to convince him that he had some sort of responsibility to help them kill the creature, that it was both a symbol and a symptom of the imbalance of nature, and that destroying it would somehow begin to put things right again. They had upped their ante to a point where, if Darling had a mind to take them out on his boat for up to ten days, he could clear $100,000. His response had been simple enough: What good is $100,000 to a dead man?

It hadn't been difficult to refuse their bait, for as he saw it, each of them was, in his own way, the next thing to nuts. Manning was crazed by his personal vendetta,

Talley by a need to prove that his life had been worth something. They didn't have a full deck between them.

He understood that they had even approached the navy. According to Marcus, Manning had contacted a U.S. senator, who had contacted the Defense Department, which had asked for Captain Wallingford's thoughts on how the beast might be caught and eliminated. The request had made Wallingford extremely anxious, partly because he regarded any questions from the Pentagon as criticism, and partly because he was a coward: He didn't want to displease a senator who might someday have a say in whether or not he got to trade in his silver eagle for a silver star. And so Wallingford had taken out his anxiety on Marcus, whom he had tried somehow to blame for the entire fiasco.

But the investigation had cleared Sharp, and had laid official blame on the easiest of all targets, the dead: Liam St. John, who had concocted what, in retrospect, was now considered a reckless scheme, and Eddie, who had agreed to go along with it.

As the taxi turned onto Cambridge Road, the newscast ended, and Darling noted that the word "squid" hadn't been mentioned once.

His own concern was to find an immediate way to make a living. He had decided that the time had come at last to sell his cherished Masonic bottle, and the dealer in Hamilton had told him there was some interest in it. If a couple of collectors could be encouraged to bid against each other, he might get a few thousand dollars for it. He knew that Charlotte had written to Sotheby's some time ago, to inquire about including her coin collection, inherited from her father, in one of their auctions. He thought he might go through the artifacts in the house and see if there was anything else rare enough to be worth selling. He hated to do it, it was like selling pieces of his past, or of himself, but he had no choice.

He did have one practical hope, however: The aquarium had called, and they were interested in discussing a new retainer agreement. Now that St. John was gone, they could make decisions based on practicality instead of ego. That might pay for some fuel.

Still, he and Charlotte couldn't eat fuel.

The chain was across the dirt road to Darling's house, and he paid the driver, got out of the taxi, unhooked the chain and let it fall.

As he started toward the house, he saw Dana's car in the driveway. What was she doing here this early in the day? Wasn't she working? *Some*body had to work in this family. He grimaced, and thought: Great, you're one tiny step away from being a true parasite.

Then he heard a voice: "Captain Darling?"

He turned and saw Talley and Manning walking down the road toward him. Manning was in front, immaculate in a gray suit, a blue shirt and a striped tie, and carrying a briefcase; Talley followed, looking, Darling thought, nervous and uneasy.

"What do you want?" Darling said.

"We want to talk to you," Manning said.

"I've got nothing to say." Darling turned back toward the house.

"Talk to us now, Captain," Manning said, "or you'll talk to the law later."

Darling stopped. "The law?" he said. "What law? You got nothing better to do than threaten people?"

"I didn't threaten anybody, Captain. I stated a fact."

"Okay. Say your piece and go along."

"May we perhaps"—Manning gestured at the house—"go to the house and discuss this like—"

"I'm not a civilized person, Mr. Manning. I'm a pissed-off fisherman who's sick to death of having people tell me—"

"As you wish, Captain. Dr. Talley and I have already made you what we think is a generous offer for your help. In light of recent events, however, we are prepared to increase that offer."

"Jesus *Christ,* man, do you still not have any idea what it is you want to go up against? Don't you know—"

"Yes, Captain, we do. But the fact is, we believe we can kill the squid. Not the two of us, not you alone, but the three of us together."

"*Kill* it? You might get to see it, but it'll be the last thing you'll ever see. Kill it? Not a chance. I don't see how anyone's gonna better that beast."

"Captain," Talley said, "let me—"

"Shut up, Herbert," Manning snapped. "Words won't convince him." He turned back to Darling. "A final offer, Captain. If you will take us out to hunt for the giant squid, I will pay you two hundred thousand dollars. If we don't find it, if it has gone away, if we fail to kill it, the money is yours to keep. Your only obligation is to make a good-faith effort."

"You still think money can do it," said Darling. "Well, it can't. Go get drunk, if that'll help you. Say some prayers for your children, give your money to a good cause in their name. At least that's worth something."

Manning looked at Talley, and Darling saw Talley close his eyes and expel a breath.

"That's your last word?" Manning said.

"First, last . . . call it what you want."

"I'm sorry, Captain, you leave me no choice. We need you. You're the only person with the skill, the knowledge and the boat. So . . ." Manning hesitated, then continued. "Here it is: I must tell you that within ten days of close-of-business today, you are to deliver to me a certified check for twelve thousand dollars. If you fail to make the deadline, you will then have thirty days to move yourself and your belongings out of your house."

Darling stared at Manning, and let the words rerun in his mind. Then he looked at Talley, who was staring at the ground.

"Wait a second," Darling said. He couldn't have heard right; there had to be a mistake. "Let me get this straight. I give you twelve thousand dollars for not taking you to sea, or you kick me out of my house."

"Correct. You see, Captain, I own your house . . . or, to be precise, I will very soon."

Darling laughed. "Right. Next, you'll tell me you're my great-great-grandfather and you built it for me back in 1770." As he turned away he said, "You folks are smoking some powerful weed."

"Captain . . ." Manning had taken a manila folder from his briefcase, and he held a piece of paper out to Darling. "Read this."

The paper was in legalese, full of *wherefore*s and *party of the first part*s, and the only elements Darling could parse were the name of the house, its location, an assignment of something or other to Osborn Manning, and some numbers. Maybe Charlotte could make sense of it. "I'll have to get my specs," he said.

"By all means. But why don't I tell you the substance? Your wife has been borrowing money, using the house as collateral. She is nearly three months behind in the payments and has twice been notified that she is in danger of default. I bought the note from the lender. In ten days, I will foreclose on the note."

"Bullshit," Darling said, staring at the paper. The paper couldn't say all that, because it couldn't have happened. "Piece of paper doesn't mean a thing. Charlie wouldn't have done that. Not ever."

"She did it, Captain."

"Bull*shit*," Darling said again, and he turned back toward the house, clutching the paper.

Charlotte and Dana were sitting together at the kitchen counter.

The screen door slammed behind Darling, and he marched in from the hallway. "You won't believe what that . . ." He stopped when he saw their faces. They had both been crying, and now, seeing him, they began to weep again. "No," he said. "No." And then, "Why?"

"Because we had to live, William."

"We were living. We had food, we had fuel."

"We had food because Dana brought us food. How was I supposed to pay our electricity? How was I supposed to pay the house taxes? When the freezer broke and all your bait melted, how was I supposed to get that fixed? And the crack in the cistern . . . we would have had no water. Our insurance was about to be canceled. They were going to cut off our gas." Charlotte wiped her eyes and looked at him. "What the hell do you think we've been *living* on all these months?"

"But . . . I mean . . . there were things we could sell. The coins . . ."

"I sold them. And the three-mold bottles, and the Bellarmine jug, and . . . all of it. There was nothing more."

"I'll go talk to the bank. For God's sake, Derek can't just—"

"It wasn't the bank," said Dana. "They wouldn't give you a mortgage. You had no steady income. I offered to co-sign the note. They still wouldn't do it."

"Who lent the money, then?"

"Aram Agajanian," said Charlotte.

"Agajanian!" Darling shouted. "That pervert?" Aram Agajanian was a recent immigrant to Bermuda who had made a fortune producing soft-core pornography for Canadian cable-television systems and had chosen Bermuda as a tax haven. "Why did you go to *him*?"

"Because he offered. Dana had done the accounts for one of his companies, and she asked him a couple of questions about securing loans, and . . . well, he offered."

"Christ!" Darling said, turning to Dana. "You had to hang out our dirty laundry in front of that Armenian star-fucker?"

"You want me to say I'm sorry, Daddy? Well, I am. I'm sorry. There. Does that make you feel better?" Dana was struggling not to sob. "But the fact is, he offered. No strings, no payment schedule. Pay it when you can, he said. I never thought he'd sell the note. He didn't want to."

"Why did he?"

"I think Mr. Manning made him one of those offers you can't refuse. Mr. Manning owns a lot of cable companies."

"How did Manning find out about it?"

"Agajanian thinks it must have been from Carl Frith."

"*What?!* Is there anybody on this island who *doesn't* know?" Darling heard himself shouting. "How did *he* find out?"

"He was working on Agajanian's dock, and he must have overheard something."

"Wonderful . . . great." Darling felt betrayed and confused. He looked around and, for no reason, touched one of the walls. "Two hundred and twenty years," he said.

"It's just a house, William," Charlotte said. "We'll find somewhere else to live. Dana wants us to move in with her. For a while. It's just a house."

"No, Charlie, it's not. It's not just a house. It's more than two centuries of Darlings. It's our family." He looked at his wife and his daughter. "It was passed on to me, and if I have one obligation in this life, it's to keep passing it on for the future."

"Let it go, William. We're alive, we're together. That's all that counts."

"Like hell," Darling said, and he turned and left the room. "Like bloody hell."

# 42

WHEN DARLING RETURNED to the end of his driveway, he found the tableau unchanged: Talley still paced and fidgeted; Manning still stood like a Bond Street mannequin.

Darling motioned for them to follow him, and as he led them down the driveway, he imagined Manning was gloating, and he had to fight to keep from spinning on the man.

He gestured for them to sit at a table on the porch.

"You're pretty sure that beast is still around, then," he said to Talley.

"Yes."

"Why's that?"

"Because nothing's changed yet. The seasons haven't changed, currents haven't changed, there have been no major storms. I got figures from NOAA last night, and they think—it's an educated guess—that the Gulf Stream won't begin its seasonal shift for maybe a month." Talley could feel his enthusiasm returning, erasing his embarrassment at being party to Manning's extortion. "Meanwhile, *Architeuthis* is finding food— not its normal food, but food. There's been no reason for it to leave."

"There was no reason for him to come, either."

"Yes, but it did, it's here. The important thing to remember, Captain, is not to make *Architeuthis* into a demon. It—not *he, it*—is an animal, not a devil. It has its own cycles, it responds to natural rhythms. I think it's hungry and confused. It's not finding its normal prey. I think I can coax it to respond to an illusion of normalcy."

"Whatever the hell that means."

"Leave that to me."

"And you truly believe you can get the best of this thing?"

"I think so, yes."

"Before it kills everybody?"

"Yes. Yes, I do."

"How?"

Talley hesitated. "I'll tell you . . . soon."

"Is it a state secret or something?"

"No. I'm sorry, I'm not playing games. The means depend on the circumstances, on how the animal behaves. It may . . . there's a chance . . . what I want to try to do is make it destroy itself."

Darling looked at Manning, and saw him staring, stone-faced, at the bay, as if these details bored him.

"Sure, Doc," Darling said. "It may take off and fly to Venus, too, but I wouldn't count on it. I think I've got a right to—"

"No, Captain," Manning said, suddenly interested again. There was a thin smile on his lips. "You have no rights. You have a duty: to drive the boat and to help us."

"Now, Osborn . . ." Talley said, "I don't think—"

"Why not, Herbert? We're not civilized people here; Captain Darling said so himself, and I respect him for it. Politeness is deceptive, and it wastes time. Better that we all know exactly where we stand, right from the start."

Darling felt a sharp pain behind his eyes, sparked, he knew, by rage and a feeling of impotence. He pressed his temples, trying to squeeze the pain away. He wanted to hit Manning, but Manning was correct: He had found Darling's price, and had bought him, and there was no point in pretending otherwise.

Darling said, "When do you want to go?"

"As soon as we can," Manning replied. "All we have to do is load up the gear."

"I'll have to get fuel, food. We could go tomorrow."

"Fuel," Manning said, and he reached into his brief-case and brought out a banded packet of hundred-dollar bills. "Ten thousand enough for starters?"

"Should do."

"Now, the terms." Manning snapped his briefcase shut. "Dr. Talley is confident that he'll be able to locate and attract the squid within seventy-two hours, so you'll provision the boat for three days. Whether or not we catch the animal, on our return, I'll destroy the note and pay you the balance of the two hundred thousand. Your net, after securing your house, should be somewhere over a hundred thousand." He stood up. "Agreed?"

"No," Darling said.

"What do you mean, 'No'?"

"Here are *my* terms," Darling said, looking at Manning. "You'll burn the note now, in front of me. Before we leave the dock, you'll give me fifty thousand dollars in cash, which will stay ashore here, with my wife. The balance in her name in escrow in the bank, in case we don't come back."

Manning hesitated, then opened his briefcase again

and took out the note and a gold Dunhill lighter.
"You're an honorable man, Captain," he said as he held
the note out over the lawn and touched the flame to it.
"We know that much about you. But so am I. Once a
deal is done, I don't quibble. You shouldn't distrust
me."

"This has nothing to do with trust," Darling said. "I
want to provide for my wife."

Darling watched Talley and Manning walk away up
the drive and turn into the parking lot at Cambridge
Beaches, then he put the stack of bills into his pocket
and went down the path to the boat. He started the
engine and climbed up to the flying bridge, and he was
about to put the boat in gear when he suddenly remembered that it was still tied to the dock.

He felt as if somebody had punched him in the stomach, and he blew out a breath and leaned on the railing.
It was the first real evidence he'd had that Mike was
gone. He stayed there for a few moments, until the
feeling passed, then went below and untied the lines.

As he rounded the corner out of Mangrove Bay on his
way to the fuel pumps at Dockyard, Darling tried to
think of somebody he could hire as a mate. He had no
reason to believe that Talley and Manning knew anything about setting rigs or keeping the boat pointed into
the wind or any of the scores of other chores involved
in running a boat.

No, he concluded, there was nobody. He had friends
and acquaintances who were capable and might even be
willing, but he wasn't about to ask them. He wasn't
about to be responsible for another death.

He'd do it alone. Well, not quite alone. He had one
ally, in a box down in the hold, and he'd use it if he had
to.

One chance, Mr. Manning, he thought. I'm giving

you one chance. And if you screw up, I'm gonna blow
that motherfucker to kingdom come.

It took Darling almost three hours to pump two
thousand gallons of diesel fuel and seven hundred gallons of fresh water into the tanks on the *Privateer,* and
to buy six bags of groceries: fresh and dried fruits and
vegetables, corned beef, canned tuna, blocks of cheddar
cheese, loaves of bread, stew meat and a variety of
beans. By the time they'd eaten all that food, he figured,
they'd either be home or they'd be dead.

When he returned to his dock, evening was coming
on. He removed extraneous gear from the boat: broken
traps, scuba tanks, parts of a dismantled compressor.
He came across the pump Mike had been working on.
He held it in his hands and looked at it, and he thought
he could feel Mike's energy in it.

Don't be stupid, he said to himself, and he put the
pump ashore.

Charlotte was in the kitchen, doing what she always
did when things were bad and she didn't know what else
to do: cooking. She had roasted an entire leg of lamb
and made a salad big enough to feed a regiment.

"Company coming?" Darling said, and he went to
her and kissed the back of her neck.

"After twenty-one years," she said, "you'd think I
would have known what you'd do."

"I even surprised myself. Until today, I thought there
were only two things in the world that really mattered
to me." Darling reached into the refrigerator for a beer.
"I wonder what my old man would say."

"He'd say you're a damn fool."

"I doubt it. He was a big one for roots—that's why
they all loved this house. It was their roots. It's our
roots, too."

"What about *us*?" Charlotte turned to face him, and there were tears in her eyes. "Aren't we roots enough, Dana and I?"

"We wouldn't *be* us without this house, Charlie. What would we be, living in a condo downtown or taking up Dana's spare room? Just a couple of old farts waiting for the sun to set. That's not us."

The phone rang down the hall, and Darling answered it, told the caller to piss off and returned to the kitchen. "A reporter," he said. "I guess there's no such thing as an unlisted number."

"Marcus called earlier," said Charlotte.

"Did you tell him what's going on?"

"I did. I thought maybe he could think of a way to stop you."

"And could he?"

"Of course not. He thinks you walk on water."

"He's a good lad."

"No, just another damn fool."

Darling looked at her back. "I love you, Charlie," he said. "I don't say it too often, but you know I do."

"Not enough, I guess."

"Well . . ." He sighed, wishing he could think of comforting words to weave.

"Or is it *you* you don't love enough?" Charlotte said, whipping gravy into a froth.

That was the strangest question Darling had ever heard. What did it mean, loving himself? What kind of person loved himself? He couldn't think of an answer, so he turned on the television to get the weather forecast.

They left the television on while they ate, letting the local newscaster fill the silence, for they both sensed that there was nothing more to say, and that any attempts at conversation would result in words they would regret.

After supper, Darling went out onto the lawn and

looked at the bay. There was still some light—the soft violet that ushers in the night—and he could see two egrets standing like sentries in the shallows by the point, perhaps hoping for a twilight meal of mullet. A gentle fluttering sound, like the opening of a paper fan, heralded the arrival of a school of fry, skittering in flight across the glassy water.

When he was a child, he had spent his evenings watching the bay, as enraptured by it as other children were by radio or television, for from the bay came sounds, and sometimes sights, that excited his imagination as vividly as had any ever fabricated on a soundstage. Marauding barracuda slashed through schools of mackerel, and the water boiled with a bloody foam. Sharks came, too, sometimes singly, sometimes in twos or threes, their dorsal fins slicing the surface as they calmly cruised in search of prey, exercising some primal rite of plunder. Crabs scuttled on the beach sands; turtles exhaled like tiny bellows; irate kiskadees chastised one another in the treetops.

The bay was life and death, and it had given him a feeling of peace and security he could not articulate. It carried with it the reassurance of continuity.

There was still life in the bay, though less, still much to love.

The crown of a full moon peeked above the trees in the east, and cast arrows of gold that flashed on the egrets and lit them like golden statues.

"Charlie," Darling called, "come look."

He heard her footsteps in the house, but they stopped at the screen door. "No," she said.

"Why not?" he asked.

She didn't answer. Instead, she thought to herself, Oh William, you look like an old Indian, sitting on a hillside, getting ready to die.

# PART FOUR

# 43

DARLING WAS AWAKENED by the sound of the wind whistling through the casuarinas behind the house. It was still dark, but he didn't need to see to know the weather; his ears told him that the wind was out of the northwest and blowing fifteen to twenty knots. At this time of year, a northwest wind was an unstable wind, so before long it should shift, either back around to the southwest and settle down, or veer into the northeast and crank up into a little gale. He half hoped for a gale: Maybe a rough ride would make Manning and Talley get sick and decide to quit.

Not a chance, he thought. Those two were in the grip of forces they probably didn't understand and certainly couldn't defy, and nothing short of a hurricane would put them off.

Charlotte lay on her side, curled up like a little girl and breathing deeply. He bent down and kissed the back of her neck, inhaling her aroma and holding his breath, as if trying to carry the memory of her with him.

By the time he had shaved and made coffee and heated up some of last night's lamb, the sky was lightening in the east and the kiskadees were gathering in the poinciana tree to announce the advent of day.

He stood on the lawn and looked at the sky. There was still a stiff breeze on; low clouds were being shoved to the southeast. But a ridge of high cirrus was creeping northward, signaling that the wind would soon shift back to the south. By noon, the chop would be gone from the shallow water and the swell would have faded from the deep.

The boat was straining against its lines, rocking gently. He was about to step aboard, when suddenly he sensed that someone was there, in the cabin. He wasn't sure why he knew, so he stopped and listened. Over the routine noises of the lines creaking and water lapping against the hull, he heard breathing sounds.

Some damn reporter, he thought, one of those smart-ass kids who think that "no" means "try harder" and that they've got a God-given right to invade a man's privacy.

He crossed the gangplank and stepped down onto the steel deck and said, "By the time I count three, your ass better be up and ashore, or you're goin' for a long, long swim." Then he stepped over the threshold into the cabin, said, "One . . ." and saw Marcus Sharp sit up with a start and strike his head on the upper bunk.

Sharp yawned, rubbed his head, smiled and said, "Morning, Whip . . ."

"Well, I'll be damned," Darling said. "To what do I owe the pleasure?"

"I thought maybe you could use some help today."

"I'd welcome a pair of friendly hands, that's for sure, but what does Uncle Sam have to say about this?"

"Uncle Sam sent me . . . sort of. Scientists from all over the country—all over the *world*—have been trying to goose the navy into launching an expedition to hunt for the squid, but the navy claims it doesn't have the money. I think the truth is that the navy doesn't want to tackle something they don't know anything about, and run the risk of looking foolish. Anyway, they've been getting on Wallingford's case, as if *he*'s supposed to come up with some magic formula. When I told him you were going out, he thought it would look good to have the navy go too, sort of show the flag—that is, me. I'm supposed to make it look as if Wallingford is actually doing something." Sharp paused. "I tried to call. I thought you wouldn't . . . I hope you don't mind."

"Hell no. But look, Marcus, I want you to know up front what you're signing on for. These folks—"

"I've seen the beast, Whip. Or almost."

"Okay, then. You've had demolition training, right?"

"A year."

"Good. We're gonna need it." Darling smiled. "Meantime, first thing to do is make some coffee."

At six-thirty, they cast off and motored slowly across the bay to the town dock, where Talley and Manning waited beside a rented pickup truck piled high with cases. Talley wore a windbreaker, khaki pants and short rubber boots. Manning looked as if he had stepped from the pages of a catalog: Topsider boat shoes, pleated trousers, a beige shirt with a club logo on the breast and a crisp new Gore-Tex foul-weather jacket.

"What's all that crap for?" Darling asked from the flying bridge while Sharp tied the boat to the dock. "You aiming to build yourselves a skyscraper?"

Neither of them answered, and Darling realized there was tension between them. Curious, he thought: What now? They've gotten their way, everything should be peachy.

They unloaded twenty-two cases in all, placing them aboard the boat under Talley's supervision. He wanted some of them inside the cabin, protected from the weather, but most were stacked on the afterdeck.

When all the cases were aboard, Manning reached inside the cab of the truck and brought out a long case. From the way Manning carried it, Darling could see that it was heavy, and from the care he took not to bang it on anything, he could tell that it was precious.

"What's that?" Darling asked him.

"Never mind," Manning said, and he disappeared into the cabin.

Is that so? Darling said to himself. Well, we'll see about that.

A van from the local television station wheeled around the corner at the end of the lane and stopped at the edge of the dock. A reporter got out, followed by a cameraman who scrambled to assemble his equipment.

"Captain Darling?" called the reporter. "Can we talk to you, please? For ZBM."

"No," Darling said from the flying bridge.

"Just for a minute." The reporter looked behind him to make sure the camerman was ready and rolling. "You're going out after the monster. What makes you—"

"No we're not. Hell, son, nobody in his right mind would do that." He looked aft and said to Sharp, "Cast her off, Marcus," and when he saw that the last of the lines were aboard, he put the boat in gear and began to move slowly through the dozens of boats moored in the bay.

He waited until he was sure that they were out of earshot of the dock, and then he leaned over the side of the flying bridge and said, "Mr. Manning, would you come up here a second?"

Manning climbed the ladder and walked forward and said impatiently, "What is it?"

"What's in the case?"

"I told you all you need to know."

"Uh-huh," Darling said. "I see." A hundred yards dead ahead, a sixty-foot schooner lay broadside to their path, flanked by two fifty-foot fishing boats. "Okay, then . . ." He reached over and grabbed one of Manning's hands and put it on the wheel. "Here you go."

Then he turned and walked off the flying bridge and headed for the ladder.

"What are you doing?" Manning shouted.

"Gonna take a nap."

*"What!?"*

"It's your show; you run it."

"Come back here!" Manning cried, looking ahead. The schooner was fifty yards away now, and they were closing on it. He had nowhere to turn; there were boats on all sides.

Darling started down the ladder. "Call me when we get there," he said.

Manning pulled back on the throttle and spun the wheel, but the boat didn't stop; it yawed; it was aimed directly at the schooner. He jerked the throttle back, and the boat rumbled into reverse and began to back toward the stern of a fishing boat. "What do you *want*?" he shouted.

Darling said, "You want to run the show, go ahead and run it."

"No!" Manning protested. "I . . . help!" He slammed the throttle forward, and again the bow aimed for the schooner.

Darling waited for another second, until Manning, panicked, flung his hands in the air and lurched backward. Then he took two steps up the ladder, walked quickly across the deck and took the wheel. He spun it, gunned the throttle and, like a tailor threading a needle, nosed the boat between the bow of the schooner and the stern of the fishing boat, missing each by no more than six inches.

"Funny, isn't it?" Darling said when they were clear. "The things money can't buy."

Manning was angry. "That was completely unne—"

"No, it was very necessary," Darling said. "Look, Mr. Manning, we have to work together. We can't have folks running all over the boat with their own agendas. Talley knows the animal but doesn't know anything about the ocean. Marcus knows the ocean but doesn't know the animal. I know something about each, and you, I figure, don't know shit about anything but making money. So: What's in the case?"

Manning hesitated. "A rifle."

"How did you get it in? Bermuda doesn't take kindly to guns."

"Disassembled. I spread the pieces around in Talley's cases. It would have taken an armorer to put the puzzle together."

"What kind of rifle?"

"A Finnish assault rifle. A Valmet. It usually shoots a standard NATO seven-point-sixty-five-millimeter cartridge."

"What do you mean, 'usually'? You've had something done to it?"

"To the bullets, yes. The clips are loaded so that every third bullet is a phosphorous tracer, and the others are filled with cyanide slugs."

"And you think you can kill the beast with that."

"That's our arrangement. Talley will find it, do whatever studies he wants, and then I'll kill it."

"It has to be you."

"Yes."

Darling thought for a moment, then said, "Do you really think there's anything you can do for your kids at this point?"

"It has nothing to do with them, not anymore. It has to do with me. This is something I have to do."

"I see," Darling said with a sigh. "Okay, Mr. Manning, but take a word of counsel: Do it right the first time, 'cause I'm only giving you one chance. Then it's my show, I'm taking over."

"And doing what?"

"I'm gonna blow him into dust. Or try to."

"Fair enough," Manning said. "Want some coffee?"

"Sure. Black."

Manning walked aft toward the ladder, and said, "I'll tell the mate to bring you some."

"The mate, Mr. Manning," Darling said, "is a lieutenant in your United States Navy. Don't tell him; ask him. And say 'please.' "

Manning opened his mouth, closed it. "Excuse me," he said, and he went below.

At the mouth of the bay, Darling turned to the north. As he rounded the point and headed for the cut, he looked back. Between two Norfolk pines on the end of the point stood Charlotte, her nightgown billowing in the breeze. He waved to her, and she waved back, then turned away, and walked up the lawn toward the house.

Sharp brought Darling some coffee and stood beside him on the flying bridge. They looked to the northwest, to the spot at the edge of the deep where the *Ellis Explorer* had anchored.

For a moment, neither of them spoke, then Darling said, "You liked that girl."

"Yes. I even thought . . . well, it doesn't matter."

"Sure it matters."

Talley came up to the bridge and stood to one side. He looked edgy, excited.

"Spend much time at sea, Doc?" Darling asked.

"Some, years ago, collecting octopus. But nothing like this. I've been waiting my whole life for this, for the chance to find a giant squid. It's my dragon."

"It's a dragon now, is it?"

"I think of it that way. That's why I called my book *The Last Dragon.* Man needs dragons, he always has, to explain the unknown. You've seen the old maps. When they drew unknown lands, they'd write 'Here be dragons,' and that said it all. I've spent my life reading and writing books about the dragon. Do you know what a privilege it is to finally get close to one?"

"Seems to me, Doc," Darling said, "there are some dragons better left alone."

"Not to scientists." Talley suddenly pointed and shouted, "Look!"

Half a dozen flying fish scattered away from the bow of the boat, skimming over the water for fifty yards or more before splashing down again. Talley's face lit up with wonder.

They came upon a trail of sargasso weed, floating patches of yellow vegetation, unconnected and yet apparently following one another, like ants, toward the horizon.

"Does it always make a straight line?" Talley asked.

"Seems to. It's a mystery, like that spawn we saw. I can't figure out what that thing is, where it comes from or where it goes."

"What thing? What does it look like?"

Darling described the huge gelatinous oblongs, with the holes in the center, and told him about how they appeared to be rotating, as if to expose all their parts to the sunlight.

Talley asked questions, pressed Darling for details, and with every answer he seemed to grow more excited. "It's an egg sac," he said finally. "Nobody's ever seen one before, at least not in a hundred years. Do you think you can find another one?"

"Never know. I'd never seen *any* till the other day. Now I've seen two. We tried to collect one, but it fell apart."

"It would. And once its matrix broke, its cocoon, the animals inside would die."

"What kind of critters live in a sac like that?"

Talley looked out over the sea, then slowly turned to look at Darling. "What do *you* think, Captain?"

"How should I . . . ?" Then Darling paused, and said, "Jesus Christ! Little baby beasts? In that jelly thing?"

"Hundreds," Talley said. "Maybe thousands."

"But they'll die, right?" Sharp said.

"Normally, yes. Most of them."

Darling said, "Something'll eat them."

"Yes," Talley said. "That is, if there's anything left down there to do that."

HAVE YOU EVER read Homer?" Talley asked as he reached into one of his cases and passed Darling a six-inch stainless-steel hook. "Homer of the wine-dark sea."

"Can't say as I have," Darling said. He fed the barb of the hook through a mackerel, and tossed the fish onto a pile of others.

"You know, the guy who wrote the *Iliad*," Sharp said. He was attaching swivels to the eyes of the hooks, then tying six-foot titanium wire leaders to each swivel.

"The same," Talley said. "There are those who believe, and I'm one, that Homer talked about giant squid three thousand years ago. He called it Scylla, and this is how he described it: 'She has twelve splay feet and six lank scrawny necks. Each neck bears an obscene head, toothy with three rows of thick-set crowded fangs blackly charged with death. . . . Particularly she battens on humankind, never failing to snatch up a man with each of her heads from every dark-prowed ship that comes.' " Talley smiled. "Vivid, don't you think?"

"Sounds to me," Darling said as he snapped wire leaders onto one of Talley's folding umbrella rigs, "like your Homer had himself a twelve-volt imagination." He dragged the umbrella rig across the deck and placed it beside two others.

"Not at all," said Talley. "Imagine being a sailor back then, when dragons and monsters were the answer to everything. Suppose you saw *Architeuthis*. How would you describe it to the people back home? Or even in modern times, suppose you were on a troop transport during World War Two and one attacked your ship. How would you describe a great monster that rose out of nowhere and tried to tear the rudder post off your ship?"

"They did that?" Darling snapped the cap ring on one of the umbrella rigs to a length of cable attached to the nylon rope.

"Several times, off Hawaii."

"Why would a giant squid want to attack a ship?"

"Nobody knows," Talley said. "That's the wonderful thing about—"

Gunfire exploded beside them, thirty shots so fast that the sound was like fabric tearing. They spun and saw Manning standing on the stern, holding his assault rifle. Behind the boat, feathers drifted down among bloody bits of shattered petrel.

"What was that for?" Talley demanded.

"A little practice, Herbert," Manning said, and he popped the empty clip from the rifle and inserted a new one.

* * *

It took them an hour to lower the gear, what Talley referred to as Phase One of his operation. From three thousand feet of half-inch rope, six umbrella rigs fanned out at intervals on different levels, each with ten baits on titanium leaders. The wire was unbreakable, the hooks unbendable and four inches across at the base—so big that the only other animal that might be tempted to take one would be a shark. If a shark did get hooked, they reasoned, its struggle would send out distress signals that would add to the lure. And if *Architeuthis* should take one of the baits, it would flail with its many arms and (or so Talley theorized) foul itself onto many more of the hooks until, finally, it would be immobilized.

"How much is the beast likely to weigh?" Darling had asked when Talley had outlined his plan.

"There's no telling. I've weighed the flesh of dead ones; it's almost exactly the weight of water. So it's possible that a truly big squid could weigh as much as five or ten tons."

"*Ten tons!* I couldn't put ten tons of dead meat in this boat, and that thing isn't likely to be dead. I might be able to tow ten tons, but—"

"Nobody's asking you to. We'll winch it up, and when Osborn has killed it, I'll cut specimen samples from it."

"With what, your penknife?"

"I saw you have a chain saw below. Does it work?"

"You're ambitious, Doc, I'll give you that," Darling had said. "But suppose the critter doesn't want to play by your rules?"

"It's an animal, Captain," Talley had replied. "Just an animal. Never forget that."

When the rope was down, Darling and Sharp tied three four-foot pink plastic mooring buoys in a line, snapped them to the end of the rope and tossed them overboard.

"What now?" Sharp asked.

"No point in pulling it for a couple of hours," said Darling. "Let's eat."

After lunch, Talley unpacked some of his cases and set up a video monitor and tested two of his cameras, while Manning sat on one of the bunks and read a magazine. Darling beckoned Sharp to follow him outside. The boat had been drifting with the buoys, but slightly faster, so by now the buoys had fallen a hundred yards astern.

"Doc's right about one thing," Darling said as he watched the buoys from the stern of the boat. "Anything tangles with that rigmarole, it'll know it's hooked."

"I don't think Talley wants to kill it."

"No, the silly bugger just wants to see the damn thing, learn about it. That's the trouble with scientists, they never know when to leave Nature the hell alone."

"Maybe it'll beat itself to death on the line."

"Sure, Marcus," Darling said with a smile. "But just in case the beast has other ideas, let's be ready. Get me the boat hook."

"What for?"

"We're gonna make ourselves a little insurance." Darling climbed down the ladder through the after hatch and disappeared into the hold.

By the time Sharp had found the boat hook on the bow and brought it aft, Darling was standing beside the midships hatch cover and opening a cardboard carton about twice the size of a shoebox. Stenciled on the side of the carton was a single word in a foreign alphabet.

"What's that?" Sharp asked.

Darling reached into the carton and pulled out what looked like a six-inch-long salami, roughly three inches in diameter, covered with a dark red skin of plastic. He held it up to Sharp and smiled. "Semtex," he said.

"Semtex!" said Sharp. "Jesus, Whip, that's terrorist stuff." He had heard of Semtex but never seen any. Manufactured in Czechoslovakia, it was the current explosive-of-choice of the world's most sophisticated terrorists, for it was extremely powerful, malleable and, best of all, stable. It would take a stupid man, and clumsy as well, to set it off by mistake. The cassette player that had blown up Pan Am 103 had been packed with Semtex. "Where did you get it?"

"If people knew what was flying around the world with them, Marcus, they'd never leave home. It came with a shipment of compressor parts I'd ordered from Germany; it must have just been an accident in packing. Lord knows where it was supposed to go. I didn't know what the hell it was at first, and neither did the customs inspector, but I figured why give away something that might be useful someday, so I told him it was a lubricant. He didn't care. It wasn't till a couple weeks later that I saw a picture of Semtex in a book and realized, holy shit, that's what I had stowed up in the garage." Darling turned the end of the salami toward Sharp. It was the color of eggnog. "We've got enough here to blow the end off Bermuda and send it all the way to Haiti. But we do have one little problem."

"What's that?"

"No detonators. Mike must have put 'em ashore and forgot to bring 'em back. Mike doesn't"—Darling paused, took a breath, then corrected himself—"*didn't* like sailing with things that might sink us."

"We may be able to make one," Sharp said.

"What do you need?"

"Benzine . . . regular gasoline."

"There's a can for the outboard down below."

"Glycerine. You have any Lux flakes?"

"In the galley, under the sink. That it?"

"No, I need a trigger, something to ignite it. Phosphorous would be best. Maybe if you've got a box of kitchen matches, we could—"

"No problem. Manning's got a couple hundred rounds of phosphorous tracers. How many?"

"Just one. A little bit goes a long way. But, Whip . . . I've never done this before. I've read about it, but I've never actually done it."

"I've never chased a ten-ton squid before, either," Darling said.

"It doesn't look like a bomb," Sharp said when they had finished. "More like a piece of cheap fireworks."

"Or a butcher's idea of a practical joke," said Darling. "Think it'll work?"

"It better, hadn't it."

"One consolation, Marcus: If it doesn't, there'll be nobody left around to chew you out."

They had blended the gasoline and the soap flakes into a thick paste, which they pressed, like a wad of gum, to the end of the stick of Semtex. Then Sharp had pried open one of Manning's phosphorous tracer bullets. He worked with his hands in a pan of water, for phosphorous ignites on contact with air, and when he had discarded the lead slug, he had poured the residue of phosphorous and gunpowder and water into a small glass pill bottle, which he had then sealed off and embedded in the paste.

Now they used duct tape to affix the contraption to the end of the ten-foot-long boat hook. Darling lifted the boat hook and shook it to make sure the bomb was secure. "What happens if he swallows it before he breaks the pill bottle?" he asked.

"It won't go off," Sharp said. "If air doesn't get to the

phosphorous, it won't ignite. If it doesn't ignite, it won't trigger the rest of the detonator. It'll be a dud."

"So you want me to make the thing bite it."

"Just for a second, Whip. Then jump, or—"

"I know, I know. With any luck, Talley's plan will work and we won't need it." Darling paused. "Of course, with *real* luck, we won't find the bastard to begin with."

He climbed to the flying bridge, went forward to the wheel, turned the boat to the south and began to look for the floating buoys. It had taken them an hour to rig the explosive and bolt a rod holder to the railing in which to stow the boat hook upright, out of harm's way. He hadn't worried about the buoys, hadn't thought about them.

He was surprised to find that he didn't see them right away. The boat couldn't have drifted more than half a mile from the buoys, and on a clear day like this, those big pink balls should have been visible for at least a mile. Still, he knew exactly where they were; he had taken landmarks when he dropped them. There was probably more of a swell on than he'd realized, and they were in a trough. He'd pick them up in a minute.

But he didn't. Not in a minute or two or three. By the time he had been heading south for five minutes, he knew from his landmarks that he was beyond the spot where he had left them.

They were gone.

He picked up the binoculars and focused them on a trail of sargasso weed. If the buoys had drifted with the tide, they'd be going in the same direction as the weed, so with his eyes he followed the trail all the way to the horizon. Nothing.

He heard footsteps behind him, then Manning saying, "Have you lost them?"

"No," Darling said. "I just haven't found 'em yet."

"God dammit! If you hadn't wasted so much time—"

Darling held up a hand, suddenly tensing; he had heard something, or felt something, sensed something.

The feeling was coming through his feet, he realized, faint and far below, a weird thumping sensation. Almost like a distant explosion.

"What in God's name are you—"

Now Darling recognized it, even though he could hardly believe it. "Sonofabitch!" he said, and he shouldered Manning aside and went to the railing and looked down into the bottomless blue.

It came into view then, the only one left intact, and it was rushing for the surface like a runaway missile. It broke water with a loud, sucking *whoosh* sound, and flew half a dozen feet into the air, spraying them, before it settled back onto the surface and bobbed there, trailing beneath it the burst tatters of the two other buoys.

Talley and Sharp had heard the commotion and come out of the cabin, and by the time Darling reached the deck Sharp had snagged the rope with a grapnel and was hauling the buoy aboard. Darling unsnapped the buoy, tossed the rope aside, then wrapped the rope around the winch and turned it on.

"Is it him?" Manning said. "Is it the squid?"

The rope was quivering and shedding drops of water. Darling felt it with his fingertips. "I can't say, Mr. Manning, but I'll tell you this much: Anything strong enough to yank the stretch out of half a mile of poly rope, plus sink three mooring buoys each designed to float half a ton—sink 'em so deep that two of 'em bust— that is one humongous motherfucker." Darling leaned over the side, then said, "I can't tell if he's still there or not."

"If he was hooked," Talley said, "he's there. He can't break those wires or bend the hooks."

"Never say never, Doc, not when you're dealing with

something that's off the scale." Then Darling said to Sharp, "Get a knife, Marcus, and use the stone on it till it's like a razor. Then come and stand right beside me."

Sharp went into the cabin, and Talley followed and began to load his video camera.

"A knife, Captain?" said Manning. "What for?"

"If this is a real monster, if he's half the size Doc says he might be—and if there's even a spark of life left in him—I'm gonna cut the line and let the bastard go."

"Like hell you are. Not before I get a shot at him."

"We'll see."

"We certainly will," Manning said, and he headed down into the cabin.

Talley set a tripod on the flying bridge and mounted his video camera on it, while Manning positioned himself against the railing, his rifle loaded with a thirty-round banana clip and held against his chest. Below, Darling ran the winch as Sharp fed the rope into a plastic drum.

When the drum was half-full, Darling reached out and strummed the rope with his fingers. Then he stopped the winch and wrapped a hand around the rope and tugged on it.

"It's gone," he said. "If it was ever there. It's gone now, there's nothing on this rope but rope."

"It can't be!" Talley said.

"We'll know in a minute," Darling said, and he started the winch again.

"He wasn't really hooked, then."

"You mean he pulled those buoys down just for sport?"

The first of the umbrella rigs came up, and Sharp lifted it aboard. The baits were there, whole, untouched. A moment later the second rig came up, then the third. Nothing had eaten any of them.

As the fourth umbrella rig came into view, Sharp held up a hand, and Darling slowed the winch.

"Lord," Sharp said, reaching for the rig, "this thing looks like it was run over by a train."

The rig had been crushed, and its wires had been wrapped tight around the rope. Intertwined with the rope and wires were strands of a white musclelike fiber. Two of the baits were whole, still secured to the hooks, but the other baits were gone, and nothing was left of the hooks but a couple of inches of gnarled shaft.

Talley's camera was running, his eye pressed to the viewfinder. Darling held one of the hooks up for the camera. "Can't bend 'em out, huh? Can't bust 'em off? Well, Doc, whatever's down there didn't just bend 'em out, he *bit* 'em off."

Sharp plucked some of the white fibers from the rig, and they left a pungent stench on his fingers. He grimaced and wiped his hands on his trousers.

"It's *Architeuthis*," Talley said. "Smell the ammonia. He left us his calling card." He turned off the camera.

"Don't other things stink of ammonia?" Darling asked.

"Not like *Architeuthis* does, Captain. It's his signature, and it's the main reason we know anything about him. Nobody has seen a live one, not in this century, except for one that killed some people in the 1940s, and that was in the dark and they never really saw it. But people have seen dead ones; two washed up off Newfoundland in the sixties. The reason they washed up instead of sinking—they're not like fish, they don't have swim bladders—is that their flesh is full of ammonium ions, and the specific gravity of ammonium ions is slightly less than that of seawater. It's one-point-oh-one against one-point-oh-two-two, if you care. I saw the dead ones, Captain, and they didn't just smell of ammonia, they *reeked* of it." Talley turned to Manning and grinned. "It's him, Osborn. He's here, no question. We've found him."

"Listen, Doc," Darling said, "either you're crazy or you've been holding out on us. You can't catch a giant squid on a hook. You can't catch him with a submarine. So how in Christ's name do you plan to catch him?"

Talley said, "Living things are driven by two primal instincts, Captain, isn't that correct? The first one is hunger. What's the other?"

Darling looked at Sharp, who shrugged and said, "I don't know. Sex?"

"Yes," Talley said, "sex. I intend to capture the giant squid with sex."

# 45

TALLEY HAD NUMBERED his cases, and had included detailed descriptions of their contents in the customs manifest. Now he consulted the manifest and, with the help of Sharp and Darling, sorted the cases and arranged them on the afterdeck in a precise order.

Manning stood aside, and stared out at the water. To Darling, he seemed to be reducing himself to a single core, with a single purpose, stripping away the layers of social conditioning and leaving only a naked compulsion to kill. Darling had known people like Manning in the past, people who had lost all regard for safety; there was nothing more dangerous on a boat.

When Talley was satisfied with the arrangement of his

cases, he beckoned Darling and Sharp over to a long aluminum box the size of a coffin, which was secured with snap locks. He undid the locks and lifted the lid.

"Admit it," he said proudly. "Isn't this the sexiest thing you ever saw?"

Cushioned in foam rubber was what looked to Darling like a six-foot-long bowling pin, made of one of the new plastics and painted bright red. Hundreds of tiny stainless-steel hooks hung from swivels all over it, and a three-inch stainless ring was embedded in its top.

Talley lifted the thing by the ring and passed it to Darling. It couldn't have weighed more than ten pounds, and when Darling tapped it, he heard a hollow sound.

"I give up," Darling said simply, and he handed the thing to Sharp.

"It's genius, pure and simple," Talley said.

"Obviously," said Sharp. "But what *kind* of genius?"

Talley took the thing from Sharp and put a hand on either end and held it up before him. "Think of this," he said, "as the main body, the head and torso, what we call the mantle, of *Architeuthis*. As a general rule, the body of a giant squid—whatever its species, whether it's *dux, japonica* or *sanctipauli*—constitutes about a third of its total length. So this represents an animal whose total length, counting the tentacles and whips, would be about eighteen or twenty feet."

"A baby," Sharp said. "A squirt."

"Not necessarily. In any case, that's not important; the sex drive doesn't notice size. Even if our animal is, as I think it is, four or five times as big as this thing, its impulse will be to breed with this. If the beast is a male, it will want to deposit sperm in here; if it's a female, it will want its eggs fertilized."

"Why the hell would it want to do *any*thing with a piece of plastic?" Darling asked.

"That's where the genius comes in." Talley began to unscrew the steel ring. "I've spent years developing a chemical that perfectly replicates the breeding attractant of *Architeuthis*. Over time, I've been able to collect tissue samples from two dead specimens. I removed the oviduct from a large female that had stranded in Nova Scotia, and then two years ago I heard that part of the mantle of a male had washed up on Cape Cod. By the time I got there, there wasn't much left; birds and crabs had been working on it. But part of it had been buried in the sand and protected, and I was able to recover the entire spermatophoral sac. It was over three feet long. For months, I analyzed both parts, male and female, with microscopes and spectrographs and computers. Finally, I was able to synthesize the chemical trigger."

"You're positive?" Darling said. "Have you ever tried it?"

"In the field? No. But in the laboratory, yes. It makes perfect sense scientifically. I won't burden you with the specifics of the science, but just as a dog in heat emits a musk, just as human beings respond to testosterone and the pheromones and all our other hormonal signals, a giant squid responds to chemicals released by others of its species during a period similar to what we mammals call estrus." He put his finger in the hole left by the steel ring. "A vial of liquid poured in here and diluted with seawater will seep out through tiny holes behind each hook. It will create a spoor that will travel for miles. *Architeuthis* will perceive that one of its kind is ready for breeding, and it will be a call of Nature that the beast won't be able to resist."

"Won't he know it's a phony?" Sharp asked.

"No. There's almost no light down there, remember, so it doesn't depend on its eyes for much. We know it can change colors, but we don't know if it can *see* colors, so just to be on the safe side I painted the surrogate

red, which we know is one of the colors of excitation.
And the surrogate's shape is correct. We'll hang chemical lights beside it, so in case the animal is accustomed
to using its eyes for confirmation, they should cast
enough of a glow to be convincing." Talley paused. "It
may be overkill," he said. "The spoor might work if I let
it leak out of a bottle. But making the lure the right
shape and the right color didn't cost much and can't
hurt. When you play cards with the unknown, it's good
to hold as many trumps as you can."

"Okay," Darling said. "So he comes and screws the
bejesus out of this thing. Then what?"

"The beast has eight arms and two whips, and it will
wrap all of them around the object. It will press its body
to it." Talley flipped a few of the little hooks, and they
tinkled. "Each one of these will set into its flesh—not
enough to alarm it, certainly not enough to cause it
pain. But when it tries to get away, it won't be able to.
That's when we bring it up, just close enough on the
surface for me to take pictures of it, and for Osborn to
kill it. Then I'll cut some specimens." Talley looked
from Sharp to Darling, and smiled.

"Well, one thing's for sure," Darling said. "By the
time he gets up here, that's gonna be one pissed-off
squid."

"I don't think so. I think it will be concerned with
only one thing: survival. The rapid change in water
temperature may stun it, the change in pressure may kill
it before it reaches the surface. It may be so exhausted
it can't respire. But whatever happens," Talley said,
turning and gesturing at Manning, "that's when Osborn
takes over."

Manning acknowledged Talley with a curt nod, and
gestured with his rifle.

"You know what scares me?" Darling said. "You're
too sure of all this. I've seen too many perfect plans go

ass-upwards." He turned to Sharp. "Marcus, I'm damn glad we built ourselves that bomb."

"You won't need explosives, Captain," Talley said. "You'll see."

"I hope so. But from what I've seen, this is not a critter to underestimate."

It took them more than three hours to set Talley's rig, which was a masterpiece of complexity, involving thousands of feet of rope, hundreds of feet of cable and a low-light surveillance video camera housed in a Plexiglas sphere the size of a fortune-teller's crystal ball. Talley hadn't realized that objects on long lines underwater tend to spin unpredictably, and had mistakenly assumed that his camera would hang beside the lure and focus on it, so Darling had to fetch his chain saw from below and find a two-by-four, cut it and lash it between the camera and the lure as a connecting brace.

"How long does the camera run for?" Darling asked as Talley plugged the power cord into the battery pack.

"The tape is a hundred twenty minutes long," Talley said, "and the lithium battery in the base will run camera and lights for all of that. But we won't turn it on and leave it—a timer will set it off for one minute every five minutes. Or, I can turn it on whenever I choose from up here."

It was twilight when at last the rig was ready. The wind had died, and the sea was a meadow of steely swells.

Sharp watched a pair of gulls wheel over the stern, looking for an offering of bread or baitfish, and then fly off. As his gaze followed them toward the sunset, he saw something in the distance, something on the surface of the sea. At first he thought he was seeing the splashes of diving birds, but they didn't act like splashes: They lasted too long, and the water flew too high, more like spray. Then he knew.

"Look, Whip," he said, pointing. "Whales."

"Nice," Darling said. "At least there's *some* left."

"What are they, humpbacks?"

"No. Sperm whales. Humpbacks don't linger like that, they keep moving. Sperm whales always gather at twilight, I don't know why, maybe to get together for a gam."

Talley looked at the whales, then cupped his hands together and shouted at them, "Go away!"

Darling laughed. "What've you got against whales, Doc?" he asked.

"Nothing. I just don't want them to scare off *Architeuthis*. They eat squid, you know."

"I wouldn't worry about it," Darling said. "I don't know anything God ever made that would scare that beast away. Whales aren't as stupid as us—they know when to leave well enough alone."

Talley went into the cabin, and by the time he came back, the whales had sounded, and the sea had closed over them.

In his hands Talley held a six-ounce vial of clear liquid. At Talley's direction, Darling and Sharp held the lure upright and poured in buckets of seawater. Then Talley unscrewed the cap from the vial, and he held it out to them. "For science," he said.

Darling hesitated, then shrugged and said, "What the hell . . . it's not every day I get to sniff a randy squid." He held Talley's wrist and put his nose to the vial—and felt as if the lining of his nose had caught fire. His eyes watered, his stomach heaved; he staggered backward, coughing.

Talley laughed and said, "What do you make of it?"

"*Make* of it!" Darling choked. "Holy shit! Ammonia, sulfur . . . that stuff the freaks use to give their hearts a trumpeting—amyl nitrate—and something, I don't know, something purely *bad*."

"Bad?" Talley said. "You mean bad as in evil? There's no such thing as an evil animal."

"That's what *you* say, Doc. Me, I'm beginning to think different."

Talley emptied the vial into the water in the lure and screwed the steel ring tight. They shackled the ring to the cable and then, with Darling holding one end of the two-by-four and Sharp the other, they lowered the rig over the stern and let it go. It floated for a moment, until the last of the air inside the lure was expelled, and then it slipped away in a flurry of bubbles.

Darling and Sharp manned two hand-crank winches clamped on either side of the stern. Simultaneously, they fed first the cables, then the ropes, over into the sea, pausing every twelve feet to allow Talley to secure the camera's cable to the rope.

Then darkness fell; the stars strewed silver glitter on the still ocean, and the rising moon cast a golden path from the eastern horizon to the stern of the boat. From behind them came the warm glow of the cabin lights.

Finally, at nine o'clock, the 480-fathom marks on the ropes slipped through their hands, and they halted the rig, wrapped the ropes around the winches and tied them off to an iron towing post that ran down through the deck and into the keel.

"Want some food, Mr. Manning?" Darling asked as he and Sharp started forward.

Manning shook his head and continued to stare at the water.

Talley sat at the table in the cabin, adjusting the video recorder and the monitor and the control box. Darling walked behind him and looked at the monitor: The lure was in frame, swaying back and forth, and from the hundreds of holes in its skin, shimmering strands of spoor trickled out and trailed off into the blackness.

Darling noticed that Talley was sweating and that his hand shook as he turned the dials on the control box. "Is it getting to you, Doc?" he said. "Sometimes it's better if our dreams don't come true."

"I'm not afraid, Captain," Talley said sharply. "I'm excited. I've been waiting thirty years for this. No, I'm not afraid."

"Well, I am," said Darling, and he stepped up into the wheelhouse. He looked through the windows at the calm night sea. There were no other lights out here, no fishing boats, no passing ships. They were alone. A little frisson passed up his back, and he shook it off.

He turned on the fathometer. A stylus traced a pattern on a sheet of graph paper, and Darling read the depth. The bottom was 3,000 feet away, so if he and Sharp had measured the lines correctly, the lure and camera were suspended 120 feet above it. He started back down into the cabin, then stopped, reached over and switched on the fish-finder and calibrated its reading depth to five hundred fathoms. As the screen warmed up, the bottom glowed as a straight line. Otherwise, it was blank.

"That spoor's driving everything away, from here to the Azores," Darling said as he stepped down into the cabin. "There isn't a porgy or a shark between us and the bottom."

"No," Talley said, "there wouldn't be. They know to stay away." He turned off the camera and set the timer.

Darling walked to the door and flicked a switch beside it. The halogen lamps mounted on the flying bridge flashed on, and the afterdeck was flooded with light. Through the window Darling saw that Manning didn't budge, as if he hadn't noticed the sudden explosion of light. He sat on the midships hatch cover, his shoulders hunched, his rifle cradled in his lap.

Sharp passed Darling a sandwich. He nodded toward Manning and said, "Should I take him one?"

"He's not interested in food," Darling said. "The man's eating himself up inside."

"Osborn is unfortunate," Talley commented as he reached for a piece of bread and some cheese. "He's lost his perspective. Three weeks ago, he was a man who had power and knew how to use it. We made a deal that would give him revenge. He regarded it as a good deal. But now the project has become an obsession."

"Can you blame him?" Sharp asked.

"Of course. He's being irrational."

"Worse than irrational," said Darling. "He's dangerous."

"It'll pass. We'll let him shoot his gun at *Architeuthis*, and he'll be what he has always been: a winner."

"That simple, is it?"

"Animals are predictable, Captain, even the human one."

"Including *Architeuthis*?"

"Oh yes. It's programmed as surely as any machine. Once we know the codes, its behavior is predictable. Absolutely."

By ten-thirty, the timer had activated the camera a dozen times, and each time they had gathered around the monitor and seen the lure swinging back and forth across the frame, leaking ribbons of spoor. Up-current from the lure, a few tiny crustaceans flashed like fireflies across the screen, leaving afterglows of phosphorescence. Down-current there was nothing but black.

The boat drifted on the calm sea; even lying beam-to, it didn't snap-roll but seemed to rock gently, like a baby's cradle. The cabin lights were a snug orange co-coon that added to the illusion of peace.

"Suppose he doesn't come tonight," Darling said to Talley.

"In the morning, then, or the afternoon. But it will come."

"We might's well get some sleep, then."

"If you can."

"Better had. You too."

Sharp went to the bunk room below. Talley watched the monitor through one more cycle, then lay back on the bench seat and closed his eyes. Darling went outside.

Manning was still sitting on the hatch cover, but he was slumped over, asleep.

Darling checked the ropes; they hung straight down, unmoving, untouched. Then he looked toward shore. The loom of Bermuda was a rosy glow against the black sky, and he could make out the light pattern of the huge Southampton Princess Hotel and the sweeping beam of the lighthouse on Gibbs Hill. They were ten miles away, but he took comfort in the knowledge that home was still there. He thought of Charlotte, in their house, in their bed, and suddenly he was suffused with loneliness.

When he went back inside, the television monitor was running again, casting pale gray shadows on Talley's sleeping face.

Darling climbed up into the wheelhouse and stood quietly, listening to the sounds of the night. The genera-tor purred; the stylus on the fathometer hissed as it tracked the boat's drift along the five-hundred-fathom line; the fish-finder hummed, its screen still showing desolate emptiness. He heard the sound of the water softly caressing the steel hull, and the sound of Talley breathing.

He went into the cabin and lay down on one of the bunks. He longed for sleep, for abstraction from himself, but, exhausted though he was, he was sure that his mind would refuse to retreat into the comfort of numbness. Ever since he had first gone to sea as a boy, whenever he slept on a boat a part of his brain had always stood watch, alert to any change in the wind, to the slightest alteration in the rhythms of the ocean.

The watchman in his head had been on duty in the best of times, when the boat had floated over an apparently infinite resource of life, when being woken in the middle of the night usually signaled promise rather than threat. The watchman hadn't flagged even in recent bad times, when nights were filled mostly with vain hopes.

Darling knew that the watchman would be on duty now, when, for the first time in his life, his most fervent hope was that the sea beneath him would remain a barren, lifeless plain.

His breathing slowed; his brain succumbed to fatigue. The watchman stood guard, a lonely sentry.

# 46

THE GIANT SQUID expanded its mantle, drew water within and expelled it from the funnel in its belly. It propelled its great mass through the night sea with a force that pushed pressure waves before it and left eddies behind.

Driven by the most basic of all impulses, it rushed in one direction, then stopped, then rushed in another, extending its many senses to gather in more and more of

the scattered signals that were exciting it into a frenzy.
Its body chemistry was confused, and the chromatophores it triggered changed the creature's flesh color
from pale gray to pink to maroon to red, reflecting
emotions from anxiety to passion.

The signals it was receiving were partly alien and
partly familiar, but its brain registered only that they
were irresistible.

And so it rushed on, soaring up and down and side to
side, like an aircraft out of control or a gigantic raptor
gone berserk.

Suddenly it encountered a stream of the signals; it was
a trail, strong and true.

The creature homed in on it, excluding everything
else.

# 47

DARLING AWOKE, WITHOUT knowing what
had woken him. He lay quietly for a moment, listening
and feeling.

He heard the familiar sounds: the hum of the refrigerator, the scratch of the stylus across the fathometer
paper, Talley's breathing. He saw the familiar sights:
darkness, relieved only by the faint red glimmer from
the binnacle in the wheelhouse. But he felt a difference
in the motion of the boat. There was a reluctance, as if
the boat were no longer going with the flow of the sea,
but rather fighting it.

He rolled off the bunk, walked to the door and stepped outside. The instant his eye caught the movement of the water, he knew what had woken him: The boat was going in the wrong direction.

Something was pulling it backward.

Then he looked at the stern, and saw little waves slapping against it, casting spray. The ropes still angled straight downward, but they were trembling, and even from a distance he could hear the high-pitched squeak of straining fibers.

So, he thought. Here we go.

He ducked back inside and shouted, "Marcus!"

Talley sat up on the bench seat and said, "What?"

"Turn your TV monitor on, Doc," Darling said, then called again, "Marcus! Let's go."

"Why?" Talley was still groggy. "What . . . ?"

"Because we've hooked the sonofabitch, that's why. And he's dragging us backward." Darling reached across Talley and pressed the switch. The monitor flickered, then glowed.

The image was without definition, a swirl of bubbles and shadows, light flashing against darkness—a scene of chaos and violence.

"The lure!" Talley said. "Where's the lure?"

"He's got it," said Darling. "And he's trying to run with it."

Just then, Sharp came up from below, and Darling beckoned to him and went outside.

Manning was standing in the stern, soaked with spray, staring at the thrumming ropes. "Is it . . . ?" he asked.

"Either it's the beast, or we've hooked the devil himself." Darling directed Sharp to the starboard winch while he took the one on the port side, and together they began to wind in the ropes.

For a minute or two, they made no headway; the

weight on the winches was too great for them to get traction, so the winch drums skidded under the ropes. The boat continued to move backward, splashing spray as the stern dug into the waves.

Then the ropes suddenly eased, and the boat stopped.

"The strain's gone," Sharp said. "Did it get off?"

"Could be. Or else he's just turning, I can't tell. Keep cranking."

They wound in tandem, retrieving a foot of rope every second, ten fathoms a minute. The muscles in Darling's arms ached, then began to burn, and he switched hands every few turns.

"Whip, he's got to have busted away," Sharp said when the two-hundred-fathom marks on the ropes rolled over the winch drums and tumbled into the coils at their feet. "Must have."

"I don't think so," said Darling. He had a hand on the rope and was feeling it, trying to read it. There was weight to the rope but no strain, pull but no action. "It feels like he's there but not pulling. Maybe taking a breather."

"Or maybe dead," Sharp said, sounding hopeful.

"Keep cranking, Marcus," Darling said.

Talley came out of the cabin. "I can't see anything on the video," he said. "It's a mess."

"Leave it run anyway," said Darling.

"I am." Talley took a position behind them, pressed against the cabin bulkhead. He had taken another video camera from one of his cases, and he hurried to load a tape and attach a battery.

Suddenly, Sharp said, "Whip! Look . . ." and he pointed. The ropes no longer hung vertically; they had started to move slowly out, away from the boat. Still there was no stutter on the winches; the rope kept coming aboard.

"He's coming up!" Darling shouted, and he thought:

He's just like a billfish on a run to breaching; he pulls, stops, gathers strength, and now he's gonna make his move. He looked at Manning and said, "Cock your gun. This is what you've been waiting for." Then he said to Talley, "If you want any pictures, Doc, you better get 'em fast. The beast isn't gonna stay long."

For the next few minutes, no one spoke. To Darling, the silence was like the false calm in the eye of a hurricane.

Darling and Sharp cranked the winch handles, and the rope flowed aboard, then ended, and the big shackles rattled over the bulwarks, followed by the first lengths of cable. "Fifty fathoms, Marcus," Darling said. "Another minute or two."

The cables angled out behind them, not quite horizontal, taut and quivering but still coming aboard. The creature must be nearing the surface now, but they couldn't tell for sure, or how far away it might be, or how far out in the darkness.

They stared at the water off the stern, trying to follow the silver threads of cable, to see beyond the edge of the pool of light cast by the halogen lamps.

"Show yourself, you bastard!" Darling called, and he realized suddenly that his fear had changed. What he was feeling now was not dread or foreboding or horror, but the galvanic fear of meeting an opponent more formidable than any he had ever imagined. It was almost like an electric charge, a healthy fear, he thought, and it blended with the fever of the hunt.

Just then the winches jolted, skidded, and the cable that had just come aboard leaped from its coils on the deck and began to snake overboard.

"What's he doing?" Sharp shouted.

"He's running again!" Darling cried, and he grabbed the winch handle and leaned on it, but the winch refused, the spool spun, the cable kept backing off into the water.

"No!" Manning screamed. "Stop him!"

"I can't!" Darling said. "*Nothing* can."

"You mean you *won't*. You're afraid. I'll show you how." Manning dropped his rifle, reached down into the coil of cable at his feet and grabbed a length of slack.

"Don't!" Darling yelled, and he took a step toward Manning, but before he could stop him, Manning had flung the cable at the iron post that ran down into the keel, looped it around the post and tied it off.

"There," Manning said. The cable continued to run off the stern, buzzing as it passed over the steel bulwark. Manning turned to face the stern, raised his rifle and waited for the creature to rise into his sights. But as he was turning, he slipped, and just then the creature must have accelerated, for suddenly the coils of cables jumped off the deck and flew. As Manning staggered to regain his balance, one of his feet stepped through a snarl of cable, and the cable snapped tight around his thigh, and he was lifted off the deck like a puppet. For a fraction of a second he hung suspended in the lights. He made no sound, and the rifle fell away from his hands.

Then a great force slammed the cables taut, and Manning seemed to fly backward, pulled by his leg, his arms out as if he were doing a swan dive.

Light flashed on Manning's face for an instant, and Darling saw no horror, no agony, no protest—only surprise, as if Manning's last sensation were amazement that fate had had the temerity to thwart him.

The rifle struck the deck and discharged a bullet, which ricocheted off the bulwark and whined away overhead.

Darling thought he saw Manning's leg pull away from his body, for something seemed to fall from the cable. But he heard no splash, for all sounds were overwhelmed by the *sproing!* of the cable setting against the iron post.

Instantly the cable rose to the horizontal, and the boat was dragged backward. Waves splashed against the transom, soaking them.

Then Darling saw the cable rise above the horizontal, and he yelled, "He's up!"

"Where?" Talley cried. "Where?"

They heard a splash then, and a sound like a bellows, and they smelled a stinging stench. The spray that fell on them suddenly became a rain of black ink.

Darling got to his knees and started to stand, but then he saw, ten or fifteen feet behind the stern, a little flicker of silver, and instinctively he knew what it was: The threads of the cable were snapping and rolling back on themselves.

He shouted, "Duck!"

"What?" said Talley.

Darling dove at him and tackled him to the deck, and as they fell, there was a booming sound from behind the boat, like a magnum pistol being fired in a tunnel, followed instantly by a high-pitched whistle.

A length of cable screamed overhead and shattered the windows in the back of the cabin. The second length followed immediately, and they heard the crash of Talley's camera housing disintegrating against a steel bulkhead.

The boat pitched and yawed for a moment, then settled back into the sea.

"Jesus God . . ." Talley said.

Darling rolled away from him and stood up. He looked aft, out into the darkness. There was no sign that anything had ever been there, no roil of water, no sound. Only the soft whisper of breeze over the silent sea.

# 48

TALLEY'S FACE WAS the color of cardboard, and as he got up off the deck, he trembled so badly that he could barely stand. "I never thought . . ." he began, but his voice trailed off.

"Forget it," Darling said. He and Sharp were pulling in the skeins of rope that littered the surface beside the boat.

"You were right," Talley said. "All along you were right. There was no way we—"

"Listen, Doc . . ." Darling looked at Talley and thought: The man's in despair; in about a minute, he's gonna collapse. "When we get to shore, there'll be time enough to piss and moan. We'll say nice words for Mr. Manning and do all the proper things. But right now, what I want to do is get us the hell out of here. Go inside and lie down."

"Yes," Talley said. "Right." And he went into the cabin.

When they had hauled the last of the rope aboard, Sharp leaned over the stern and said, "I hope none of that rope's wrapped around the prop."

"You want to go overboard and have a look?" Darling said, starting forward. "*I* don't." Then he added, "Talley was right about one thing—the bastard sure was drawn to the lure. But now, who knows? All I know

300

is, I want to be somewhere else when he figures out he's been had."

In the cabin, Talley was sitting at the table. He had rewound the videotape, and he looked at the monitor as he started to play it back.

"What are you looking for?" Darling asked.

"Anything," Talley said. "Any images at all."

Darling took a step up toward the wheelhouse, and said over his shoulder to Sharp, "Check the oil pressure for me, Marcus."

Sharp opened the engine-room hatch and started below.

Suddenly Talley jolted in his seat and shouted, "Jesus, Mary and Joseph!" His eyes were wide as he stared at the monitor, and he groped blindly for the controls for the recorder.

Sharp and Darling crowded behind Talley as he found the tape controls and pressed the "pause" button.

On the monitor was an image of froth and bubbles. Talley pressed the "frame-advance" button, and the picture jumped. "There's the lure," he said, pointing to a flicker of something dense and shiny. On the black-and-white screen it looked dark gray. In the next frame it had disappeared, then it reappeared at the top of the screen. Talley pointed to the bottom of the screen, and he said, "Now watch."

A grayish hump rose from the bottom of the screen, and, in the staccato pulse of the frame-advance, it seemed to march upward until it covered the entire screen. The frames kept changing, and the gray shade kept climbing. And then the bottom of the screen was invaded by something off-white, curved on top. It moved upward, as if to cover the screen.

The thing must have moved away from the camera, for gradually the image widened out, and the thing showed itself as a perfect off-white circle, and in its center was another perfect circle, blacker than ebony.

"My God," Sharp said. "Is that an *eye*?"

Talley nodded.

"What kind of size?" asked Darling.

"I can't tell," Talley said. "There's nothing to measure it against. But if the focal length of the camera was about six feet, and the eye fills the whole frame, it has to be . . . like so." He held his hands two feet apart. For a moment he gazed at his hands, as if unable to believe the size of the span he had created. Then, in a voice barely above a whisper, he said, "The thing must be ninety feet, perhaps more." He looked up at Darling. "This could be a hundred-foot animal."

"When we get home," Darling said, "we're all gonna get down on our knees and give thanks that we never got any closer to that fucker." Then he turned away and climbed the two steps up into the wheelhouse.

Dawn was breaking. The sky in the east had lightened to a grayish blue, and the advancing sun cast a line of pink on the horizon.

Darling pushed the starter button, and waited to hear the warning bell from the engine room and the rumbling cough as the engine came to life.

But all he heard was a click, then nothing.

He pushed it again. This time, nothing at all. He swore to himself several times, and then whacked the wheel with the heel of his hand, for as soon as he knew that the engine wouldn't start, he knew why it wouldn't start. There was no generator noise: The silence told him that sometime during the night, the generator had run out of fuel. The batteries had taken over automatically, but eventually, after being drained for hours by the lights and the refrigerator and the fathometer and the fish-finder, they had run down. They were still putting out some power, but they couldn't muster the juice to fire up the big diesel engine.

After he had calmed down, he considered which of the two fully charged compressor batteries would be easiest to shift over to the main engine, selected one, and reviewed in his mind the procedure for removing it from its mounts and sliding it through the tangle of machinery in the engine room and mounting it beside the engine.

It was nasty work, but not the end of the world.

As he crossed the wheelhouse on his way down to the engine room, it occurred to him that he should turn off the instruments, to save power. All the kick in the new battery should be directed to igniting the engine. He turned the knob on the fathometer, and the stylus stopped moving. The switch on the fish-finder was farther away. As he reached for it, his eyes glanced at the screen.

It wasn't blank anymore. For a moment, he thought: Good, life is coming back. Then he looked closer, and he realized that he had never seen an image like this on the screen. There weren't the little dots that signaled scattered fish, or the smears that showed schools of larger animals. The image on the screen was a single, solid mass, a mass of something alive. Something rising toward the surface, and rising fast.

# 49

THE BEAST SHOT upward through the sea like a torpedo. An observer might have thought that it was in retreat, for it moved backward, but it was not retreating. Nature had designed it to move backward with great speed and efficiency. It was attacking, and its triangular tail was like an arrow point, guiding it to its target.

It was over a hundred feet long from the clubs on its whips to the tip of its tail, and it weighed a dozen tons. But it had no concept of its size, or of the fact that it was supreme in the sea.

Its whips were retracted now, its tentacles clustered together like a trailing tail, for it was streamlined for speed.

Its chemistry was agitated, and its colors had changed many times, as its senses struggled to decipher conflicting messages. First there had been the irresistible impulse to breed; then perplexity when it had tried to mate and been unable to; then confusion when the alien thing had continued to emit breeding spoor; then anxiety as it had tried to shed the thing and found it could not, for the thing had attached itself like a parasite; then rage as it had perceived a threat from the thing and proceeded, with its tentacles and its beak, to destroy the threatener.

Now, what remained was rage, and it was rage of a

new dimension. The beast's color was a deep, viscous red.

Before, the giant squid had always responded to impulses of rage with instantaneous explosive spasms of destruction, which had consumed the rage. But this time the rage did not abate; it evolved. And now it had a purpose, a goal.

And so the hunter rose, driven to cause not only destruction but death.

# 50

A THOUSAND FEET, Darling guessed as he calibrated the fish-finder. The thing was at a thousand feet, and it was coming up like a bullet. They had five minutes, no more, probably less.

He jumped down into the cabin. "Get the boat hook, Marcus," he said. "And make sure that detonator's ready to fire."

"What's wrong?" Talley asked.

"The bastard's coming up at us again," said Darling, "and my bloody battery's dead." He disappeared down into the engine room.

Sharp climbed up to the flying bridge, lifted the boat hook and examined the bomb. The paste of glycerine and gasoline had hardened, but it was still moist, and he smeared it evenly over the top of the explosive. Then he pressed the little glass bottle deeper into the paste, so it couldn't fall out even if the end of the boat hook was waved around.

The device was simple; there was no reason it shouldn't work. As soon as air got to the phosphorous, it would ignite and start an instantaneous chain reaction, setting off the Semtex. All they had to do was make sure that the beast bit down on the bottle, or crushed it in one of its whips.

All they had to do was feed an explosive to a hundred-foot monster, and jump out of the way before they were blown to tatters.

That was all.

Sharp suddenly felt sick. He looked out over the calm sea, dappled by the rising sun. Everything was peaceful. How did Whip know the creature was coming up? How could he be sure? Maybe what he had seen on the screen was a whale.

Stop it, he told himself. Stop fantasizing and get ready.

It would work. It had to.

Darling crawled across the engine room and pushed the heavy twelve-volt battery in front of him. His knuckles were bloody and his legs cramped. When he judged that the battery was close enough for the cables to reach it, he unbolted them from the dead battery, without bothering to remove the dead battery from its mounts. He didn't care if the fresh battery tore itself loose and tumbled around; once he got it to kick over the engine, he wouldn't need it.

He paused long enough to be sure he was attaching the cables to the proper poles—positive to positive, negative to negative—and bolted it down.

Then he got to his feet and raced up the ladder.

# 51

ITS PREY WAS directly above.

It could see it with its eyes, could feel it with the sensors in its body. It did not pause to analyze the quarry, did not seek signs of life or scent of food.

But because the prey was alien, instinct told the creature to be wary, to appraise it first. And so, as a shark circles unknown objects in the sea, as a whale emits sonar impulses and deciphers the returns, *Architeuthis dux* passed once beneath the quarry and scanned it with its eyes. The force of its passage cast a pressure wave upward.

Then suddenly the prey above it erupted with noise, and began to move.

The beast interpreted the noise and movement as signs of flight. Quickly, it rotated the funnel in its belly, turned in its own length and attacked.

# 52

WHEN DARLING HAD felt the boat surge beneath him, he had held his breath and pushed the button, and then, a second later, had heard the rumble of the big diesel. He didn't wait for the engine to warm up—he rammed the throttle forward and leaned on it.

At first, the boat leaped forward, and then suddenly it stopped short, as if it were anchored by the stern. It tipped backward; the bow rose, and Darling was thrown back against the bulkhead. Then the boat fell forward again, and nosed into the sea. But still it didn't move.

The pitch of the engine had changed from a roar to a complaining whine. Then it began to sputter. It coughed twice, then died, and the boat lay dead in the water.

Sweet Jesus, Darling thought—the beast has wrecked the propeller, either jammed it or bent it up against the shaft. He felt suddenly cold.

He dropped down into the cabin and went out through the door onto the afterdeck.

Talley was standing by the midships hatch, staring numbly at the sea. When he saw Darling, he said, "Where is he? I thought you said—"

"Right underneath us," Darling said. "He's screwed us good and proper." He went to the stern and looked down over the transom into the water. A few feet beneath the swim step, snaking out from beneath the boat, was the tip of a tentacle.

Standing beside Darling, Talley said, "He must have tried to grab the propeller."

"Now he's lost an arm," said Darling, "maybe that'll discourage him."

"It won't," Talley said. "All it will do is enrage him."

Darling looked up at the flying bridge and saw Sharp standing at the railing, holding Manning's rifle. As he started up the ladder, he heard Talley say, "Captain . . ."

"What?"

"I'm sorry," Talley said. "This was all my—"

"Forget it. Sorry's a waste of time, and we don't have much time. Put on a life jacket."

"Are we sinking?"

"Not yet," Darling said.

The boat hook stood vertically in a rod holder, and Darling removed it and felt its heft.

"I'll do it," Sharp said, gesturing at the bomb on the end of the boat hook.

"No, Marcus," said Darling, and he tried to smile. "Captain's prerogative."

They both looked out over the water then, and as they watched, the sun cleared the horizon and faded from orange to gold, and the color of the sea changed from dead gray to steel blue.

The beast writhed in the darkness, berserk with pain and confusion. Green fluid seeped from the stump of its missing tentacle.

It was not disabled—it sensed no loss of power. It knew only that what it had perceived as prey was more than prey. It was an enemy.

The creature rose again toward the surface.

\* \* \*

Darling and Sharp were gazing off the bow, when suddenly from behind them came Talley's voice, screaming, "No!"

They whirled around and looked at the stern, and they froze.

Something was coming over the bulwark. For a moment it seemed to ooze like a giant purple slug. Then the front of it curled back like a lip, and it began to rise and fan out until it was four feet across and eight feet high, and it blocked the rays of the sun. It was covered with quivering circles, like hungry mouths, and in each one Darling could see a shining amber blade.

"Shoot it, Marcus!" Darling shouted. "Shoot!"

But Sharp stood agape, mesmerized, the rifle useless in his hands. Then, below them, Talley heard something, and he turned to his left, and screamed. Amidships, slithering aboard, was the beast's other whip.

The scream startled Sharp, and he spun and fired three shots. One went high; one struck the bulkhead and ricocheted away; the third hit the club of the whip dead center. The flesh did not react, did not bleed, twitch or recoil. It seemed to swallow the bullet.

More and more of both whips came aboard, writhing like snakes and falling in heaps of purple flesh, each atom of which moved and pulsed and quivered as if it had a goal of its own. They seemed to sense life aboard, and movement, for the clubs bent forward and began to move ahead on their circles, like searching spiders.

Talley seemed paralyzed. He did not flinch, made no move to flee, but stood still, frozen.

"Doc!" Darling shouted. "Get the hell out of there!"

When both whips were heaped in the stern, they stopped moving for a moment, as if the creature were hesitating, and then suddenly both whips expanded with muscle tension, and the stern was pressed downward. Behind the boat, the ocean seemed to rise up, as if giving birth to a mountain. There was a sucking sound, and a roar.

"Jesus Christ!" Darling yelled. "It's coming aboard!" He backed away, holding the boat hook at shoulder level, like a lance.

They saw the tentacles first, seven thrashing arms that grasped the stern and, like an athlete hoisting himself onto a parallel bar, pushed downward to bring the body up.

Then they saw an eye, whitish yellow and impossibly huge, like a moon rising beneath the sun. In its center was a globe of fathomless black.

The stern was forced downward until it was awash. Water poured aboard and ran forward, flooding into the after hatches.

It's gonna do it, Darling thought. The bastard's gonna sink us. And then pick us off one by one.

The other eye came up now, and as the creature turned its head and faced them, the eyes seemed to fix on them. Between the eyes the arms quivered and roiled, and at the juncture of the arms, like a bull's-eye on a target, the two-foot beak, sharp and protuberant, snapped reflexively, looking to be fed. The sound was of a forest falling in a storm, like great trunks cracking in a roaring wind.

Talley suddenly came to. He turned and ran to the bottom of the ladder and began to climb. He was half-way to the flying bridge when the creature saw him.

One of the whips recoiled, rose in the air and sprang forward, reaching for him. Talley saw it coming, and as he tried to dodge it, his feet skidded off the ladder, and he hung by his hands from one of the rungs. The whip coiled around the ladder, tore it away from the bulk-head and held it suspended over the flying bridge, with Talley dangling from it like a marionette.

"Drop, Doc!" Darling shouted, as the other whip hissed overhead and slashed at Talley.

Talley let go, and fell, his feet struck the outboard lip of the flying bridge, and for a second he teetered there, his arms cartwheeling as he groped for the railing. His eyes were wide, and his mouth hung open. Then, almost in slow motion, he toppled backward into the sea. The whip crushed the ladder and cast it away.

Sharp fired the rifle at the beast until the clip was empty. Tracer bullets streaked into the oozing flesh and vanished.

The tail of the creature thrust forward, driving the body farther up on the boat, driving the stern farther down. The bow rose out of the water, and from below came the sounds of tools and chairs and crockery crashing into steel bulkheads.

"Go, Marcus!" Darling said.

"You go. Let me—"

"*Go,* God dammit!"

Sharp looked at Darling, wanted to speak, but there was nothing to say. He dove overboard.

Darling turned aft. He could barely stand; the deck sloped out from under him, and he crouched, bracing himself with one foot on the railing.

The creature was tearing the boat to pieces. The whips flailed randomly, clutching anything they touched—a drum of rope, a hatch cover, an antenna mast—and crushing it and flinging it into the sea. As it drew air into its mantle and expelled it through its funnel, the creature made sounds like a grunting pig.

And then its rampage ceased, and as if it had suddenly remembered something, the great head, with its face like a nest of vipers, turned toward Darling. The whips lashed out; each one fastened on a steel stanchion on the flying bridge. Darling saw the flesh balloon as the muscles contracted. The whips pulled, and the creature lunged forward.

Darling balanced one foot on the railing and one on the deck, and he raised the boat hook over his head like a harpoon. He tried to gauge how far he was from the beak.

The creature seemed to be falling toward him. The arms reached out. Darling focused only on the gnashing beak, and he struck.

The boat hook was torn from his hands, and he was thrown back against the iron railing. He saw one of the whips raise the boat hook, and drop it into the sea.

His only thought was: I am going to die.

The arms reached for him. He ducked, his feet slipped out from under him, and he fell, skidding over the edge of the flying bridge and dropping onto the sloping after-deck.

He found himself in waist-deep water. He started to slog toward the railing. If he could get overboard, away from the boat, maybe he could hide in the wreckage, maybe the creature would lose interest, maybe . . .

The beast appeared around the edge of the cabin then, looming above him, its whips waving like dancing cobras. The seven shorter arms, and even the oozing stump of the eighth, reached for him, to push him into the amber beak.

He turned and struggled toward the other side of the boat. One of the arms slapped the water beside him, and he dodged to the side, stumbled and regained his footing. How many steps to go? Five? Ten? He'd never make it. But he kept going, because there was nothing else he could do, and because something deep inside him refused to surrender.

An obstacle blocked him. He tried to push it out of the way, but it was too heavy, it wouldn't move. He looked at it, wondering if he could dive under it. It was the big midships hatch cover, floating. Lying atop it was the chain saw.

Darling didn't consider, didn't hesitate, didn't think. He grabbed the chain saw and pulled the starter cord. It caught on the first try, and the little motor came to life, idling with a minatory growl. He pressed the trigger, and the saw blade spun, shedding drops of oil.

He heard himself say, "Okay," and he turned and faced the beast.

It seemed to pause for a moment, and then, with a grunt of expelled air, it lunged for him.

Darling squeezed the trigger again, and the sound of the saw rose to a shrill screech.

One of the writhing arms flashed before his face, and Darling swung the saw at it. The saw's teeth bit into flesh, and Darling was bathed in a stench of ammonia. The motor labored, seemed to slow, as it might when cutting wet wood, and Darling thought, No! Don't quit, not now!

The pitch of the motor changed again, rose again, and the teeth cut deep, spraying bits of flesh into Darling's face.

The arm severed, and fell away. A sound burst from the beast, a sound of rage and pain.

Another arm assailed Darling, and another, and he slashed with the saw. As the teeth touched each one, the arms flinched and withdrew and then, as if goaded by the creature's frenzied brain, attacked again. A shower of flesh exploded around Darling, and he was drenched with green slime and black ink.

Suddenly he felt something touch one of his legs underwater, and it began to crawl up his leg and circle his waist.

One of the whips had him. He turned, trying to find it, wanting to attack it with the saw before it got a secure grip on him, but in the mass of curling, twisting tentacles he couldn't distinguish it from the arms.

When the whip had circled his waist, it began to squeeze, like a python, and Darling felt a stabbing pain as the hooks in each sucker disk tore into his skin. He felt his feet leave the deck as the whip picked him up, and he knew that once he was in the air, he was as good as dead.

He twisted his body so that he faced the snapping beak. As the whip squeezed and drove the breath from him, Darling leaned toward the beak, holding the saw before him. The beak opened, and for a second Darling could see a flicking tongue within, pink and studded with toothlike rasps.

"Here!" he shouted, and he drove the saw deep into the yawning beak.

The saw stuttered as its teeth failed to slice through the bony beak, and skidded off. As Darling raised the saw again, one of the arms flashed before his face, circled his hands and wrenched the saw from them and flung it away.

Now, Darling thought, now I am truly dead.

The whip squeezed, and Darling sensed that the mist that dimmed his eyes was signaling the onset of oblivion. He felt himself rising, saw the beak reaching for him, smelled a rancid stench.

He saw one of the eyes, dark and blank, relentless.

Then suddenly the beast itself seemed to rise up, as if propelled by a force from below. There was a sound unlike anything Darling had ever heard, a rushing, roaring noise, and something huge and blue-black exploded from the sea, holding the squid in its mouth.

The whip that had him contorted violently, and he felt himself flying, then falling into nothingness.

# 53

PULL!" SHARP SHOUTED.

Talley reached into the water and groped for Darling's belt. He found it and pulled, and with Sharp hauling on his arms they brought him aboard the overturned hatch cover. It was awash, but its wood was thick and sound, and it was large enough to hold three of them.

Darling's shirt was in tatters, and streaks of blood crisscrossed his chest and belly where the creature's hooks had torn at his skin.

Sharp touched an artery in Darling's neck. The pulse was strong and steady. "Unless something's busted inside," he said, "he should be okay."

In a dark fog, Darling heard the word "okay," and he felt himself swimming up toward light. He opened his eyes.

"How do you feel, Whip?"

"Like a truck ran over me. A truck full of knives."

Sharp lifted Darling up and supported his back. "Look," he said.

Darling looked around. The motion of the hatch cover made him nauseated, and he shook his head to clear it.

The boat was gone. The animal was gone.

"What was it?" Darling asked. "What did it?"

"One of the sperm whales," said Sharp. "It took the whole damn squid. Bit it off just behind the head."

There was sudden movement in the water, and Darling started.

"It's all right," Talley said. "Just life, just Nature."

The surface of the sea was littered with flesh, masses of it, and each one was being assaulted. The tumult around the boat had been like a dinner bell, summoning creatures both from shallow and from deep. The dorsal fin of a shark crossed the debris. The head of a turtle poked up, looked around, then submerged again. Bonitos rippled the surface as they swarmed on fresh and helpless prey. Triggerfish, yellowtails and jacks ignored one another as they darted through the rich broth.

"Nice," Darling said, and he lay back. "That's the kind of life I like."

"I don't know where we are or where we're going," said Sharp. "I can't see land. I can't see a thing."

Darling wet a finger and held it up. "Home," he said. "Northwest wind. We're going home."

# 54

IT HAD BEEN created in the abyss, and had remained there for weeks, adhering to a rock overhang on the mountainside. Then it had broken away, as Nature planned it should, and, buoyed by a concentration of ammonium ions, it had begun slowly to drift toward the surface. In times past, it might have been eaten on the way up, for it was a rich food source.

But nothing had attacked it; nothing had shattered its integrity and permitted a rush of seawater that would have killed the tiny creatures within, so it had arrived safely on the surface and bathed itself in the sunlight vital to its survival.

It floated on the still water, oblivious to wind and weather, so thin as to be nearly transparent. But its jelly skin was remarkably strong.

It was oval, with a hole in its center, and it followed eons of genetic instructions and rotated itself in the sun, exposing all of itself to nutrients sent from almost 100 million miles away.

Still, it was vulnerable. A turtle might have fed on it, a passing shark might have slashed at it. Nature had ordained that many of its members would die, feeding other species and maintaining the balance of the food chain.

But since nature itself was out of balance, the gelatinous oblong rotated through days and nights until its cycle was complete. At last, ripe, it broke apart and scattered into the sea thousands of little sacs, each containing a complete creature. As each creature sensed that its time had come for life, it struggled free of its sac and immediately began to search for food.

They were cannibals, these creatures, and those that could turned on their brethren and ate them. But there were so many, and they dispersed so fast in the water, that most survived and dove for the comfort of the cold abyss.

Almost all should have been eaten before they reached the bottom, or the safety of the crevices on the submerged volcano's slopes; at most, one creature in a hundred should have survived.

But the predators were gone, and while a few lone hunters did appear, and took their toll, there were no longer the great gatherings that had once acted as natural monitors. The vast schools of bonito and mackerel, the swarms of small white squid, the pelagic jacks, the herds of tuna, the voracious wahoo and barracuda, all were gone.

And so, by the time the creatures had crossed three thousand feet of open water and taken shelter in the cliffs, nearly ten percent—perhaps a hundred individual animals, perhaps two or three hundred—still lived.

They hovered, each alone, for each was completely self-sufficient, and drew water into their mantles and expelled it from the funnels in their bellies. Their confidence grew with every respiration. Their bodies would mature slowly, and for a year or more they would be wary of other predators. But the time would come when they would sense their uniqueness, their superiority, and then they would venture out.

They hovered, and they waited.